Rapunzella, Or, Don't Touch My Hair

A Love Letter to Black Women

ELLA MCLEOD

YELLOW JACKET

🐝 **YELLOW JACKET**

New York, NY
Text copyright © Ella McLeod, 2024
Cover illustrations by Alex Cabal
First published in the UK in 2022 by Scholastic
All rights reserved, including the right of reproduction in whole or in part in any form.
Yellow Jacket and associated colophon are
trademarks of Little Bee Books.
Manufactured in China RRD 0224
First U.S. Edition

10 9 8 7 6 5 4 3 2 1

Library of Congress Cataloging-in-Publication Data is available upon request.
ISBN 978-1-4998-1611-2 (hc)
ISBN 978-1-4998-1633-4 (pb)
ISBN 978-1-4998-1612-9 (eb)
yellowjacketreads.com

For more information about special discounts on bulk purchases, please contact Little Bee Books at sales@littlebeebooks.com.

For Celina, who always knew.
And, of course, for You, who witnessed and endured.

Ella McLeod is a proud South Londoner, Pisces, and daydreamer. She lives in Peckham with her partner, Michael, and their cat HRH, Princess Persephone.

Part One
Seed

The Prophecy

In a garden, beneath a tower,
where dwelled witches, robbed of power,
gave breath and life to an avo-pear tree,
all fruit will ripen and set them free.
A son born of witch and might,
a thief who will learn to fear the night,
if witches' magic he steals and drains,
the King will Persea with darkness stain.
One girl will be more powerful than all the rest;
two girls will in dazzling white be dressed;
three girls will fight, two will stand,
the other of us, and yet not of this land.
Keep them secret, and all will return;
say it's a story, say it's a game,
listen to our whispers, the truth you'll learn.
Do not let him take her name.

The Seer

The Seer from Persea was friends with the trees.

Well, as friendly as one could be with trees. It was this that made her so good at her job. The great stretch of forest at the edge of Kingstown was the same stretch that had lined the horizon, just visible from the King's palace and its surrounding estate, where she and her coven had worked for many years. She had often stared at that great, dense expanse, leaves stretching towards the sky as though trying to claim some part of it. Had often wished that she too could reach for the clouds, brush her fingertips against the sun and suck in the cool mossy air that surely tasted of freedom.

She had covered her crudely shaven head against the heat of the sun and left her coven that morning, headed deep into the forest looking for the right one. Long had her people known of the wisdom held in that age-old bark. Other plants had their own power, but willow trees were her favorite. The interconnected network of roots growing beneath the damp, fragrant soil had the capacity for far more than mere water absorption. This earth magic was what gave her coven power—power harnessed by the King.

Sneaking away from the palace was never without the quick two-step of anxiety in her breast, but her dreams had never steered her wrong before and it was worth the risk. There was a message for her today. The trees were calling to her. She could feel their whispers prickling along her skin. She walked among the willows, pressing her hand to their barks in a sign of respect and she felt, rather than saw, them bow in response. Eventually, after several minutes of treading carefully over fallen branches, stepping lightly over the sweet-scented mulch of dead leaves and decaying fruit, the Great Forest opened into a wide clearing and a river.

The great River Aphra was the most powerful source of magic in all of Xaymaca, guarded by the River Mumma, a mermaid of terrible wrath and beauty, who protected the river and the land that sourced it. The Seer bent her head as she ducked under the tree branches, before crawling into a cross-legged sitting position at its base. Touching her hands to the place where bark, roots, and earth all meet, she tipped her head upwards. Smiled. Breathed. And began to sing:

> There's a Brown girl in the ring
> Tralalala
> There's a Brown girl in the ring
> Tralalalalala
> Brown girl in the ring
> Tralalala
> She looks like the sugar in the plum

The trees, her friends, sang with her in their soft whispering way. She felt the magic ebb and flow, until she was part of every willow in the land. As they sang, she felt her body thin and dissolve. Become liquid and gas and sparkle as the tree wrapped itself around her, absorbed her until she and the tree were one. And when she opened her eyes, she saw the great truths that the magic would only show to her.

And she was afraid.

Her people had not been free for a long time. They worked in service of the King, within his palace and its grounds. For generations he had bent their backs, bruised their skin, blistered their hands, bled them dry. The Seer was the only one who knew how old the King was, the only one who remembered a time before his darkness, before her sisters had been forced into submission.

Now, though, the Seer, lingering in the half-place between the

Great Forest and truths brought to her by the land, could see change on the horizon. She summoned the dregs of her magic—what little had been left to her after the King had stolen the core of Persea all that time ago—and sent a message back through the tree. The willow understood, and as the Seer returned once again to solid flesh and bone, she felt her prophecy zinging through the roots and fibers of every plant and tree and flower around her. Hope and terror combined to hurry her footsteps to the path beyond the pines, which eventually would meet the road to Kingstown, and so she chased her warning, back to her sisters.

THE SALON

The beautiful lady is turning in a circle, slowly, slowly, in the empty window of the empty storefront.

She eyes each exposed brick, touching her fingertips to some. She studies each damp patch as though it is precious, as though she is a queen in her kingdom. She has reddish curling hair, almost as dense as yours, tied up with a colorful scarf, and she is adorned with many glinting gold necklaces. She is goosebumps-excitement, her smile is tired from dreaming, now brightened by the joy of acquisition, the warmth of accomplishment. A boy runs around her feet, enjoying the vast space, cluttered with an assortment of boxes, bags, and various lumpy packages containing mysteries. A kingdom all to himself. A young princeling with broad, bony arms and scuffed swagger.

You recognize him.

Recognize the scrawny limbs and lanky frame of someone riding the high-energy wave of a growth spurt as he mock-boxes an imaginary friend, lighter on his feet than any dancer in your class. He manages to make every swing of his arm look graceful.

Maybe he feels your fascinated gaze on him, maybe hairs go up on the back of his neck, maybe he senses your still shade, your small half-smile, and he turns.

He smiles. There is recognition, there is joy, and with it an unfamiliar swooping inside you.

Like missing an expected step.

Your palms tingle and you bury your face in Mum's dress, but you're laughing.

He waves a half-greeting. His mother looks from him to you. You can sense her questions and you see the boy's mouth form your name through the window.

"You know him from school?" Mum asks, her expression curious. You shake your head. "You're six years old. You don't know any other boys."

You clasp her hand tighter. Her manicured nails graze your skin. "He boxes at the rec center at the same time as ballet. I've seen him."

His is the first smile to outshine your mother's.

"Well, it looks like his mum is opening a salon there." Your mum points as movers unload a van, dragging decapitated steam dryers into the room. Amid all the chaos, the queen is unmoved. "Let's go and help them."

"What?"

This is too much, really, too much for her to expect of you.

"No, no, we can't, we should go home, we should . . ."

"Come on, you can talk to your friend and I can find out what her prices are. It's right around the corner from home, maybe I can finally make it to a hair appointment."

You squirm, wishing you were loose-tongued and lovely, not sulking, matching sleeping Saffy in her stroller. Mum tugs you with one hand, pushes the stroller with the other. "Don't be shy!"

The queen is carrying a box of rollers, cradling them like a child, when your mum stops her. They talk and you look at the boy, who looks at you.

"Hi!" he says at last. "I'm Baker, I seen you at the rec center with the dancers." His accent is a beautiful lilting thing, with strangely curling vowel sounds, partway between sounding like your little patch of city and somewhere else entirely.

"Yeah, I know who you are." You are rude in your shyness but he smiles anyway.

"These are my girls," your mum is saying and the queen smiles down at you. She is laugh lines and frown lines in equal measure. She places her hand on your head and gently tugs a pigtail. There is a mild crackling, like an electric shock. Even Mum notices. "Ooh, static! Must be all the packing material!"

"So, little one." The queen's eyes hold yours and you don't know if it's your childish imagination, but they seem to flash like lightning. "What will it be?" Her accent is soft but stronger than Baker's.

Mum tuts. "You're so busy! It doesn't have to be today; we can book it for when you're set up?"

But the queen shakes her head, earrings catching the light and sending gold dancing across the walls. "No, please. It would be my pleasure."

You look up at her and quickly look away, squinting because looking at her is looking at the sun without glasses. You mumble something about just wanting to look like Mummy and both women laugh.

"You can't relax your hair like mine yet, Mush, you're too young."

You wince at the private pet name in public, stare at the pavement.

"Cane row would be nice; all little girls look cute in cane row," says the queen.

"But they'll take a long time," Mum warns. "You'll have to be a very good girl and sit patiently."

"I don't have a book," you say, horrified.

"You like stories?" Baker says. "Mum tells the best stories!"

Baker is looking at you, but you can't look back at the son of the sun; his smile is too bright for your mortal eyes.

"Yeah," you mumble. "I like fairy tales—but the long ones, not the ones with the pictures we read to Saffy before bed."

You gesture contemptuously to your sister in her stroller, who is clutching a blonde Barbie beauty with a big pink dress.

"Oh, fairy tales, yuh knuh?" The queen's accent reminds you of your grandma's. It warms you inside out, and you find the courage to look at her again.

"Yes." You are eager now. "I like *Jack and the Beanstalk* best.

9

Or *Hansel and Gretel.*" And now you're on your favorite subject, the words come tumbling out. "When me and Saffy play, I'm always the witch because imagine being able to do magic and living in a house of sweets! Those kids should have never just taken them without asking. They deserved what they got. But Saffy likes the ones where the girls just sleep and have shiny gold hair and get kissed."

Baker *ewww's* in agreement and the mothers chuckle again.

"Right," says the queen. She smiles at you. "No kissing. No sleeping. No girls with shiny gold hair."

She holds out her hand. You hesitate—a life, a minute, a nanosecond—then take it. She smiles wider.

"I think I have just the thing."

Cytnhia and Ama

The sun was hot where they stood in the soil,
as they labored on in an endless toil.
Cynthia's sympathy hummed in her voice,
"We don't have a choice."
Ama and Cynthia, two witches,
weeding and seeding and
sewing and mowing
while ruled
by a bejeweled tyrant,
an indolent king.
Their rosebush-green fingertips granted life
to his gardens, buds brimming with color everywhere they walked,
they tasted the red and smelled the blue and saw the scent bathe the air
in an arousing rush of synesthesia.
But this was a mere fraction of what they could do—
their creation did not fill them with elation,
instead a frustration,
knowing that they were trapped in so many ways,
but knowing that they had the power to *slay*.
Out of all the fruit they grew, only one,
a pale green pear,
would not ripen.
They respected its defiance,
its refusal to ripen and grow,
to put on a show
for another's benefit.

They wondered if they'd made an error
in its planting,
but that was unlikely.
They were rarely wrong when it came to plants.
Cynthia chanted as she worked,

There's a Brown girl in the ring
Tralalala
There's a Brown girl in the ring
Tralalalalala
Brown girl in the ring
Tralalala
She looks like the sugar in the plum

Ama had been practicing her magic from the time she was born,
magic that defied the royal's structured norms,
turning herself from "Amos the boy" that they misnamed her,
witchcraft feminine power soon claimed her,
and she found in Cynthia a half of her whole.
They fell in love,
bonded as one soul.
But they did not want to labor
from dawn to the grave,
would cast off their shackles with the hope of the slave.
They worked beneath the shade of the avo-pear tree—
and then, through the roots—a prophecy . . .

AVOCADO OIL

The queen leads you inside, through the maze of boxes and bags and bits and bobs, saying over her shoulder to your mum, "We finally just had the hot water turned on today. It's been a to-do acually. . . . "

"You've been living upstairs with no hot water?" Mum's voice is horrified.

"We've had to fill the bath using the kettle." The queen is cheerful enough, but Mum grabs her wrist, her carefully manicured nails a blush pink vice.

"Listen, we're basically neighbors now! If that ever happens again, you come to me." Mum is scrawling her phone number on a page torn out of the planner she is never without.

"Ah now." The queen is bright proud, palms protesting. "We 'uh fine."

But Mum just kisses her teeth and stalks over to a stack of boxes, officiously imposing her organizational methods on this warm stranger, ordering everything into "zones."

Baker shows you around.

"And over here is where Mum says the till will be and she says she'll show me how to use it so I can help, and over there is where all the dryers will go and over here will be a big cupboard and drawers so Mum says I can help her organize all the rollers and oil jars—"

"I'd suggest this for her," the queen says, holding out a jar.

"Oh, we never normally use avocado oil!" says your mum.

"I don't use this often; it's a homemade recipe," says the queen. She tugs your pigtail again, and again the same jolt of electricity surges

13

through your skin like a current. "Special. But for you I'll make an exception. My first customer."

She swoops down on you, her firm hands appearing beneath your arms, and the ground vanishes beneath your feet. You are placed gently into the lone chair in front of the lone sink. She wraps a gown around you with a "Superwoman!" and places a towel round you with a flourish.

You face the ceiling, propped up on a mountain of cushions so that your neck reaches the basin. The queen undoes your pigtails and begins to run the warm water over your hair. You feel your scalp being gently massaged by expert hands, with just the right amount of nail. You are happy like dessert before dinner, like summer playdates, like Mum coming home early from work. The queen pours three different potions into your hair, each smelling more wonderful than the last, until you can feel how shiny your hair must look. She dries it and begins to braid, running each thick curly section through with the avocado oil and your damp scalp is warmed. You feel almost immediately sleepy.

"Stay awake." Mum gently nudges you. "Val's going to tell you a story, remember."

The queen's name is Val, you realize slowly, ploddingly.

Val is piling up yet more cushions, adjusting the back of the chair so you semi-recline deliciously, saying, "It's okay, let the chile' doze off if she wants tuh. Good stories give good dreams."

"Why don't you use it often?" you ask. "The avocado oil."

"Because it's a magic potion and I don't want to waste it."

You giggle. You never forget that.

As your mind stumbles inevitably towards nodding heavy restfulness, you hear her begin,

"There was once a witch,
on the run . . . "

*

Later, you are woken. Mum pays. You're hungry, you realize, and still tired, eyelids drooping. Mum and Val talk and talk; they can't seem to say goodbye. It's nice. Mum doesn't usually have time for small talk or friends.

As they chat, Baker says, "Mum said the avocado oil was only for her." He is puzzled. "She said it was the only thing she had of home and she doesn't have much of it left. But she gave it to you." He reaches towards you and then hesitates.

"Can I feel your hair?" The intimacy of the question startles you, but you don't mind. You nod.

He lightly touches the end of your fresh braid. "You're special. I can tell."

"Oh." You mouth the word.

Baker grins.

It was that night that the dreams started.

King Charming

Once upon a time there was a king.
A king who ruled his land
with a hand tyrannical.
An abundant land of water and wood,
every day the King, he stood,
and asked,
"Mirror, Mirror, on the wall, who is the fairest of them all?"
Mirror, with dark power contaminated,
shudders to life, opens mouth, is animated, says:
"Mate, I won't lie to you—you are fit. Charming, even.
See your beard and your nose and your ears and your chin,
see your brow, your jaw, your eyes, your skin—
why, you, my old friend, are the ivory tower,
the snow-capped mountain, the alabaster power,
and—quite frankly—I fancy you.
But in your kingdom, you have dissent.
There are women who are not meant
to conform to your way of doing things.
Dark eyes see things that we cannot,
they hear the whispering of the leaves,
the murmuring of the trees.
These women are sorceresses.
On this morn, one of these witches,
called forth a prophecy—
the shadows heard and whispered to me:

"A son born of witch and might,
a thief who will learn to fear the night,
if witches' magic he steals and drains,
the King will Persea with darkness stain.
One girl will be more powerful than all the rest;
two girls will in dazzling white be dressed;
three girls will fight, two will stand,
the other of us, and yet not of this land.
Keep them secret, and all will return;
say it's a story, say it's a game,
listen to our whispers, the truth you'll learn.
Do not let him take her name."

"They're tired of you touching their hair,
they'll want it back, they'll feel no fear—
so be afraid, Your Majesty. Of this
Black Girl Magic.
Unlike everything else in your kingdom,
it owes you no pleasure."
The mirror told the King what the prophecy decreed,
but he did not the warning heed.
Instead, in his hubris, he sought to bend
the prophecy of the witches to his end.
"Stolen Xaymacan magic I will employ
to grant myself a baby boy—
a babe born of magic and might,
my own champion in this fight.
Persea may think this prophecy will save her,
but he'll turn the tide in my favor."

17

The First Dream

You are in a garden, illuminated by the silver-gold electrum of the moon and stars. Neatly ordered flowerbeds, herbs with leaves familiar and strange, tendrils of green climbing the high fences, which dissolve into the dense thicket on either side. It is as though this garden has been carved out of the forest around you. You think of the Eden in the picture book Bible your grandma gave you. Clear, vivid, sharp, sharp cutting colors, like turning the brightness and the saturation up on the TV. The air is pure, the birds are loud, the trees are the greenest green. It is nighttime, you know it is, there is no light—but it isn't dark. You know this is wrong, wrong, wonderfully wrong.

From somewhere, far away on the horizon, however, there is darkness that is at odds with the bright blue-black of the sky, a pulsating void that consumes even the bright pinpricks of stars. You turn away, back to the garden.

The flowers are pure vermillion, rich cerulean, deep violet, blooming before your eyes, and you can smell the warm salty skin smell of a day in the sun even though there's no sun anywhere—

"Where am I?" you ask aloud, not expecting a response.

"In my garden. My garden is in Persea. And Persea is in Xaymaca."

"Xaymaca?"

"The Land of Wood and Water."

Two girls are standing behind you, leaning against a broad white swing seat. The girl who spoke could be a night-blooming flower or a comet dashing across the vivid sky. Her eyes are aflame with curiosity, and her night dress is spangled with stars. She is your height but her hair—her magnificent elaborate twisted and wrapped crown—gives her several centimeters' advantage. She steps towards you and you see round, ripe features on her broad, full face.

The second girl is her opposite but no less striking. Smaller, bonier, darker-skinned, with a face made of straight lines and clean edges. Her hair is shorter but coiled looser and spun into many small braids that hang in neat precision to just below her ears. Her eyes are deep-set and seem to swallow the not-quite light of the garden around them. She is warier than the first girl, hanging back against the swing, twisting her long, thin limbs around it like a tree clinging to a stake for support.

They are simultaneously strange, these children of this night garden, and familiar. You know them, you think. But that is impossible.

"Did you hear us singing?" the first girl asks. "Is that why you came?" Her accent is lilting and musical.

"I don't know why I'm here. I'm dreaming, I think. What were you singing?"

"It's the song we have always sung," she says. "My sister and I." She gestures to the girl behind her. "We are most powerful when we use our voices."

"Will you teach me?"

She grins at you, then looks at her sister. "What do you think, Kam?"

The girls eye each other in silent conference. A powerful current seems to pass between them, seems to charge the air around you, and the first girl asks, "Do you mind if Kam touches your hair?"

You are startled. Before Baker, no one had ever asked for permission. You nod.

Kam reaches towards you and gently touches the end of your braid. Up close you see how kind her eyes are, how her hand shakes slightly. She gives a sharp intake of breath. Releases it. Looks at you. Really looks at you. Sees you.

"Yes. Yes, we will teach you."

She nods to her sister, waits a beat, and then,

There's a Brown girl in the ring
Tralalalala
There's a Brown girl in the ring
Tralalalalala
Brown girl in the ring
Tralalalala
She looks like the sugar in the plum

Though your bed is far away, this is a homecoming.

The song is like sinking into a perfectly temperate bath, sugared plums and smiling. The charge between you swells in time with the music. You all hold hands, palms warm and smooth beneath your own. When Kam squeezes your fingers, you feel it—something like an electric shock.

You stand with them, pulsating with the life around you. Your feet are bare in the grass, like theirs, fronds settling between your toes, but you feel no cold. You had often wondered why moths, if so attracted to brightness, didn't simply emerge during the day instead of waiting till night. But you understand now. Understand the magic of a vivid bright spark, shining among the dark.

You feel a low tug inside and the vivid dark night around you begins to blur. You're waking up, you can feel it.

"What's your name?" you ask the taller girl, the girl with the hair that seems to breathe all on its own.

"Zella," she says.

"Will I see you again?" you call out as wakefulness claims you, pulling you towards the surface of your consciousness like a large buoyancy aid.

The other girl, the quiet one called Kam, calls, "Often, I think."

*

As you linger between the hazy half-wakefulness of morning and the deep pool of sleep, you try to catch it before it escapes you. That sweet dream, those half-forgotten friends. It's like trying to cling to a melting snowflake. When you strain to remember, it vanishes. They leave something behind, though. A lingering, warm glow.

And then Mum opens the curtain and daylight pours in.

The Ripening

"I won't live this way any longer!" said Ama, angry and proud.
"Working until we cannot stand,
living every day mouth to hand,
watching the King's power infect this land,
beat and quell our people into submission.
I've not seen my own sister
since the King summoned her
to serve him in the palace.
Twelve moons have yet passed since Yvane did see
the prophecy—
how much longer will it be,
until the pear tree sets us free?"
But soothing Cynthia said, "Sing with me."
So Ama sat by her woman and
sang the Brown girl song.
And as they felt this internal stirring,
a great warmth came from the avocado tree.
Through the power of this great shift,
Cynthia and Ama felt Xaymaca's gift,
and when Cynthia plucked, peeled, and tasted,
she knew the prophecy would not be wasted.
For lover, mother, growing babes alike,
knew the time had come for the witches to strike.

A Little Magic

In the years that follow, you visit your friends in the garden often: three or four times a week. Most of the time it is the garden you appear in, sometimes the little side alley of the house or on the street in front of it. Never inside.

Zella always finds you, barefoot in your old pajamas. You never remember to put on something nicer. Sometimes you come in your bonnet too, if it hasn't slipped off in the night, as it so often does. You think about how embarrassed you used to be, at the thought of people seeing you in your bonnet. You're never embarrassed in Persea, though.

Returning is safety and comfort and exhilaration. A strangeness that is not truly strange. There is a power to this place. You feel it caress the hairs on your arms and the back of your neck, see it ooze from your friends—out of the tips of Kam's fingers, electric currents sparking between Zella's curls.

This power does not frighten you. Quite the opposite. You are at home here. Even the gathering darkness on the horizon doesn't scare you. After all, it's just a dream and nothing in a dream can hurt you.

Kam avoids you sometimes.

"Why doesn't your sister like me?" you ask Zella one night and her eyes widen.

"She does like you! Very much!" Zella insists, reaching out to clasp your hand. "It's just . . . actually, she is a bit afraid of you."

"Afraid of me?" You gape. "Why? I don't have power like you two!"

"Exactly," says Zella. "You are the first girl we've met that is not of magic. And yet here you are. In our garden. Which is strange." Tact is unnatural to Zella. "But I am not afraid of you!"

The two of you sit together, cross-legged and crinkle-eyed, under a tree at the back of the garden with wide, expansive arms like a roof to a small forest house. From each branch hangs a succulent-looking green fruit with a dimpled surface reminding you of your mother's thighs as you sit between them while she does your hair.

"Magic?" you say, although of course there must be magic here.

"Our mothers are very powerful witches," Zella explains. "Which makes us powerful too. Years ago they fled from a terrible king, so you can imagine how strong they are. Kam's magic means she sees the roots of things. The truth of people, if she can touch their hair."

"Why does she have to touch hair?"

Zella shrugs. "I am not sure exactly, but we Persean witches . . . our hair is special to us. It is the doorway that lets the magic in. That's what Mum says."

This amazes you, and you twist the ends of your skinny, messy braids round your little finger in wonder, thinking of the tender ritual of Val washing, combing, oiling, drying, braiding. Zella notices the wistful expression in your eyes and smiles at you, poor, magicless creature.

"What about *your* magic?" you ask. "Can you see things too?"

Zella shakes her head. "Oh, no. My magic is different than Kam's, even though it actually comes from the same place. All of us have magic that comes from the energy of living things. It flows from the source in the River Aphra, through Xaymaca, and into us. But *my* magic is very special."

Zella thinks quite a lot of herself, you think. Her eyes glow in the not-black of the bright night. "What can you do with your magic?" you ask.

"I do not know yet," she says reluctantly. "I am too young. But sometimes I feel it tingle over my body, right up into the roots of my hair. Mum says, *Magic isn't exact, but it's always intentional*. It chooses how and where to come alive. And it has chosen me."

You think for a bit. "Have you not got a dad?" You don't have a dad, or at least you haven't for a long time. There is a girl at school who has two dads.

"What's a dad?" asks Zella.

"Like a mum that's a man," Kam replies, melting into solidity from the lush shadows behind you. "There are dads in some of our stories. There were dads here too once. Remember, Zella? Mama told us. Then they all left. And anyway, our mothers made us."

"Mum and Mama stole a pear!" Zella says, with wicked delight. "The Seer heard a prophecy, which told them that when the pear tree ripened they would know it was time to strike. When they got belly with us, the tree ripened and they ate from it. They grew strong, stronger than ever, and began feeding their sisters with the pear too, until they were all strong enough to rise up and march for freedom." Zella's eyes are shining, her hair crackling from some internal blaze. "The earth helped them escape. Mama says that when they said goodbye to the garden, the pear tree rained fruit down upon them, and it was as though Xaymaca was saying—"

"*All fruits ripen*," Kam repeats, finishing her sentence. "That means it is going to be okay."

"So you don't know any boys? Any at all?"

"No," said Zella, rather wistfully. "Maybe we did when we were small. But I cannot remember any now. I have never known anything else."

You digest this. A world without boys.

You think of Baker.

"Have you . . . have you never ever *seen* one?"

"No!" Kam's face is serious.

"What would happen if you did see one?" you ask.

"I'd run, I expect," says Zella, eyes wide again.

25

"I wouldn't run from a boy!" you say scornfully.

"It's different for you. Boys are dangerous here," says Kam firmly, "because of the prophecy."

"I wonder if it would hurt their feelings," you muse, staring into the rich brown center of the nearest bud. "The boys. Knowing your prophecy is saying bad things about them and making you run away."

Zella's eyes fix on you. "You know a boy, then?"

You think of Baker again. His smile and his eyes, the way he can reduce you to helpless laughter or fierce indignation. Baker always listens to you. You think he would be hurt if you ran away from him. "Yes. Well, one. He's called Baker."

Kam shushes you dramatically. "We have to be careful when we name things here."

"Oh, please," says Zella impatiently. "He is not from here; saying his name does not matter. He does not have magic."

"Everyone has a little magic," says Kam. "And boys are dangerous."

"Well, this boy is nice," you say stubbornly. You wince internally. *Nice* is feeble sun after an April shower and Baker is . . . Baker. He is hot sun, ice pops after school on the last day of summer term.

The others just shake their heads at you and you roll your eyes. "Anyway, I know *your* names."

"But not our true names." Zella laughs. "Our full names."

"Oh." You are caught short, you had only ever known honesty from them. "You don't trust me?"

"No, we do!" Zella insists. She looks at Kam. "It is just that . . . we must be very careful." The look they exchange is a powerful, tangible thing.

Then Kam slowly nods. Zella turns and, picking up a stick, writes a name in the rich, fragrant soil of the flower bed. Points at herself. Writes another name. Points at Kam. She makes sure you've seen, and then scratches over both with the stick, obliterating the letters.

You raise your eyebrows at Zella's haste. "Do sticks and dirt have magic too?"

She cuts her eye in response.

But maybe fear is catching, because as you feel yourself beginning to rise to the surface of your consciousness, you turn and see the darkness on the horizon and it looks as though it is vibrating. As though whatever lurks there is stirring sleepily.

There's a Brown girl in the ring
Tralalalalala

And you resolve, in that washed-up place between rest and waking, not to mention Baker to Kam and Zella again.

The King's Command

The King's breakfast table is laden
    with piles of scones and croissants and jams,
    eggs and bacons and hams,
and in the center—the King could only stare,
ripe and sliced, an avocado pear.
For almost two years he'd chosen to ignore
the growing power outside his door;
instead he had cracked his whip,
and summoned another bargaining chip.
To his staff he had said, "Send the Weaver to me,"
and threatened to harm one of her sisters
when she begged, when she pleaded,
then he told her what was needed.
He told her what he wanted,
she didn't have a choice,
a Persean witch without a voice,
and once she'd under duress consented,
the King believed his future cemented.
But now, the hard fruit was ripe—
what did this mean?
Ripe avocados had not been seen
since he'd stolen the Persean witches'
magic.
"Send the Weaver to me," he cried once more.
"The Persean witches must never be free!"
But the Weaver was gone.

And with her the babe,
And so the King began to rage.
The King did not know
that every tree and flower in the castle
had a message sent through its roots,
that every witch tired of working,
should pack a bag and don their boots.
And now, echoing through the palace halls,
he heard their song rattle the walls,
he tasted change in the air
and for the first time—felt a prickle of fear.

There's a Brown girl in the ring
Tralalalalala
There's a Brown girl in the ring
Tralalalalala
Brown girl in the ring
Tralalalala
She looks like the sugar in the plum

BAKER AND
THE SECRET

As the years pass, Val and Baker become constant fixtures in your life: *part of the furniture*, as your grandma would say. Mum and Val become best friends.

You like to think of Val as a comfy, if slightly too firm, mattress. The kind that's good for your back. She is tough, solid, but quick to soften, her hands gentle on your scalp as she tells you and Saffy and Baker a story. Saffy's favorite is the one about the whispering willow trees with secrets to share. Yours is the one about the good witch who ran away from an evil wizard, that she told you on that first day in the salon.

"There was once a witch," she would say, drowsy in the half-light, Baker beside you, learning to braid, "on the run."

If Val is tough support, Baker is light. Sometimes blazing sunlight and sometimes gentle warmth. A bedside table lamp. The one you read by when Mum has said, "Lights out." A soft glow, burning secretly beside you.

Val's salon is a second home. But Baker is never a sibling.

You drive each other wild laughing. The teasing, the fighting, the games that made your sides hurt laughing. He is everything. You're fully comfortable around him, and yet uneasy. You have butterflies in your stomach every time Mum drops you off for Val to mind while she goes to work at the rec center. But not seeing him is worse.

It's a Friday, about six o'clock. You are ten and Baker is eleven. It is a sweet age, these, your gobstopper days. Childhood looms large initially, almost chokes you in your rush to get through it and then, in no time at all, it will evaporate on your tongue. You don't know this yet.

Mum is at the salon. Again. Half the time Mum doesn't actually need her hair done, she just wants to gossip with Val. You once heard Grandma say to Mum that Val was an "expensive friend." Mum had just laughed and called herself a "patron of small businesses." You didn't know what that meant, but liked the way it sounded.

It is July, still warm and sunny. You are in Mrs. Goss's community garden, opposite the salon, sucking on the bright blue ice pops that Mum doesn't know Mrs. Goss gives you. The golden joy and additives of the day have melted, faded into something muted, and now you're in a mood. Today is the last day of school before summer, which means it's also the last day that you and Baker will walk back to the salon together afterwards. He will be starting secondary school in September. He's got a place at the all-boys' high school, the one that only accepts the top students.

He'd gone to an orientation the week before. His new English teacher had given him a piece of summer homework—to write about a childhood memory. He'd been pestering Val ever since, pressing her to fill in details he couldn't remember, but Val had not been forthcoming.

The grass is scratchy against the backs of your knees; your sticky, cold, ice pop hands are bothering you. You don't like being sticky. Or dirty. Or messy. You didn't even like finger-painting as a toddler.

You carefully spread out your cardigan on the grass and lie back. It's not that comfortable and the ground is dusty. Baker takes the books out of his book bag and hands the empty nylon satchel to you. Now you can prop yourself up on your forearms without them coming into contact with offensive grass and dirt.

"Thanks," you say.

But Baker is far away and somewhere else, flipping through a notebook, saying for the hundredth time this week, "Mum says we came from Jamaica the summer before I turned seven. So I should remember,

31

right? I remember everything *here*. I remember the salon and the rec center and boxing." He glances at you. "I remember seeing you."

You squint at the serious expression on his face. You wriggle free from his gaze, lying back and trying to ignore the thought of bugs scurrying into your dense mass of dark curls, now in contact with grass and soil and plant life.

"Of course you remember seeing me," you say. "I'm very memorable."

He laughs then and pulls off a dandelion stem, blowing its feather-light dustings in your face. You squeal about "bacteria" (your new favorite word) and "allergies," but you're laughing too. You always laugh when Baker laughs.

"You can make wishes with those, you know!" Saffy calls from a few paces away, where she is watering flowers with Mrs. Goss's watering can—a little too enthusiastically. Mrs. Goss herself is sitting on the other side of the flowerbed, lovingly tending to her geraniums and smiling indulgently.

"No, you can't," you say with a forced, elder-sisterly calm. You've noticed how patient Baker is with your younger sister, and strain for maturity with Saffy when around him.

"Yes, you can!" Saffy insists. "It said so in the books you used to read me at bedtime."

"Well, those were just fairy tales. They're not real, Saffy."

"They are too!" Saffy stamps her foot crossly, the precursor to a temper tantrum.

Baker, noticing the warning signs, takes Saffy's hand, and says, "I believe in fairy tales, Saffy. And so does your sister, she's just being silly."

"Am I?" You're ten and too old for this childish nonsense.

"Yes." Baker is calm and unwavering. "You are."

"Yes, you are," parrots Saffy. "And it is silly. If you believe in magic, you believe in fairy tales."

"Who says I believe in magic?" You glare at your sister, imploring her with your eyes that she not embarrass you in front of Baker, but Saffy is too young for such looks and ploughs on determinedly.

"You said you believe in magic! You said!"

"Of course she believes in magic." It's Baker's turn to eyeball you. "She believes in the tooth fairy and Santa's magic at Christmas—"

"Yes, and she has magic dreams!"

Silence.

You are breathless.

Your dreams are a half-forgotten secret that you'd half-forgotten sharing with Saffy.

"Magic dreams?" Baker asks. He is smiling.

"Saffy," you hiss. "That was a secret! A special sister secret!"

She claps her hand, still dimpled like a baby's, to her mouth, her big eyes widening with horror. Her voice muffled by her fingers she says, "Sorry, sorry! But"—looking rapidly from you to Baker and back again—"Baker can keep secrets, can't he?"

"Yeah, yeah, I definitely can." He is playing along, his eyes bright with amusement. You're surprised he can't see your stomach doing backflips through your shirt.

"See?" says Saffy, eager to undo the damage, and you concede, nodding your forgiveness.

Saffy beams and turns back to Mrs. Goss, who pats her on the head saying, "Very good, Saffy. Why don't you pull up some dandelions for me? They grow without help and there are far too many."

"You should keep them, Mrs. Goss. If you have lots of dandelions, you'll have lots and lots of wishes!" she declares, but does as she's asked.

"So," says Baker, grinning, "magic dreams, huh? When did these start?" You study him, contemplate lying, search Baker's eyes, Baker's face, Baker's eyes, Baker's eyes, Baker's eyes. "When did these start?" he says again.

Beat. You are held in the pre-truth. You savor the simplicity. Then you say, casually, although your heart is beating a mile a minute, "Just after we met actually. So about five years ago."

His grin broadens. "You've been having magic dreams for five years?"

You don't smile. "Yeah."

His eyes change, he can't tell if this is a game any more. "How do you know they're *magic* dreams?"

"Well . . ." You hesitate. "I always go to the same place. A garden, with two girls in it. One has loads of hair. It's a place that I mostly forget when I'm awake but remember when I'm dreaming. It's a place that feels like home, but looks nothing like here."

You don't remember sitting up but you are. You lie back down again. Gooseflesh raises along your arms and your hair is standing to attention.

"I've heard of . . . of people having the same dream over and over," Baker says hesitantly. "Maybe it's just something like that?"

"Maybe." You feel the lie thicken your tongue. The absurdity of it all hangs in the air, the bright sunlight, the honks of horns and revving of motorbikes making it all the more ridiculous. "It's weird, though, right? You don't remember anything before about five years ago, don't even remember coming here. And five years ago, we meet and . . . and I start having these dreams." You had never given it much thought before. Your hazy memory of your dreamland combined with the bright sparkle of childish obliviousness had prevented you from connecting these dots. Or maybe you simply hadn't been ready yet.

"You think it has something to do with me? Or me and Mum?"

Something like the truth brushes against you, like a purring cat.

"I dunno. I just think it's strange."

"But I don't have these dreams," Baker says. "So they can't be anything to do with me."

You shrug. "It's probably nothing. I have weird dreams and I tell my baby sister they're magic, that's all."

Baker frowns into the lap of his favorite football shorts. His fingers work away, braiding a daisy chain, with delicate, agile movements, into a bracelet far neater and prettier than anything you or your friends had ever made on the playground. You wonder at how quickly he's learned.

You turn and watch Saffy, busy with her bouquet of dandelions.

"Wishes don't actually come true," you say meanly. "You know that, right?"

She looks up at you, eyes shining. "Um . . . if you can have magic dreams, then dandelion wishes can come true, I think!"

You roll your eyes and Baker laughs.

His face is lit vividly by the sun as it drifts westward.

"I think it's the avocado oil, you know." The words form as if on someone else's tongue, but you know they are true when you hear them. "That your mum puts on me. I think that's why I have those dreams."

The silence is not silent. The birds chirp, Saffy chatters to Mrs. Goss, the cars and their horns rev and blare. But there is silence between you.

He doesn't say anything, so you go on. "Maybe there's . . . there's something in avocados in Jamaica. Like when my mum eats cheese too close to bedtime. It can't be magic, can it?"

Baker is still frowning at the daisy bracelet in his lap. "Nah. I guess not." He sighs. "So Mum won't tell me anything about where we came from and she's never put the avocado oil on me." He forces a smile. "Maybe she doesn't trust me. Maybe you really are special." He shrugs, then says, "Hey, maybe I should take a bit of this oil. See if I dream too."

You can't articulate the feeling of foreboding that the thought of Baker's presence in the dream world elicits. For some reason—and you can't quite remember why—you know it's a bad idea. Forbidden. He sees the expression on your face and you rush in, wanting to make it all better. "Yeah, maybe you should! It's not stealing, is it, not really? It would be . . . so cool to see you in my dreams!"

It's the first time you've ever lied to him.

"Is it scary, in the garden?"

You think about this. "No. I'm never alone. I don't think anything could really hurt me. I always know that I'm going to wake up, after all."

Baker grins. "Maybe I'll meet you for a midnight feast, then. But don't tell your dream friends, okay? I don't want them thinking I'm . . . butting in or something."

The quiet blooms like the daisies in the grass beside you. The sun-drenched nylon of the book bag is warm against your skin. Baker's thigh is solid beside yours. He passes you the bracelet. You take it wordlessly, slide it onto your wrist.

You say, "You're special too, you know." Your response feels inadequate. He cannot know how much you mean it.

The Strike

The King stood looking down from his window
at the witches before him.
"We're leaving you," said Cynthia, her voice deep and
unafraid, surrounded by her coven.
"We have eaten the fruit, we are soon to be mothers
and we will not let you steal our babes' freedom too."
He roared, "You think you can revolt, with your plant magic and
your talking trees?"
"Oh, we have power you'll never see,"
replied Cynthia. "When we're united, you don't stand a chance."
His response was only a contemptuous glance.
The King rose in a fury, put his hand on the handle—
but the door was locked and he, imprisoned.
His magic suppressed by the witches' spell,
his gilded palace became a cell.

*

The witches marched to the woods and sheltered within.
The trees shared their magic and knew them as kin,
but one last change must be made before their fresh start—
their men said farewell and prepared to depart.
The prophecy had warned of a son of Persea.
"It could be any of you," so said the Seer,
"who may help the King return to his might."
And so the men left in the night.

Knowledge

For a time, after your talk with Baker, your dreams are permeated with worry. You never remember enough when you wake to warn him against attempting to join you, but memories of your day-lit world remain clear every time you arrive in the garden. You occasionally wonder if you should relay what you and Baker had speculated upon to your nighttime friends. But any mention of Baker's name dies on your tongue and evoking Mrs. Goss's hard-labored flowerbeds in Persea seems . . . wrong somehow. You imagine, also, what Kam and Zella would say if they knew you might have invited a "dangerous" boy into your lush moon-bright haven and find yourself looking over your shoulder. But weeks go by and you don't see him, and after a while you start to relax.

And yet, in the garden, something feels off. A new current in the air aside from the usual electricity. A chill. The pulsating black spot on the horizon seems to ripple wider with every visit. You had asked Zella about it once. Her eyes had grown serious and wary. "We don't talk about that," she had said.

You didn't ask again.

"Don't you get bored?" you ask Zella, one drowsy summer night. The air is thick and scented, the velvet sky a wash of purples and blues and studded with silver. Magic leaps and sparkles between her curls. "Stuck here in the garden, all the time?"

"There is more to Xaymaca than our garden, you know," she says scornfully. "It is not like your city, I am sure, but outside of Persea there are mountains and rivers and villages on the Kingstown estate."

"Will you tell me about it?" you ask, and she looks at you thoughtfully.

"Maybe," she says at last. "But it would be rude to ignore the stars when they are putting on such a show for us."

The summer drags by in your waking world, hours to days to weeks of humid city air and sharp thunderstorms that seem to roll in out of nowhere, but in Persea you are as likely to find the ground crisp and white with frost or snow. The plants in the garden never wither and die. They are evergreen and perpetual in their pinks and purples, and thrum with the magic of life given by the witches who mothered them.

One night, Kam drags a heavy trunk out onto the lawn in front of where you and Zella sit on the grass, before the swing. There is frost on the ground tonight and it sparkles like diamonds in the glossy light from the moon, icing the bushes and tree trunks like shimmering marzipan. The flowers echo the drop in temperature; each petal subtly changes its hue, vivid purples subduing to indigos, scarlets darkening to wine, as though this garden is a song, each element meeting in pitch-perfect harmony. Here, in this place, you can feel the cold but are unbothered by it and this delights you. The sting of icy shards is pleasant against your bare skin. You pity your friends, wrapped against the cold in fleecy pajamas, scarves, and woollen socks.

"Books," says Kam. She flips the fastenings and opens the lid. "Maps. Charts. Scrolls. Zella said you were asking questions about Xaymaca. Well, all the history is here."

The trunk itself would be enough intrigue for one night; it is finely carved and engraved in the same runes and swirls as the botanical definitions on the map. You run your fingertips over the rough surface, the pads of your prints grazing the calloused wood and goosebumps leap to the surface of your skin. You shiver.

"Cold?" Kam asks, but Zella regards you knowingly and runs

her fingers over the runes as you have, and then through her hair. She closes her eyes, breathing deeply, and says, "It is not the cold, but the brush of magic."

Kam unrolls a map, her long, slim fingers tracing the ridges of a mountain range. "That is Carrion Ridge in the far east, a dangerous and barren place. They say the mountains themselves possess the same dark magic as the King. He traveled over those very mountains to get to Kingstown." Her finger trails a line down the mountains to where a castle is marked on the map. "He wasn't a king then at all, just a merchant sailor shipwrecked on the far side of the island. When his ship went down he had the only floating belt and chose to save his riches, not his men. He knew that wherever he went, his riches would buy him more men and more loyalty."

"That's horrible," you say.

"Our people have often whispered that the dark mountains saw this wicked act and recognized him as kin. Some of the mountain's magic seeped into him. As he traveled over the mountains with his bags of treasure, he got lonely. He would talk to himself in his most prized possession, a beautiful golden mirror. And one day, in those strange and dark mountains . . . the mirror began to talk back."

You shudder and Kam grins fiendishly, looking almost unlike herself.

Zella pushes her lightly. "Kam, don't scare her!"

"I'm not scared," you say defiantly. "So the King has magic? What sort?"

"He uses the shadows. He can make them tell him their secrets. And fear. Pure fear. And loneliness and despair." Zella points to the dark spot on the horizon and raises her eyebrows significantly.

You shudder again.

"There is more good magic here than not good," Zella reassures you. "Like the River Mumma. She's a mermaid." She points to a silvery line that cuts through the dark green inked trees, the map's rendition of the very forest where you now sit.

"A *mermaid*?" You are awed, envious. You wish you had a local mermaid.

"Yes. She guards the River Aphra, which runs through the Great Forest not far from here. It is said to be the source of all of Xaymaca's magic, as water is the source of all life. Even the rainbows start there."

Kam says, "Our people say that all things of the water, water spirits and nymphs, fishes and frogs, reeds and weeds, are the River Mumma's children. But you must never look at the River Mumma without her permission. She is very shy and has a terrible temper and if you try to catch her, all of the rivers and streams in Xaymaca will run dry. The fish will die, the willow trees will wither, and our magic will wilt and fade along with it."

You gaze down at the map in wonder, run your fingers over the inked crosses that mark the homes of many magical forest-dwelling creatures, *Here Be Spiders, Here Be Nymphs, Here Be Faeries*. Symbols indicate elevations and glens and there is a list written in a swirling strange ancient language that you can only assume must be a guide to Xaymaca's plant life because of the carefully drawn images beside it.

Zella passes you a glass jar with thick, creamy liquid inside. It is a very pale green, almost white, and when you open it a warm, familiar scent hits your nostrils.

"I know this," you say. Even in your dream you can recall strong fingers kneading your scalp. "Val puts it on my hair. Avocado oil. Maybe that's why I have these dreams."

Kam turns to look at you, her eyebrows raised, faint amusement glimmering on her face. "You still think we are in your dreams? That we are not real?"

"No, I . . ." You swallow again. "Why can't you be in my dreams *and* real?"

41

Kam snorts. "We are not inventions of your imagination. Your imagination is not that good."

To change the subject, you turn to Zella, who is taking a book out of the trunk. It is heavy and leathered and ancient looking. The cover is embossed in that same gold swirling script.

"What is this language?" you ask.

"It is Ancient Persean. The old tongue of our people," Zella explains. "This book contains all of our history, the story of where we came from."

"Can you read it to me?"

"I was going to, silly," says Zella, grinning. "We're hoping that there might be something in the stories that can help with *that*." She jerks her head at the swirling blackness on the horizon, that they won't speak of. You take the opportunity to find out more.

"What is it?"

They look at each other. Eventually Zella says, in hushed tones, "It is what is left of the King's evil, high above his tower to the east. He was imprisoned at the same time that our people freed themselves. At first, our mothers say, it was a small, dark cloud. But it gets stronger every day. We can't ignore it anymore, even if our mothers want to."

You feel suddenly vulnerable, standing there in the dark, barefoot, in your *Avatar: The Last Airbender* pajamas.

"You think it might be dangerous?"

"We know the King was dangerous," said Zella firmly. "It stands to reason he still is."

"But if there is something in that book that could help, wouldn't your mothers have found it already?"

"Our mothers are very brave and very strong," says Kam, "but they fought to be free, and now they want to think the battle is over."

"But you two, you think they're wrong?"

Kam and Zella exchange a glance and Zella answers. "Grown-ups do not always know best. Ah! I've found it. This is the story of our ancestors—the first, most powerful witch, who the King subdued."

You and Kam gather round as Zella lies the book flat on the frost-hardened ground, smooths out the pages, and begins to read:

The First Fairy Tale

Once, on this land, bush fire burned,
and from it rose the First Witches,
who gave the land its name—
Xaymaca.
And it became an abundant, fruitful place.
The first two of our kind, two powerful lovers,
bore fruit and together did Persea discover,
a family, a coven without crowns or thrones,
and so the sun seeped into our flesh and our bones,
our hair. We, like flowers in a dark room,
grew towards the light. Until, one day,
after the earth's longest summer,
a rich merchant came.
He found the land and liked it,
except for the strange wild magic,
decided the world is better if everything is the same,
so he asked his mirror how he might control it and the
     mirror gave him a name.
He spoke it, the name of their most powerful witch,
in his mouth it twisted and mangled,
and from Persea, the merchant wrangled
control of the land.
He shaved their hair
to remain young and fair,

used each strand in a mixture,
a powerful elixir.
The most powerful witch perished,
her name lost to history,
and Persean freedom became a mystery,
as witches waited centuries long,
for another witch to become as strong.
So the merchant called himself King,
tried to silence the witches, but yet they could sing,

Swing low,
Sweet Chariot,
Coming forth to carry me home.
Swing low,
Sweet Chariot,
Coming forth to carry me home.

I WANT TO BE
A MERMAID

The thin wispy July clouds and the prospect of occasional rain are blasted by an inferno of August heat as summer rolls on. The mercury rises and so do the vibes, the familiar packed high street around Val's salon thrumming with activity, teeming with life. Everywhere you go, every footstep that beats the worn, littered pavement, every word in a language you don't understand sings with the song of summer.

In the day, the various vendors stand outside their stores: Dr. Pillai, paused outside the halal butcher's bantering with Mr. Patel, who is leaning outside his grocer's, pouring bright red and yellow Scotch Bonnets into brown paper bags, a pound a bag. A frailer child might have balked at the sight of all that meat hanging upside down, raw pink and white flesh, might have blanched at the tang from the fishmonger's. But you are not frail. You are of this messy imperfection. You pound the streets with Baker, dodging tumbleweave blowing in the pedestrianized parts of the road, causing mischief in your official capacity as patrons of small businesses, and chatting to Giles, the old boy with no home.

Mum and Val fight about Giles sometimes. Val gets him money from the ATM, which makes Mum cross. "Val, really, who knows what he'll spend that on?!"

You didn't know what she meant—what might Giles spend it on?

But Val had just kissed her teeth and said, "Me nuh care if the ol' boy craves a bit a' oblivion. An' sure a rum jacket is better for the col' than anyt'ing I could buy him."

Giles always gives you small presents, brings them round the salon and leaves them with Val if you're at school—little plastic rings or socks patterned with fairies. He gave Baker a miniature wooden brush and comb set after you had told him how good Baker was getting at braiding, how fast he was learning from his mum. Baker had been chin-lowered, all bashful delight, and proudly displayed them on a shelf at the salon later that day.

"Does old Giles give you many things?" Val had asked. You and Baker had nodded and she had smiled a little sadly.

You showed her the little bracelet of pink, blue, and purple beads that he'd given you earlier that week. She took both your hands and looked into your faces and said, her accent more pronounced in her solemnity, "These t'ings may naht seem like much. But from a man who has so little, they are treasure. So treasure t'em."

If you're not at Val's, you're with Mum at the rec center. You love your dance classes, especially ballet, but you don't love performing in front of an audience. It is Saffy who is the extrovert; you are most content in your lessons when no one is really watching, thrive off the *one-two-three, first-second-third* position repetition.

One balmy August afternoon, the cool breeze a gentle kiss on your sticky face, you stand in your leotard at the center waiting for Baker. Mum is in management meetings all afternoon and doesn't want to leave the three of you in her office because, "Who knows what trouble you'll cause!" Last time, you and Baker had persuaded the reception staff to let you sit with them behind the giant desk in the lobby. They had given you the blue uniform shirts and name badges and let you answer the phones. Saffy had loved the opportunity to use her "grown-up" voice and luckily the customers had all found the sight of you in your oversized uniforms hilarious, but Mum wasn't pleased. "It's not a joke," she had said. "You'll distract the staff." She told you to wait here until Val came at three.

Baker is out first, strut-swaggering alongside his friends from under-thirteens boxing, all mock-jabbing and laughing at each other.

"Did you see my right hook?"

"Yeah, it weak, man, it was weak!"

"Well, did you see how I nearly clocked Baker in the face?"

"Nah, man, it's hard to miss that fat forehead!"

Baker kisses his teeth, laughing. "None of you mans will ever even lay a finger on my fine-ass face!"

"He thinks he's so dope!"

"Who says you have a fine face?"

"Bet it was his mum!"

"Nah, it was YOUR mum!" Baker retorts loudly to a chorus of hype, mock-horror, more laughter.

You observe quietly from your corner next to the door, against the wall. He hasn't seen you yet and this is fine. You like seeing him like this, it is unfamiliar in a pleasant way. With you he is someone different, not entirely, but there is less boyish bravado, something special and separate. With you, he is Baker of the braids, whose nimble fingers dance along a doll's head or a flowerbed and you suspect his love of hair and hydrangeas is something his boxing boys don't know. You would never tell them. You will always keep Baker's secrets.

The boy on the receiving end of the "your mum" line spies you then and, grinning wickedly, crows, "Yo, Baker, ain't that your girlfriend?"

Baker's eyes meet yours and you see him, caught between two versions of himself. So you save him. You thrust your chin and cock your head, impersonating Saffy at her sassiest, "He wishes I was his girlfriend!" and the boys crow with laughter and shake your hand, bump your fist. You have passed the test.

Baker's eyes dance as he falls into step beside you, free in their approval to sling an arm around your shoulders. They're still heckling him, as the two of you proceed round the side of the building together, heading to the side exit where Saffy's arts-and-crafts class lets out. But then you hear, "Nah, she's chill, she's chill," from the group at large and feel a pooling of warmth in your stomach that you've never felt before.

You like it, you realize. This new kind of attention.

"Sorry 'bout them." Baker smiles, as you turn the corner and head to the side entrance of the rec center where the kids' clubs are. "They think all girl friends are *girlfriends*, you get me?"

"I didn't mind," you say. You think it wouldn't be so bad, being Baker's girlfriend. Your face grows warm.

The hubbub from the assembled group in front of the side entrance drifts over to you. A few hundred paces further down the side alley, you can see Val, emerging from the blue gate that connects the path to the rec center to one of the paths from the park behind it. She is running, which isn't like Val. She can see something you can't. You can hear someone screaming and you realize it is Saffy.

Val is now sprinting at top speed and, after a stricken look at Baker, you follow. You're small but fast and you reach the group before Val does, just as Saffy launches herself at another little girl, tackling her to the ground. Saffy is wearing a wig that you haven't seen before. It's somewhere between strawberry blonde and ginger, long and slightly matted. It's much too large for Saffy, swallowing her appley cheeks and cute little snub nose and her large, round eyes, which, right now, are shining headlights of fury.

The wig sits askew and is dripping, down the left side, with bright green paint. She flies at the girl who, though still small, is definitely bigger than Saffy. Staff and children alike stare, shocked but passive, holding up their hands to protect themselves from the shards of shamrock-green staining their T-shirts.

You stride into the fray, hauling your sister off the other girl and spinning her round to face you. Val and Baker stop behind you, panting, seconds later. "Saffy! What are you doing? What's going on? Mum said no fighting!"

Her tiny face is smudged with green paint, reddish hair sticking to her cheeks. She has a scratch under her eye. You watch the red blood mix with the green and you think, absurdly, of Christmas. She looks so angry while also being so small, that, for a fraction of a second, you want to laugh. But the urge quickly dies as Saffy's screwed-up glare crumples. Beat. A suspended silence before the howl of sound and then she is wailing in your arms.

"I . . . WANTED . . . TO . . . BE . . . A . . . MERMAID." She is wracked with such bone-shaking sobs that she struggles to get her words out. "BUT SHE"—she flings a devastated finger at the girl, still lying crumpled on the floor—"SHE . . . SAID . . . BLACK . . . GIRLS . . . CAN'T . . . BE . . . MERMAIIIIIIIIDSSSS!"

The last world is a howl of despair and rage and you feel the sounds reverberate in your chest, in your bones, in your core. Val turns on the staff member, a teenage girl, who hustles her quickly into the lobby. You catch phrases like "anti-discrimination policy" and "duty of care" all in the "Queen's English" voice Val uses when she means business, but can barely hear them over the roaring in your ears. You fish a tissue out of your bag and dab at the cut on Saffy's cheek. It is shallow and has stopped bleeding, but the wobbling of her bottom lip beneath her determined fierceness breaks your heart and you stand, take her hand, Baker flanking you both.

"Listen to me," you say to the girl on the floor. Your voice is low and you are satisfied by the sight of her pale face going even paler. "I don't know what it's like at other places you've been. But people who say things like what you said, don't fit in here." You step towards her. "Touch my sister again, throw paint at her again, and I will fucking throw hands, all right."

You think it might be the first time you've ever sworn out loud. The effect is impressive. The surrounding kids go deathly quiet. This girl, this disdainful stranger whose face you would forget almost immediately, had not picked on someone her own size. She had chosen your little sister, and even the sight of the bruise Saffy has given her blossoming like a dark, ugly poppy on her cheekbone is not quite satisfying enough.

You look down at Saffy, still paint-smudged, blood-smeared but now grinning up at you. You tug her hand and the two of you turn away, Baker at your side.

"Come on," you say. "Let's go to the salon. Val can catch up."

Saffy trots at your side. "Mummy will be angry, won't she?"

You know what she's worrying about. What if Saffy gets kicked out of arts club for fighting? What if Mum gets into trouble with work? What if she loses her job?

"No." You are firm in your reassurance. "She'll understand. It wasn't your fault at all, Saffy-baby."

She smiles through her tears at the old nickname.

"Your ma basically runs that place." Baker is confident. "Our rec center, it's not like others, man." He grins. "This is our turf, innit?"

You both grin back. "Yeah! It's our turf!" you say in unison. "Our turf, ours."

*

Val catches up with you just before you turn the final corner into the high street. You're sucking on blue ice pops Mrs. Goss gave you. Baker is regaling Saffy with stories of his great boxing victories.

"So then I went *pow pow pow*, and he ducked like *that*."

"Yeah, like that?"

"Yeah, right, Saffy, and then I went *pow smack* like *this*!"

"Like *this*?"

"Yeah, perfect. Wow, Saffy, thassa *sick* uppercut right there!"

You hear a low laugh behind you and Val is there.

"Was everything okay?" you ask. "Mum's not going to get in trouble, is she?"

"Oh, no." Val smiles. "I made it clear it wasn't Saffy who was at fault." She scoops Saffy up. "Saffy, you are not in trouble. But in future, if you punch people, you probably will be. This place"—she gestures around her—"and the rec center, the people there, they're your community, but not everywhere is. So you haffa be careful, y'un'erstand?"

Saffy nods solemnly. Then says, "What's community?"

Val thinks, then says, "Like a family. But you're not related by blood or name. You're related by place and time an' a . . . a sorta understanding of each other because you share a lickle slice of the world."

Beat. The words hang. You and Baker look at each other. You sit in your shared little slice of the world.

Saffy nods again. "Okay, Val. I promise I won't punch anyone outside of the community." You all laugh then and Val says, "Good. And that girl was wrong, ya knuh?" She squeezes Saffy once more before letting her go. "Black girls *can* be mermaids."

Saffy sighs. "I don't know, Val. None of the ones I see on TV or in my books are."

"Is that why you were wearing that wig, Saffy?" you ask.

She nods.

"Well, you're just not looking in the right places," Val says. "Remember my story about the witch?"

"The witch who ran away from the evil wizard?"

"Exactly! See, it's a mermaid who tells the witch where to run to. And actually"—she lifts the matted now green-and-ginger wig off Saffy's head—"she has green hair, not red." She drops the wig into a bin.

You are outside the salon now. Val unlocks the door. "How about this, Saffy? I tell you this story I know about a mermaid, and if you t'inks it's as good as the stories you've read or the ones you've seen on TV, I'll help you dye a wig mermaid color."

"Yes, please!"

The four of you head into the salon, unpack, and settle. Val puts the kettle on, takes warm water to a damp cloth, and starts gently sponging down Saffy's face, neck, hands. You and Baker open juice boxes and sink into the worn leather sofas at the front of the shop, tired and ready. You love Val's stories. Her lilting voice is the soundtrack to your comfort, to the restful place you drift to before dreaming.

Val wrings out the cloth. Takes a sip of her tea. Begins: "She is called the River Mumma."

Where our Great Forest lies,
a river quietly burbles by.
Willows drape the earth and skies,
weeping and with magic cry,
as dawns the sun of summer.
Underwater, over stones,
the land's power will pulse on loam,
fishes swim, nymphs they roam,
all things return to the watery home
     Of the River Mumma.

She guards the magic of the land,
she protects its treasures from violent hands,
all our fears she understands.
She watches all from the sands
and basks in heat of summer.
She is neither foe nor friend,
you will find her at the rainbow's end.
The land's source she must defend
while mortality she must transcend.
     Beware the River Mumma.

Many foolish men have tried,
have ignored the mermaid's wrath and pride,
have pulled and hauled against the tide,
when on hot days her beauty spied,
at the surface in the summer.

But they have suffered for their greed,
of my warning they did not heed,
and though they beg, though they plead,
down into the river they are heaved
    By the River Mumma.

Her skin is dark, her hair is green,
her eyes are gray and silver gleam,
but if you see her, hear her scream,
darkness descends, a watery dream,
and death forgets the summer.
Do not catch her, do not try,
the earth will brown, the river will dry,
her children, all the fish, will die,
she is older than the sea and sky.
    Respect the River Mumma.

After the Strike

Once upon a time,
the King had maintained order rigid and neat,
hedges clipped into angles on every street,
men in trousers,
women in dresses,
locs slicked and shiny,
hanging in his preferred golden tresses.
Each person slick, coiffed, groomed,
not a smudge on a face.
Each person perfumed,
not a leaf out of place.
All shops bore his sigil,
and so the King's magic had kept silent vigil.
But after the Strike,
after the ripening,
what the King saw unfolding below
was frightening;
for even those of the upper class,
loyal to the King trapped in his tower,
noticed how tall grew the trees and the grass,
saw the swift, bright bloom of every flower.
And though those minor nobles
still took the tithes monthly demanded,
soon those without magic
would not be commanded.
The King was still handsome but

without the witches' magic
his split ends frayed,
he sickened and decayed.
He looked in his mirror,
watched as his hair grayed.
But the King knew he was not forsaken,
the witch's name would once more be taken.
Help would come from the Weaver's son,
Persea would once more be won,
and so a dark cloud of his rage he cast,
a warning that this stalemate would not last.

Coven

Zella stands before you, eyes closed, focusing. A golden halo of light encircles her thick, softly curling hair, which crackles and dances with energy.

You yawn. "Saffy kept me up," you tell her. "She wanted to come into my bed."

Zella's eyes are kind. "Well, she loves you. It is a powerful thing, a sister's love."

As she speaks, her hair seems to expand, as though it has released a breath, shooting tendrils of gold light into the sky. The light becomes suspended there, imitating the shape of her hair and holding it, like a golden crown.

A golden butterfly flutters into view. It flickers and suddenly there are two gold butterflies, and then three and then four until a flock of them are dancing around her head, glistening like a coronet in the glow of her magic.

"Amazing," you breathe.

Zella sighs, opens her eyes and looks up at the gold light, the dancing butterflies. "It is a pretty trick, I suppose. But I cannot imagine that butterflies will help me against the dark arts of the King."

You can't help agreeing. In the nights and weeks that had followed your reading of Persea's history, you, Zella, and Kam had spent much time speculating about what the King was up to in his tower. You settle on a few key details.

"He knows our hair is powerful," Zella says. "He knows that out of all the witches, I am probably the most powerful. Like the first witch." She looks smug, and Kam rolls her eyes. "I am! Everyone knows it. But he cannot control me. And when I turn sixteen and come into my full power, I'll make sure he never bothers my family ever again."

"When you turn sixteen?"

Zella nods, "You think this is impressive?" She points at her glittering Afro, shining a bit brighter every day. "You wait until our sixteenth birthday, on the Sankofa. Then you will *really* see what I can do."

Her hair blazes like her eyes and you believe her.

"What is the Sankofa?" you are curious, sounding the syllables out on your tongue.

"It is our special holiday." Kam is basically an encyclopedia of Persean culture. "We celebrate our magic and thank the great goddess Yaa and honor the land as the year begins to change."

Zella's eyes gleam. "It is a particularly witchy time."

Halloween, you think with a thrill of the familiar.

"But what if he finds out your name before then? What if his shadows hear and whisper it to him?"

Kam snorts. "You don't think that Kam and Zella are our true names, do you?"

"Oh. Aren't they? Well . . . what are they? Your true names?"

Kam looks at you blankly. "Obviously we cannot say."

Zella reaches for your hand, squeezes it as she dimples at you. "You will know when it is safe to know, when the time is right."

Silence.

Zella leans back into the dark cobalt of the night, running her fingers through the grass beneath her outstretched palms. She is quiet for a while.

"The King"—she, as usual, whispers the word—"is getting stronger. We do not know how or why or why now. But he is. And he will stop at nothing to rule the land once more. To steal the magic from our hair and be young and beautiful again." She looks towards the looming darkness on the horizon. "If there is something I can do to prepare myself, to prepare our people, then I must do it."

"How?" you ask, awed.

She smiles. "Practice. Because butterflies won't be enough."

*

You work your way through the books in the chest over the weeks and months that follow. Zella's hair is an expanding force, and she learns to manifest a hundred tiny jewel-bright winged things, shimmering vivid flowers, life itself beams radiant from her Afro.

Kam struggles. Occasionally, she will touch a petal and murmur something about the land that its seeds had drifted from, sharing those strange flashes of origin granted by her root magic.

"Do you think she's scared to try?" you ask Zella one night, as you watch Kam, shoulders hunched, as she whispers to the roots of an ebony sapling, ripped, splintered, and felled in a wild Xaymacan storm. Occasionally the roots quiver beneath Kam's trembling palm, but that is all.

Zella thinks for a moment. "You see that tree behind us?" she says at last. You turn and look. It has thick, leathery leaves and creamy white flowers. "It's the avocado tree." Zella's voice is quieter still. "Remember I told you that our mothers stole a pear from the tree in the King's garden?"

"Yeah." You nod. "They ate it and fed it to the other Persean witches and it made them strong enough to break free of the King and take back their magic."

"Exactly. Well, when they left, they took one single fruit with them—and using its seed they planted that tree."

"Just one fruit? I'd have stuffed my pockets if it were me!"

Zella raises her eyebrows and for a moment looks exactly like Kam. "You still know so little of this world," she says. "It is like the child, given three wishes by the faerie, wishing for three more wishes. Our goddess Yaa does not bless the greedy. One fruit was enough."

You think for a moment. "Maybe if Kam used her root magic on that tree, we could learn more about what the King is planning."

"She's too nervous to try."

You walk over to Kam. "You know, Kam, my sister Saffy, she's only five but she's never ever nervous or afraid. And one time, I asked her why, and she said she just doesn't think about what she's doing very much. So . . . so maybe you should . . . should think less."

Your voice tails off as Kam turns, slowly, so slowly, eyes meeting yours with a flat glare, as empty of warmth as it is full of a tar black resentment.

"I do not need a five-year-old's advice. Bring your *own* sister next time if you want someone to boss around. You understand nothing!"

You blink. This is hostile, even for Kam. "I understand some things!" you say. "Your world is not so different from mine. We have fear and danger and wicked kings and queens. We even have some of the same stories. My hairdresser, Val, she told me a story about the River Mumma too!"

The world around you seems to ripple at this, as though a rose-gold-touched breeze brushes the grass, the air, kisses your skin, ruffles Zella's hair. It might just be a trick of your eyes, but for the briefest moment Zella's halo seems tinged with a pinkish red. The light fizzles and dies. Zella's hair is its normal lush dark brown once more.

Kam looks unsettled—scared, even. "How can your hairdresser know of our River Mumma? Does she know of our coven?"

You laugh. "You really call yourselves a coven?"

"What else would we be?" Zella is proud, defiant. "A group of witches. Magic singing in harmony like our voices."

Kam sighs. "Not always in harmony. Some of the witches don't like our mothers. Or they don't trust them. But they have to follow them because they are the most powerful."

"And because the avo-pear tree only ripened for them." Zella puffs out her chest importantly. "For us."

You have met Kam and Zella's mothers, but from a distance. You can see them now, in the kitchen of the house that overlooks the garden. In many ways the house is something out of one of the fairy tale books you used to read Saffy: moderate-sized with a thatched roof with enough windows to indicate four upstairs rooms and one wide, open downstairs room. Creepers and climbers adorn the outside so as to turn the painted white green, but reach and spin without the help of a trellis. As though the house is a living thing, as though it contains life itself, with flowers and herbs seeming to bloom out of its core. In the years you have been coming to this garden, you have peered inside often enough to make out the solid, engraved wooden staircase that twists out of the main room to the upper landing, the piles of books, the careful clutter that seems never to increase or decrease. A family's home, yes, but radiating some internal light every bit as warming as it is fierce, protective. As though the house itself is a member of the family it shelters.

You've never been invited inside.

Both women know you are here—they have caught sight of you a few times, sitting in their garden in your pajamas, but they never speak to you, and only wave and smile polite hellos. "Kam? Don't your mums think it's strange? Me just appearing like this, in their garden at night?"

"They are witches," Kam had explained patiently. "They have seen much stranger things. Besides, they think you're here for a reason. Magic is not exact but—"

"—it is always intentional," you had finished solemnly.

Standing now, watching the two women inside, talking by a roaring fire, it is hard to imagine anything being beyond their power. The one who looks most like Kam is the taller, with walnut-bronze skin half-lit by the glow of the flames, long hair twisted into thick dreadlocks and hanging heavy to her waist. Maybe it is the quick-step flicker of light in her eyes, but she pulsates with an innate power. Someone to be feared and loved passionately. Dressed in something you might have found in one of those fairy tales, but you might also have seen in one of your mum's magazines. A loose, pale-pink gown, that comes in slightly at the waist, emphasizes her elegant, willowy frame.

Next to her, her wife is warm darkness, almost in shadow, but radiates a quiet presence, a subtle force. She is Zella but older and softer with hair as tall and curling as her daughter's but braided into an elaborate crown atop her head. Her skin is brown-gold mahogany, she is slighter, softer but more solid than her partner, with lightness to her gaze that makes you think of someone who laughs readily and often. Her simple blue shirt hangs past her knees over thick woollen leggings, to protect them against the night's chill. It is mostly warm here, but you've known seasons to change in a day or last a year. You can't count how many times you've watched the two of them together. Through this window. Watched their every touch and smile and, at ten years old, you begin to wonder if your own mother is ever lonely. Wonder if you'll ever smile at anyone like that. For some reason, you think of Baker.

"Why doesn't the coven trust your parents?" you ask.

"Mama says that when she was young she was known as Amos," Zella is saying now, and you tear your eyes away from the pair in the kitchen to focus on what she is saying. "Amos the boy. But even witches make mistakes. Mum says that who we are is more than just the body we are given at birth. Mama said she always knew she was not a boy. When she was sixteen, and gained her full power, she was able to use creation magic to show everyone the powerful witch she would become. Then everyone started calling her Ama and she was much happier."

"So that is why some do not like her?"

"Yes," says Kam. "The prophecy said that a boy whose mama was a witch would hurt us all, remember. And if boys are bad omens and Mama was thought of as a boy once—well, some do not like that."

You lapse into a thoughtful silence. Memories surface. You think about the kids at school who say mean things sometimes, the girl at the rec center. "It sounds like they were jealous of your mum's power. And looking for a reason to be unkind."

"I think so too," Zella agrees solemnly. "It's not all the witches. Most are not so short-sighted. But there are a few. And they are very noisy. We are better when we are united."

She looks towards the horizon and you follow her eyes. To the roiling blackness on the horizon. A king, growing in strength.

"I do not like it," Kam whispers. "The winds are changing."

Her voice is fading as the light of day drags you away from her. You feel your corporeal body making a conscious effort to stay asleep, to squeeze your eyes tight shut, to not leave them in their worry.

"Let's sing the Brown girl song!" you cry and they smile at you.

> *There's a Brown girl in the ring*
> *Tralalalala*
> *There's a Brown girl in the ring*
> *Tralalalalala . . .*

Their voices fade and you feel light above you but you sing along, hoping your words are carried back down to them as you return to reality.

The Weaver's Son

At the heart of the forest Ama found her sister,
the Weaver.
She rushed to embrace her,
hugged her, kissed her,
cried, "Where have you been?
Have you heard? We are free!"
Her sister replied, "Oh, the things I've seen,
and look who I have here with me!"
In her arms, her babe who waited and cried,
a knavish stranger's bastard, the Weaver lied
to the witches.
The prophecy's warning was clear,
while men remained in Persea,
the witches had cause for fear.
But Ama and Cynthia,
the most full of the pear's power,
decided that the King, locked in his tower,
would not look for a babe,
still too small to be by the dark blighted.
They would keep him safe until then
and delight, a family united,
for babies in Persea were a rarity
and now, at once, it seemed there'd be three.
Only Yvane the Seer felt a tremor of unease,
as though she could smell on the breeze,

a dark cloud shifting, a malevolent humming,
as the witches danced and sang of their winning,
Yvane could see a storm was coming,
could sense this end was just the beginning.

I WANT TO BE
A PRINCESS

Saffy is screaming. Properly screaming. She is rage-paralysis gasping between sobs and then raw-throat yelling her defiance as you and Mum stand by the door, waiting it out.

Mum wants to take you both back-to-school shopping today with Val and Baker.

You avoid her gaze, these days. There are many things your mother misses, you realize. She will always see a scraped knee, a torn shirt, a spelling mistake. She is polished, beautiful. Her nails are always manicured, her trainers are always shiny and white, she always smells of fresh laundry. When she's not wearing a jacket with trousers and a skirt, she is in casual two piece sets, matching athleisure, pastels. She has never given you a permission slip late or forgotten to pack your PE kit. Your packed lunch is the mirror image of the balanced diet poster on your classroom wall.

But, still, she misses things. Misses the way you awaken rested but restless. Misses the pattern in your reading habits—faeries and witches. Misses the glow every time you so much as hear Baker's name. It is probably unfair of you to define her as what she is not. She's your mum and you love her. You've just realized that perhaps she is a person all of her own.

Your sister shows no sign of stopping the tantrum—if anything she is building to a sharp crescendo. She is face down at the top of the stairs, the contents of her dress-up box strewn around her.

"I . . . WON'T . . . TAKE . . . IT . . . OFF!"

The fight had begun nearly forty minutes earlier when Mum, hurrying the two of you to get dressed, had ordered Saffy out of the giant pink tulle princess dress and ringleted golden wig.

"Saffy-baby." Your mum is dry and patient. "You cannot wear that dress out shopping. It's impractical. It's too big and will drag on the ground and get dirty. And that wig was your sister's and probably hasn't been washed since she was your age. Come on now. Stop with this silliness."

This only enrages Saffy further and she yells even louder, "I . . . WANT . . . TO . . . BE . . . A . . . PRINCESS!"

Mum rolls her eyes and looks to you appealingly. You sigh and put down the book on magical plants you've been hiding behind. Your stomach hurts. You wish Mum would just give in and let Saffy wear the stupid dress. What does it really matter? You wonder if your mum would be so steadfast were Saffy to have insisted on wearing her doctor's costume, or her firefighter's.

"Saffy." Your tone is placating. "You look so cool, but can you imagine what it'll be like going round the shops in that dress? Everyone will be bowing and curtseying to you and we'll never get our shopping done!"

You feel Mum's eyes roll behind you, but Saffy's heaving hysteria has already quieted as she follows your logic. It stops altogether when you say, "What if you just wear the wig?"

Mum tenses, reluctant shifting of her weight, but you know she'll agree. It was she, after all, who taught you the meaning of compromise.

"Okay. Jus' the wig." Saffy hiccups, and retreats into her room to change.

*

Twenty minutes later you're strapped into the back of Mum's car. The high street glides by as you drift in stop-start traffic. Mum is very proud of her car. It's shiny and silver, but other than that you're not sure what the fuss is all about. You pass Val's salon, closed for the afternoon. You take in the rest of the street, so familiar to you and the comfort of it eases your motion sickness.

You can see your GP, Dr. Pillai, going into Mr. Patel's grocer's, reaching out to flip through the magazine rack. A few doors down, Miss Annie, whose Caribbean takeaway boasts the best bulla cake your grandma swears she's tasted outside of Jamaica, is flirting with Mr. Feeney, the landlord of the Irish pub on the corner. Mum honks her horn and they wave at you. Miss Annie is big-breasted and big-bottomed and Mr. Feeney is big-bearded and big-bellied and they have been flirting like this for years.

"I heard Mr. Feeney cooks all the food at the pub hisself," Baker had whispered to you once, as you waited for Val. She'd gone into the thrift store for a browse and gossip with Ife, the sharp-eyed Nigerian woman who ran it.

"So?" you'd replied.

"Soooo," Baker said archly, wiggling his eyebrows suggestively, while jerking his chin towards where Mr. Feeney stood outside Miss Annie's shop, taking several greaseproof paper bags from her. "If he's such a good cook, why does he go to Miss Annie's for breakfast, lunch, and dinner?"

You had caught his meaning then, and giggled. You watched as Mr. Feeney turned as red as his hair and backed away from Miss Annie. Miss Annie hadn't smiled, but her eyes sparkled as she sashayed back inside, throwing a coy glance over her shoulder. Baker's chuckles turned into outright cackles as you imitated Miss Annie, hand on hip, bum wiggling, down the street in front of him.

You liked making Baker laugh. Even as Miss Annie and Mr. Feeney realized, at the same moment, that they had an audience, and had chased you back down the street, yelling in lilting, accented English and admonishing Val through Ife's window for permitting such disrespect, you and Baker had laughed yourselves dizzy.

Your stomach tightens again with that unfamiliar pain.

You pass the community garden. Mrs. Goss runs it and many afternoons you and Baker have plagued her, Baker in particular asking endless questions about how to sow seeds and identify plant species, until his rows of tulips and foxgloves were almost as neat as the cane rows Val has been teaching him to do on a hairdresser's doll head.

You would mostly sit with Giles on these occasions, the homeless man who, in the warm summer months, sleeps on a bench in the garden and washes in the small backroom that Mrs. Goss left him keys to. He would help Mrs. Goss with the heavy lifting and show you where a finch had built its nest among the hedges or point out where foxes had burrowed beneath the fences to make their dens.

"What about your den, Giles? Where do you sleep?" you had asked him.

"I'm like a fox, small girl." He had smiled a gap-toothed smile at you. "I make my den anywhere!"

The traffic lights at the end of the high street are a speck in Mum's mirror now. She turns the corner and it's gone. Saffy is speaking along to the audiobook, propped up in her booster seat. The behemoth of the old shopping center looms ahead of you, stark grubby white against the bright-blue sky.

There's a billboard outside, showing a caterpillar fighting free of its membranous cell and stretching its wings for the sky, while the copy stamped across the bottom reads: *New School Year! New School You!*

You think of shimmering butterflies in the dark. You glance back at the flickering ad, the dim image of a blue butterfly now bigger than Mum's car. You are grasped by a fervent desire to pull those gossamer strands back around you. To robe yourself in a permanent childhood. To always be a caterpillar.

The Weaver's Departure

Half a dozen years passed
and the witches lived in peace.
Deep in the forest's heart,
they felt the King's power decrease.
But the Witch-Weaver's son,
a boy true and kind,
showed magic precocious,
and his coven, gripped by fear ferocious,
considered it essential
that he and his mother
should leave Persea, for the common good.
So the Weaver sought out a powerful force,
who dwelled in the forest by a powerful source,
the River Mumma, who told her where to run,
to keep the King from her son.
She took with her very little,
for she did not need very much,
but most prized of all—a comb and a brush,
for hair always softened under her magic touch.
And so she took her son that night,
stowed away her sadness and fright
as across the ocean her course was set,
she felt her boy and her family fast forget,
began to sing, began to cry,
the song of her sisters as she waved them goodbye.

Power Nap

You close your eyes in the car. The steady hum of the engine is the only lullaby you've ever known. Saffy is snoring quietly. All is peaceful. All is warm and comfortable. The sun caresses your face through the window of the passenger seat. As you float there, just underneath the surface of your consciousness, you think you can hear yelling. You strain your ears and sink deeper; yes, yelling, and, underneath the yelling, the quiet calling of your name.

Your name.

You've never visited Persea in the daytime before. But they have called you and so you have come.

You are back in the garden. The same garden you've been coming to for years. But the white-gold light of day dazzles you and you look around at your surroundings. At night the garden is wondrous, a dreamscape that you could never have imagined. In the day it is paradise. You think now of Eden as you did on that first night, of a holy land in a child's picture book, of the first garden that belonged to the first people, and all the people who would come after.

The sky is a rich cerulean and the green of the grass matches the emerald of the parakeets that sing joyfully, soaring above you. And the flowers! At night they are lush creatures of the dark, but in the day they are great shining jewels, rich amethyst buds shaped like peonies but with petals that sharpen to a fine point; clusters of ruby and amber gathered in the hedges as though they've been mined or stolen from the crown of some queen and left there, for you to marvel at. You take a step towards them, move, hand outstretched, to graze a petal with your fingertips, but halt as your name is called again.

You see Zella and Kam then, hunched against the back wall of the cottage, knees tucked beneath them. You run over, marveling as you do so at the new warmth of the sun, this strange twenty-four-carat golden sun, on your bare skin.

"What's going on? Did you call?"

Kam nods and Zella says, "Yes. Were you asleep? We could see you drifting here but we were not *actually* sure."

"I'm napping in the car, I probably won't be here long—" You're cut off by the holler of raised voices inside. "What's going on?" you ask again.

You survey their tight little faces, brows clenched and furrowed. In all your years of friendship you've never seen them so anxious, so fearful, and you glance reflexively towards that place in the east. In the day, set against the bright lightness and the smells of tropical sunshine, the blossoming cloud is even more menacing.

Zella clasps your hand in hers and pulls you to a crouching position between her and her sister. There are thuds from inside the cottage and the very earth beneath you seems to shudder. The ground is hot against your bare feet, the air ripples in the heat.

"They are fighting," she murmurs, jerking her head upwards, towards the window. "Our mothers never fight."

You risk a quick glance into the kitchen before they tug you back down. Your view into the kitchen through the window is obscured by dense jungle, a thicket of vine leaves, a wild and angry imitation of the forest around you.

"What's with all the trees?"

"It's what happens when they lose their temper," Kam explains in a low voice. "It's why we live on the edge of the village, just in case." You sneak a glance again, awed. All that life. Contained, but barely.

"What are they arguing about?" you whisper.

71

"It started a little while ago," Zella explains. "They sent us to the village center for cloth. Kam and I grow so fast Mum is having to make extra dresses."

You realize this is the first time you've seen them wearing anything other than pajamas. Zella is wearing a sundress, in a soft, lilac cotton, scattered with embroidered white flowers. Kam is in a short-sleeved tunic of baby blue with narrow green stripes, flecked with shimmering silver thread. Her green three-quarter length pedal pushers stop halfway down her calves.

"But then the earth started to heat and shake and we knew something was very wrong." Kam's eyes are grave. "They never fight," she says again.

Sweat is beading on your forehead, running down your spine and pooling in the small of your back. Voices are raised inside. The windows of the cottage seem to shriek and shimmer, the inside a greenhouse as the climbers and branches begin to force their way out of the cracks in the plaster and the walls. Then a terrible groaning sound that reverberates your bones. Kam covers her ears and Zella shrieks and flings herself to the ground; the world erupts. The enormous kitchen windowpane shatters. Glass rains down on the three of you and the ground cracks, shudders, cracks again; the branches reach from the window for the sky. Birds' nests appear, the clusters of twigs seeming to morph out of the wood, and then the birds themselves, with feathers of jewel tones fluttering and tweeting into being, before fleeing the wreckage. Squirrels emerge, bees, beetles, and bugs, as well as tiny flocks of woodland creatures you've never seen before, creatures you know are not of your world, creatures of moss and nettle and bark.

You can make out words now.

"I did not mean it like that, and you know it!"

"*It might be easier if we left.* That's what you said, no? Because of the prophecy, we should scurry away, tails between our legs? For years

I have endured the mutterings, quiet mutterings, growing quieter, and have ignored them like you told me to do! And now you want to what? *Run away?*" A pause and then, in a ragged voice, "I never thought that you, Cynthia Striker, were a coward."

"And I never would have imagined you, Ama Liberator, to put your pride before your children's lives!"

Another flash of that bronze-gold light, met with a yell of fury; the ground shakes again.

Zella is sobbing quietly beside you. Kam has her arm in a vice-like grip so tight her knuckles pale. You reach out to both of them, take one of their hands in each of your own. *Squeeze. Squeeze.*

When Cynthia speaks again, her voice is quieter. "Some of these old witches have lived through things, Ama. Have seen things in their years that we have not. They say they cannot remember two girls ever being so powerful so young. Especially Zella. They say they can see magic being pulled towards her, like currents in the sea or dust in rays of light."

You and Kam turn to look at Zella. She has closed her eyes but her hair is glowing fiercely with a blinding white-gold light. Tears continue to run down her face, to stain her pretty purple sundress. You squeeze her hand tighter.

"Of course they are powerful!" Ama's voice rings with pride. "They are ours! Created of our magic and our flesh and our blood! They came into being as the pear tree ripened, as freedom and magic was restored to our people! Of course those old hags are afraid of them! They've never seen anything like our daughters before!"

Cynthia's voice is low. "You know it is not just that. The prophecy, Ama—it said *three girls*. Zella and Kam are two. And then, as if called to them by the wind, by the currents of our rivers, a child arrives, from another world, to make a third. If the King discovers them, if he learns Zella's name, then all is lost."

Your palms are sweaty as they clasp the fingers of your friends.

Their eyes are wide on you. You do not understand. *A child from another world.*

"So what do you want to do?" Ama sounds tired. "Tell them? Burden them with the knowledge that their actions could prove to be either our making or our undoing?"

"No. We need to leave. What if any of the coven found out about their nightly visitor?"

"They will not find out. Cynthia"—Ama is pleading now—"I know the risk as well as you. The King is getting stronger and he means to come for them. But if we run, he will follow. If we hide, he will find us. The forest can only protect us so much. We are stronger when we are united, when we stand shoulder to shoulder with our coven."

"He will never give up. He and that cursed mirror—"

"We are stronger when we are united," Ama repeats. She takes a steadying breath. "It is not forever. When Zella turns sixteen, she will be more powerful than anything seen in generations. We may end him once and for all. In Persea we must trust. We must."

There is quiet. The silence rings. The air shifts. You feel the calm begin to descend, and as it does, the wild jungle that has emerged from the kitchen of the white cottage begins to recede, like a film in rewind. The leaves fall, wither, die, turn to dust and ash. The branches retreat, cavalry falling back from battle. The bright-blue sky comes into view once more, the cracked earth beneath your feet cools and heals, the grass is lusher and greener than ever before. But the birds don't return, the bugs have long since burrowed into the earth, and the strange creatures of soil and wood have melded into the forest around you, as though they are part of it. Some things, done and said in anger, cannot be taken back.

Kam and Zella relax slightly, though they still cling to each other. You hear footsteps inside, a chair scraping, and you peek again over the ledge. The two women are locked together, cradling each other.

Ama presses her lips to Cynthia's hairline. The latter closes her eyes. You look away.

After everything you have heard, it is the sudden intimacy that has unnerved you the most.

Ama says, "We'll have to get that window fixed. Who is good with broken things?" Then, softly, "So we wait, then. Wait and see, and meet the danger when it comes?"

Cynthia's sigh is heavy. "Yes. We wait."

"You are sure you do not want to tell them?"

You hear Cynthia's slow inhale, exhale. "Tell them what, my plum? We think but we do not know. They are . . . so young. The prophecy mentioned three girls; but it also mentioned a *son* of witches. He has not come yet. Maybe when he does, it will become clear."

Beat. A breath. You sit in it.

Ama's voice is resolute. "It will be soon. It will be soon, sugar. The winds are changing."

The three of you look at each other. In the distance, you can once again hear the hum of Mum's engine, the beeping of the car in reverse. You become slowly aware of the motion of the vehicle beneath you. You are leaving them behind.

And so, as the familiar riptide of your awakening drags you away from their scared faces you say, more to Zella, in a fierce whisper,

"Hey. At least you've been practicing."

IN-BETWEEN TROUBLE

You are flushed. Flushed and warm and irritable. Not actually blushing, you think. Black girls don't blush. But you feel as though you match the bright-pink frills clasped round your chest.

This feeling is new to you. You stand there, in the department store changing room, harsh fluorescent lighting burning every part of the body you had never realized you didn't like until now. The pink-and-white training bra perched on your barely there breasts. You stare at yourself with distaste. Before now your body had been a house, a car, a time-traveling machine, a magic broomstick. It had carried you around, supported the imaginary worlds that dwelled inside your brain or the books you read. It had housed your blood and organs and bones. Sometimes you designed it fantastically, donning elf ears or a witch's hat or wings. Sometimes you had experimented with versions of this person in the mirror. Put on Mum's dresses and too-big heels, posed in Baker's hats and jackets, even adorned yourself in Val's colorful scarves and gold necklaces. But you had never criticized it. Bemoaned it when you were ill, perhaps, cursed it when you were clumsy, but never *this*. Never this acrid contempt, this cold self-appraisal.

Mum pokes her head around the pink curtain. "Need any help?" You quickly fold your arms across your chest. Mum laughs. "Don't be silly, Mush! I've seen it all before, haven't I?"

"Don't call me *Mush*," you snarl. You see the flash of hurt across her face. You scowl harder, pull your vest over your chest and awkwardly unclasp the bra, flinging it on the pile of other rejected frilly and flowery things. You zip up your jacket, muttering, "Just get whichever you think is best. I think they all look stupid. I'm going to find Val."

You hurry away from the changing room, past Saffy who is dawdling behind Mum, posing in front of a mirror and singing to herself.

You wend your way through the bustling crowds of shoppers. You can't shake the feeling that everything you've ever known and loved is enjoying one last summer, basking in the warm glow of the familiar, but on the horizon a storm is rolling in. You feel it now, in your stomach again, like a clap of thunder just below your navel that radiates out, lightning hot, down your back and into your legs. It is getting worse.

You find a seat outside the ground floor of the department store. The ground floor is where many of the local schools stock their uniforms, and you watch throngs of children about your age milling around the racks of blazers and sweaters with their parents. You like people watching. You like making up stories for them as they pass you, and it distracts from the pain in your abdomen.

You watch a girl in front of you. She's about your age but taller and pale with dark blonde hair hanging in ringlets down her back, and freckles scattered star-like across her face and arms. She is straight-backed, spike-shouldered and swans with a confidence you didn't know you lacked. Her mother, dressed all in black despite the August sun, is her image in elder grace and deepened contempt. Fine lines around her nose and mouth indicate a permanent sneer. Her heels are gloriously impractical. She is pointing to the display of dark green and gray blazers and sweaters, a school crest stitched across them in fine gold threading. A gray skirt with a striped white-and-green shirt sits underneath on the mannequin beside a second one displaying a range of outerwear. Smart, hooded duffel coats with fiddly ties, fancy raincoats in the same shade of green and gray. And then, a third mannequin, dressed in a pleated skirt with a crew neck sweater and long, over the knee socks. The mannequin has strange padding over the socks on its legs, and is wielding a stick, like a wooden golf club.

The woman and her daughter stop beside this last one. "Look, Monica darling, this will be your field hockey kit."

The girl, Monica, you assume, eyes it distastefully. "I don't want to wear anything so dreadful."

Her mother rolls her eyes and, though dissimilar in every single way, in that moment she reminds you of your own mum. Maybe all mums are alike in this shared impatience. "Don't be silly, darling." And then, stroking her daughter's golden head like praising a champion breeder at a dog show: "I rather like the blazers, I must say. *Très chic!*" The woman and her daughter giggle and your stomach rolls and clenches.

You can see Val now, making her way towards you, weighed down with bags, followed by Baker. You notice the woman in black eyeing Val suspiciously, taking in Baker's height and clutching her handbag tighter to her.

Saffy chooses this precise moment to come dancing towards Val and Baker, at top speed, twirling ahead of your mum who is calling after her, "Saffy! Earth to Saffy!" She is singing to herself, entirely in her own world. She is wearing an enormous, blonde, curled wig.

You lip-read rather than hear Monica's mother mutter something like "Good god!" Thankfully Saffy doesn't notice, doesn't have her bubblegum-pink and sunshine bubble popped by a French-tipped talon.

That pain again, clenching your stomach. You stumble towards Val on trembling legs.

You grip her arm. "I think something's wrong. It hurts," you whisper, at the exact same moment that the girl, Monica, happens to walk past you and loudly—far more loudly than is necessary, you think—gasps, "Mummy! That girl's bleeding!"

Shame is an agonizing fist that joins the tight cramping below your navel. This is the first time in your almost eleven years that you actively think, *I want to die. I want to die. I want to die.* You refuse to look at Baker.

Val's hand tightens on yours in understanding. She has your jacket off, hiding the sticky blood you can feel but not see, tied neatly around your waist in seconds. "Go to the toilet," she orders. "Opposite the food court. I'll find you, okay?"

Up the escalator, across the bright white pavilion, avoid the nauseating smells of frying food, and you slam open the doors to the toilets. Normally public bathrooms turn your stomach, normally you would rather hold it, but this is not your normal. The toilets are surprisingly clean anyway and you lean against the cool metal door of the cubicle, sighing with relief at the cool metal peace. The cool metal quiet. Beat. Breathe. Just breathe. You're okay.

You brace yourself and assess the damage. Your leggings and underwear are ruined but nothing has seeped through to the jacket. Merciful. You untie it and hang it behind the door and peel off the soiled leggings and clothes. The blood is more than the teaspoon your health class teacher had promised. Dark brown in places, brighter red in others.

"Hello?"

"Val?"

You unlock the door and open it a crack. She passes things through to you—knickers, fresh leggings, and a pink squishy plastic pack of pads. You recognize them from your health class demonstration from the term before, but these are smaller, sleeker, and smell of lavender when you tear one open to examine it.

"Where's Mum?" you ask.

"She's getting the others lunch."

Mum is paying for lunch because Val can't afford to. Val and Mum. Alone but together. Each making sure that no one went without. You feel a rush of gratitude then, for their support and presence, for their consistent tag-teaming throughout your childhood. You are sure that if they had the time to breathe and the money to back them, together they could rule the world.

Tears prick your eyes. "Thanks," you mutter. Humiliation sweeps over you once more, dirty and hot and sticky, it sullies you, you can feel it clinging to the dampness at the back of your thighs, where you'd peeled your underwear away. Ire is easier.

"You don't need to wait," you say coldly. "I'll find you all in the food court."

Val sighs and says, "Okay." Then, "If you put the old clothes in this"—she passes a plastic bag under the door—"I'll throw them away for you."

You do so silently. *You want to die, you want to die, you want to die.* You thrust the bag back underneath and there is silence.

Then, "Happens to the best of us, little one. You a bit early, maybe, but don't worry too much." You say nothing. You hear her footsteps retreat, taking all comfort and reassurance with her.

*

You find them all, fifteen minutes later, sitting round a large table in the food court. Val and Mum are handing out fries and nuggets and burgers to Baker and your sister, who is focused on coloring in her kids' menu. Val eats a rice bowl and Mum spears salad leaves enthusiastically.

"This one's yours!" Val calls to you, gesturing to the brown paper bag between her and Saffy. Her voice is carefully careless, her eyes are kind, and your heart swells for her. You want to slide in next to her, tuck yourself in beside her, thank her for the clothes, have her soothe you like she did when you were smaller than Saffy. But you are prickly proud and preteen, riding the first waves of hormonal rage, and you snatch the bag away from her, and drop it on to the table next to Baker, where it lands with an unsatisfying smack.

You sit down beside Baker, still unable to look at him but needing to be near him. As you unwrap your parceled burger and dig out the carton of fries you feel his hand, warm and dry, reach out and gently pinch you, just below your elbow. The angry, heavy, roiling acid loses some of its fizz. It's still there, but you can breathe a bit better now. You tune into the conversation.

It's an old argument, between Baker and Val.

"But why can't I remember anything?"

"Me nuh know!"

It is weird, you think. You can't remember much, but you remember the important things. Old friends, a few parties. Saffy being born.

"But, Mum! We need to write our autobiography. I can't be the only one in Year Seven whose life starts at seven. Can you not just even tell me some stuff so I can write it?"

"Nuh, suh!" Val's accent becomes more pronounced when she is irate. "Issa *auto*-biography, nah? That means yuh have to write 'bout yusself—yusself! It's your story, not mine."

Saffy's tongue is poking out as she tries desperately to stay within the lines. Her blonde wig is askew as she looks up at you. You smile at her, despite yourself.

"Maybe you could write 'bout the magic avocado oil instead?" she says.

Beat. Silence. Held. Held. Saffy keeps coloring, unaware of the pause she has cleaved through the noise at the table.

"Magic avocado oil?" Val's eyes are wide, flick-flicking from your face to Baker's.

Mum laughs. "Honestly, Saffy-baby, that imagination of yours—"

Val interrupts her, "What magic avocado, Saffy?"

"The hair oil you use," Saffy says, barely looking up from where she's coloring. "You know, it makes them dream. Baker was jealous because he never gets to use it." She looks up then, sees the expression on your face and her smile falters. "Oh, no! Was that a sister secret too?"

Mum and Val turn to you both, eyebrows raised. Baker stares at the table.

"No, don't worry, Saffy," you say hastily. You grin at Mum and Val.

"You know what Saffy's like. All those fairy tales."

Mum nods, chuckling, and begins dissecting her receipts, striking through items with a highlighter, making sure she hasn't been overcharged for anything.

Val's eyes continue to search your faces. "Baker?" she asks. Baker lifts his head and holds her gaze.

"I don't know what she's talking about," he says easily. "Wild imagination that kid."

"If yuh say suh." Val's tone is wary.

Mum is beginning to gather her bags, and you pick up the pace on your munching, knowing her inability to keep still. She notices and says, "Oh, don't rush, Mush, I only need to get a few more bits and then we can go home. Though we can go look at books and stationery first?"

Mush. You hate the stupid nickname. You love that she's giving you time to eat because she knows you're upset. You hate that she knows you're upset. You love that she's offered to take you to the books and stationery shop, your favorite, because she wants to cheer you up. You hate that she feels sorry for you, that she wants to try and cheer you up. You hate her, you love her.

You turn to Val. "Val, where are you from?"

She scrutinizes you. Baker is quiet beside you, but he is listening. "You know this. Jamaica. Why?"

"Just wondering. Your accent is like my grandma's. But also different. Is it the same Jamaica?"

"There's only one Jamaica, Mush!" Mum laughs, helping Saffy tidy her crayons.

Val lowers her voice to above a whisper and says, "Almost-Jamaica. I'm from Almost-Jamaica. Just the other side of the clouds."

You open your mouth to ask more and she silences you with a look. You know that you'll always remember this conversation and later doubt that it happened.

Beside you Baker is tight-lipped and wide-eyed.

Val says, "Things are different there now, though, m'dear. My friends there are . . . worried. The winds are changing, I think."

It is only when you're leaving, hours later, Saffy now asleep in the back of the car, bags loaded into trunks as you prepare to go your separate ways home, that Val squeezes your hand and murmurs, "Dream well, little one."

The King's Heir

The King intensified his search of many years,
the source of his hope and all of their fears.
He used the darkness and the hate and the bile
to scry across the kingdom, to seek and beguile,
hoping to return to his employ,
his key to their kingdom, a little lost boy.
A weaver's son born of Persea and might,
whose magic he'd use to darken the night;
he'd rolled the dice in this game,
the prize was the witch girl's name.

Fear is Catching

"You coming here," Kam tells you. "It's fated."

A sour, ugly tang seems to ooze from the large dark ripple on the horizon. You can almost taste the fear that hangs over Persea. Whatever storm is brewing will be thunderous and dreadful.

But you don't want to believe it. All around you your world is shifting, mutating, and you are not ready. You wish you could cling to each piece of the life you have loved, but it is as though in trying to cling tighter, it slips through your fingers faster, like a bar of soap that shrinks even as it leaps away from your grasp.

"What do you mean, it's fated?"

"She means it is prophesized," says Zella, rising from where you are sitting, in the usual white swing at the back of the garden, under the avocado pear tree. "A long time ago, before we were born, the Seer was taken to the banks of the River Aphra by the willow trees, who whispered to her. She was given a prophecy, the first in a long, long time."

The parts of this story are blurred around the edges, sprinkled with clarity. The more you think, the less you can make sense of it, like trying to remember this place when you're awake. Val's avocado oil. Avocado oil that brings you here . . . but that she won't give to her own son. Her son, Baker, your dearest friend, who can't remember anything before four years ago.

"What is it?" Kam's eyes are narrow and shrewd. "You know something, don't you?"

"No!" you cry. "Except I know I'm not part of some old prophecy!"

Baker had said that you were special too. Val's words from the shopping center drift back to you on a nighttime breeze spangled with rose-gold light. *I'm from Almost-Jamaica. Just the other side of the clouds.*

"Kam!"

You feel something gently brush the end of your braids. At the same time you feel a softly fizzing feeling, a mild crackling like static, flow through your hair, ends to roots, and into your scalp. Kam's arm flies away from your head as though she has been electrocuted.

"You did not ask!" Zella is aghast.

Even you know that among the witches in Persea, unsolicited hair-touching is one of the greatest taboos.

"I am sorry," says Kam quietly. "But there is something you are not telling us. I can feel it in my hands, in my bones." She points to the sky and says, "If there is anything you have learned in your world about this one, then as our friend you must tell us."

You swallow. You go to speak, then—

You turn. Someone behind you is calling your name, in a voice that you know and love.

The fence at the back of the garden gives way to the trees of the ancient, enchanted forest. Trees that you know are older than your grandmother's grandmother stretch away, encircling the village, protecting the coven. In your years of visiting the garden, you had never seen anything other than animals hidden among the foliage, never seen a person emerge from between the trunks. Until now.

Until Baker steps out from the trees.

Your friends scramble away from where you are sitting, Zella tripping over her long nightie, Kam's bare feet skidding in the earth as she reaches to clutch her sister. The moon casts a ghostly blue light across their faces. But it is Baker who looks truly spectral.

The sun of your waking world, cast silver-blue in the moonlight, and he has brought something terrible with him. Something dark and awful.

Ignoring the girls' cries of warning and disbelief, you reach for him, stumbling towards the fence, towards your Baker.

86

"Baker! You shouldn't be here!"

"I know. I know." His voice cracks something inside you as tears begin to track down his face. "I thought I would try and come here, just once, but it's not like I thought it would be. I'm scared." He begins to cry as he looks into the dark mist. "I can see bad things, terrible things."

You reach for him again. You are so close now, leaning half your body across the fence, but Kam has shaken off her fear and has wrapped a bony arm around your waist and is pulling you away.

"Kam! Stop! Get off me! What are you doing?" You are kicking and shrieking and struggling but she won't let go and now Zella is helping her and they're hauling you away from Baker together.

"Baker!" you cry, and he calls your name, but then he is pulled by his dreads, by the darkness, back into the forest. There is a great rush of dark wind, of gale-force nothing; it writhes and swirls around you and the breeze that had been gentle before, picks up and about-turns, blowing hard towards the east.

"Baker! We can help you; whatever it is we can help!" You shout the empty words out into the empty night. Silence answers. Baker is gone.

"How could you? He needed me and you let him go!" you rage at the girls. Zella looks shamefaced, but Kam's eyes are flashing with a bright steel you have never seen before.

"How could *we*?" she challenges, her voice low but full of threat. "How could *you*? You told him how to come here, didn't you?"

"Baker is my friend! You don't know him, but I do, and I know he would never hurt anyone!"

"So you are more loyal to him, a boy, than to us?" Zella is angry too now, hair crackling by her sister's side. Kam's hands spark and flash.

"Boys, girls, both, neither, who cares?" you cry. "They were wrong about your mum; they all thought she was a boy. Well, maybe you're all wrong now!"

Kam explodes. "Could you not see the darkness around him? The evil summoned?"

Zella lays a hand on her sister's arm. "Kam——"

"No! No, Zella! I knew there was something she was not telling us! I knew she couldn't be trusted!" Fury contorts Kam's face as she whirls to face you. "Just a game to you, isn't it? Our lives and our magic and our prophecy! Just dreams and fantasy! What do you care about the kind of shadows *that boy* may have brought with him? You're not even really here!"

The words hit you like a slap. And the shock is waking you up.

"That's it." Kam's eyes are alight with contempt. "Drift away, back to your *real* life and your *real* friends and your *real* Baker. Tell him thanks so much."

You can feel consciousness tugging at you. You can't leave them this way, you can't. You turn to Zella.

"But it's a dream. You always said I could do no harm!"

Zella meets your eyes, her face drawn and pinched and older than you have ever seen her. "I guess I was wrong, wasn't I?" she says quietly.

Your stomach sinks. You swim upwards and away from the dark forest into the morning light, and the rush of cold reality is, for the first time ever, a relief to you.

The Changing of the Wind

For a decade Cynthia and Ama had lived bold and loud
with their two little girls born strong and proud—
under the caring arms of the willow tree,
guardians of the avocado pear,
the most powerful witches in Persea.
They knew a reckoning would come one day.
But why would they burden their daughters' play?
No.
Better not to tell,
to wait and see,
to hope that they would always be free.
But then one night everything changed,
their daughter awoke and acted strange.
And as the dark clouds swelled above the peat,
they saw fear in the eyes of those they would meet,
then came the clouds and the rain and the hail,
then each plant and crop began to fail.

THE PROTAGONIST

You have begun to suspect that you are not the main character of this story.

The summer holidays wind to a close, sluggish yet inevitable. You wake one morning certain that something bad has happened— an argument, you remember, Baker, a pressing darkness, and you are shivering and irritable. But as usual you can't remember much about it. You ask Mum if you can go to the salon to see Baker, but she shakes her head.

"Val called this morning. She says Baker is under the weather. She's staying home with him."

You are uneasy. Baker isn't usually sick and when he is, Val still brings him to sit in a quiet corner of the salon or leaves him at home, with a neigbor checking up on him.

"Is he . . . is he really sick or something?"

Mum is only half-listening, stacking dishes at lightning speed. "A nightmare," she said. "Probably a fever."

The days pass and September looms. You don't see Baker, and you worry. You don't visit your dreamland, and you worry. You know that something must be wrong, very wrong, but you can't remember exactly what.

And then it's the last week of the holidays. Your final year at this school. You are on the cusp of newness and you do not want it. Mum drops you at Val's and your heart thumps in your chest. It's been weeks since you saw Baker and it feels like a lifetime.

Saffy immediately sets to lovingly brushing out Val's wigs, chirruping, "Val, when I'm older, can you teach me how to dye hair mermaid colors? Blue and silver and green like the River Mumma in the story?"

The River Mumma. This question jogs something in the corner of your memory but, as usual, when you reach for it, it is gone.

"Val? Where's Baker?"

She smiles at you, but there is a tightness in her eyes. "At the garden with Giles and Mrs. Goss. Good for him to get some fresh air after being cooped up. Guh long! Find him. Just come back for lunch at one."

You leave Saffy with Val and head out of the salon and down the busy, bright high street with its hopscotch of chewing gum and litter and food waste. Mr. Feeney and Miss Annie are flirting outside the pub as usual. Miss Annie calls, "Yuh goin' tuh fin' Baker?"

"Yes, he's in the garden with Mrs. Goss, Val said!"

She goes inside, then presents you with a package of banana cake and fresh sugar water, sticky and pulpy with lime. "Enough there for Mrs. Goss and ol' Giles," she instructs.

"Aren't you looking grown-up?" Mr. Patel smiles from where he leans outside his grocery store. You have dressed carefully today. A pale-purple dress with its spaghetti straps and scalloped hem. It made you feel pretty and you wanted to feel pretty today.

You head into the park and through the second set of gates, lined with bright perennial peonies and tall bunches of lavender. You breathe deep, soothe, hold it a moment, clinging to the scent of this summer. You enter.

Baker is sitting on a stool, watering the flowerbed he's claimed as his own, tending to his tulips and talking to Mrs. Goss. It has been a long, dry summer and the earth is scorched, cracked beneath his long fingers. Your stomach swoops unpleasantly. His eyes meet yours, he smiles and you forget why you are here, are lost in the planes of that face in Baker's eyes, Baker's smile, Baker's mouth, Baker's eyes, Baker's eyes, Baker's eyes. It's been weeks. It feels like a lifetime.

"Hey," he says.

"Hey," you say. You smile. He smiles. You are both just . . . smiling.

Mrs. Goss murmurs, "I'll go fetch that new bag of compost, then. Can't be waiting on Giles to do it."

"Is Giles not here, Mrs. Goss?"

"No, pet. I've not seen him in . . . Jaysus, it must be a couple of weeks now. But you know how he is. The nights get colder and he looks for a shelter of some kind. Normally he says if he's moving on, though. I hope he's all right." She potters back inside.

You unwrap the cake and take out the sugar water. You can ask Mrs. Goss to keep Giles's for him, in case he comes by later. But as you settle opposite Baker on the bench you usually share with Giles, you feel a wave of grief rush over you. The hedges on either side seem to rustle in understanding, the daffodils that line the flowerbed on your side bow their heads in acknowledgement and for a fractured second your dream world intrudes. You know. You know you won't see Giles again.

"Everything is changing," you whisper to Baker. He watches you over the tall tips of his foxgloves and nods.

He looks at you. Takes a deep breath. "I think I did something bad."

Your insides become a bottomless abyss. Smoke, shouts, hands on you, dragging you away.

"I took that avocado oil and put it in my hair. And I . . . I think I went into your dream. I can't remember it but I know it was bad." He is quiet for a moment. "Your friends were there. I think they were scared of me."

You pick at the cake. "We should forget about it," you say. "Forget all this ever happened."

He bites his lip. "I feel like something is wrong, though."

"How could anything be wrong?" you say. "It's just a dream."

You reach through the tangle of foxglove leaves for Baker's hand, clasp it and savor the warm, dry palm, the elegant fingers weaving through yours.

"You start big school next week."

He sighs. "I know."

"I don't want you to."

"I know that too." And then, "We'll still see each other loads. I'm still going to box at the rec center. You and your ma and Saffy will still go to the salon." Beat. "It'll be okay."

It is your turn to sigh. "I know."

You're not lying exactly. But the weight of many worlds sag against both of your shoulders. You squeeze his hand tighter. A breeze picks up, blowing away the scent of summer.

The Poison

S aid the King to the boy,
   "You poor stolen thing,
   the wicked witch took you from me.
I have so much to teach you of power and might;
I have so much to show you of who you could be.
I'll tell you the secret
of who you are and why.
Just one thing you must do—
cut off your locs,
lend me your magic."
And the lost boy, ensnared
by King Charming's—well—charm,
believed the wicked King would cause no harm,
and so took a knife and cut off each loc,
then felt a wave of grief and shock
as they vanished into the black cauldron.
He felt his knees get weak,
and something vital was leached from him.
He tried to speak,
but as his vision began to dim,
he heard King Charming crow and call,
"Mirror, Mirror, on the wall . . ."

FINAL YEAR

Term starts for you and things do change. Val still collects you and Saffy after school. You still go to the salon. But Baker is there less and less often, either out with his new friends or at boxing practice. When you do see him, he is tired and heavy. Not sleeping much, he says. Despite all of his jokes about insomniacs being the most productive people, you are still bothered by it. But after a while you find that you're busy with school and you don't go to the salon as much either.

Mum works late shifts at the rec center to send you to an after-school tutor because she wants you to get a scholarship to the local all-girls' private school. The one with the uniform and field hockey kit you had seen *that* day at the shopping mall. You are too tired even to dream and, after a while, you realize the cloud light of your nighttime garden has dimmed over the last few weeks.

Just a dream, you think. A weird one, but over now.

It is the beginning of November. Petrol-blue and streetlamp-lit early winter and Mum's headlights glisten where they reflect in the rainy tarmac. The roads are busy and the heater is on. She plays a soft jazz on the radio, where the DJ announces their mellow evening show. But you are feeling anything but mellow. You are on your way to an open house at the private school with Mum, butterflies in your stomach like the giant swallowtail you'd seen in one of your books. You might meet future classmates, future teachers.

You pull up to the school. The driveway is sweeping and lined with golden lights and even the lights on the cars contribute to the feeling of the place. You and Mum are shown inside behind throngs of parents and chattering girls. The large front doors are thrown open, there are flowers everywhere, and an orchestra sounds from somewhere in the distance.

Once inside, Mum is handed a glass of wine by a middle-aged woman baring her teeth in a ferocious smile. "None for you, I'm afraid, we need you paying attention!" she guffaws at you and you force a laugh. She hands you an apple juice instead, and Mum speaks in a voice you've never heard her use, "Are you a teacher here? She's terribly excited!"

"No, I don't *teach* here," the woman laughs. "I'm Virginia, I'm the head of the PTA!"

"Oh, lovely to meet you!" your mum gushes. Virginia's perfume is strong and sweet and your head is beginning to swim.

Thankfully the girl taking your group on a tour of the building arrives. Her uniform is clean and crisply ironed, her black shoes are shiny and her coppery hair is tied off her pale, freckled face in a ponytail. Her name badge says her name is Pippa. Pippa is as shiny as her shoes.

"Hello, everyone! Right, shall we get started? If we go up the stairs here we'll find ourselves on the humanities' corridor and . . ."

Your group follows her around the school. She answers every question with ease and confidence. As you take in the amazing facilities, hear about the school trips, the exam results, you are filled with intense longing and worry. You so badly want to fit in here and you are so sure that you won't.

Mum asks Pippa question after question. "Your own swimming pool?" "Oh, so the shop class, the art room, and the pottery lab are all separate, are they?" "A school trip every term, Mush, think of that!" You bite your lip. You don't want to ruin it for her.

Framed photos line the corridor between the dance studio and the main sports hall. Pictures of past students—athletes, lawyers, politicians. Cabinets full of trophies. You don't see yourself here, reflected in the pictures on the wall, in the shiny cups and shields.

The dance studio is large and airy, with floor to ceiling windows on one side and floor to ceiling mirrors on the other. "The stage in the main hall has sprung floors," Pippa says to your mum.

"Look at this," your mum gushes. "You won't have to go to the rec center for classes any more!"

Your stomach sinks at this. You like the rec center.

Pippa smiles at you. "I'm a dancer too. Grade Six ballet, tap, and jazz. What about you?"

You swallow. "Grade Five ballet. But I do hip-hop as well."

Pippa's voice goes a bit higher. "Hip-hop! That's *totally* cool! I've never done anything like that!"

"So it's not on the list of clubs?" Mum asks, flipping through to the page in her prospectus.

"Oh, no!" Pippa laughs, and something in the laugh makes you feel silly for even mentioning hip-hop in the first place. "But we have Round the World week, where each year gets to pick a different cultural dance to do in PE."

She turns to lead the group out of the room to allow the next cluster of parents and girls into the studio. This group is led by another student, a brunette version of Pippa. Her skirt is hitched a little higher and she winks at Pippa as she passes.

"Hope your lot are better than mine," she murmurs. "I've got the mum from hell."

Pippa snorts.

An imperious voice calls, "Is this part of the tour going to take long? Some of us would like to see the *real* sports facilities!"

The woman with the piercing voice is blonde and haughty-looking. She is older than your mum, and seems more imposing, dressed in all black and impractical heels, like a glamorous bird of prey. It takes you a moment, but then you recognize her. The girl trotting beside her gives you a sly side-eye.

The mum and daughter from the shopping center *that* day.

"Come along, Monica," the blonde woman says and the girl smirks at you. She remembers you too, all right.

You duck your head, feeling warm and sick. The part of you that had been excited about this evening and this school is fading. You no longer want to stay and see the dance performance. You just want to go home.

As you hurry away after Pippa and your mum, you notice a girl at the back of the other group. Her mother is, like yours, leafing through the brochure, but the girl has her nose behind a book. You recognize it as the same book on magical plants that you have. Her face is round and dimpled and her thick, dark, curly hair is pulled into a pineapple on top of her head.

"Cat!" her mother calls. "Come on, pay attention; you can read later."

The girl catches your eye above the embossed cover and lowers it slightly. She glances at her mum and then rolls her eyes at you. You grin at her in sympathy and hurry on.

Pippa ends the tour in the hall where a dance show is about to start, pointing your group over to a drinks table. She shakes hands with the parents—"a good, firm handshake!" your mum reports—waves at the girls, and vanishes into a sea of identical uniforms.

The hall is large and brightly lit. Red velvet chairs are laid out in rows, matching the heavy, red velvet curtains that hang across the windows and the giant stage at the front. It feels surreal that this small theatre is where you might have assembly every morning. The headmaster rises to address the crowd. You don't really listen. You think it's strange that an all-girls' school has a headmaster and instead look up into the gallery above where there are more seats. The girls who had done the guiding are sat there. Some of them are watching the speech but most of them are whispering to each other, nudging each other, giggling as teachers who have gathered with the parents below throw them disapproving glares. You try to picture yourself here, as this person. Try to see how you might look in a posh uniform or what version of yourself you might become. The headmaster finishes. The curtain lifts and the dancing starts.

And as you watch them, in their leotards and tutus and slippers, you are swept away by the image of yourself up there. They are slight-bodied and slick-haired and sure, glowing under their spotlight, and you are none of these things. But you feel a joyful yearning watching them, a delicious pain, at the bright glow of the warm yellow light that dances across the stage. Beyond them, only darkness and uncertainty. But they burn on, the red-gold event horizon of your adolescence, and the inevitability of adulthood calls you forwards like gravity, swallows you like a black hole.

The Curse

T he King with his lost boy's roots,
　　returned to the height of his considerable power.
　　The residents of Kingstown were struck quite mute,
to hear him addressing the kingdom from his tower—
stating that he'd spent so many years in the sky
that he couldn't descend from up on high—
and trembled for those on whom revenge he promised.
His eyes glowed brighter than the moon,
in his reedy, nasal voice, he sang a tune:

Swing low,
Sweet Chariot,
Coming forth to carry me home.
Swing low,
Sweet Chariot,
Coming forth to carry me home.

Far away in their community,
the Perseans were stung
as they heard the song
their grandmothers had sung,
while first forced into work by the King,
a song that for them was too painful to sing.
Oh! His brazen appropriation
of their battle cry, sung to their nation.
The King's hatred rose up like bile,

yellow and green,
he poisoned their hair.
And so,
every Black woman at once ceased to know
their natural hair.
Every kink softened, every curl straightened,
until hair hung limp, women wincing in pain,
looked in their mirrors, as the King looked again
and saw himself refracted into every pore of dark skin,
each strand of keratin.
With the son of the witches now in his power,
he used the boy's magic from high in his tower,
and so withered the plants and so decayed the fruit,
as the King cut Persea's magic at the root.

*

Until the next morning when, carried to him on the wind, he heard
     that same song that he had fought so hard to mute.

There's a Brown girl in the ring
Tralalala
There's a Brown girl in the ring
Tralalalalala
Brown girl in the ring
Tralalalala
She looks like the sugar in the plum

The girl was small, aged ten and cute,
but in her hair was pure rebellion.
He hunted her down, he knew her by sight,
for the prophecy had told of a girl of might—

and the King said, "Little girl, what is your name?"
But the girl was no fool
and had learned her lessons well,
with the pride of Persea declared,
"I'll never tell!"
"Never is a while,"
said the King politely.
He gave her a smile,
addressed her brightly, "Come along with me."
And then, using all of his dark power, he banished her.
"You will tell me your name eventually,"
in her ear would his shadows whisper.
Time passed.
She closed her eyes and thought of her sister,
And, yes, she was alone and far from home and the strands of grass
    were all she could call her own,
And, yes, there was pain, but in her heart there were flames. She was
    not just the same as every other girl—
because she knew three things for certain:
one, there was magic in her roots that the King did fear;
two, this magic grew, and it grew in her hair—she was strong, not
    Snow White nor a golden Cinderella;
three, she was no damsel—

                              and her name was Rapunzella.

Stolen Salad Days

"Shall I tell you a story?"

You spin around at her voice. She is sitting in front of you. It is dark, pitch-dark, but the light that comes from her shows that the ground beneath her is mostly craggy and barren, with a few small sprouts pushing their way through the unyielding earth. The air around her glows faintly in the light shimmering dimly out from her hair like a halo. You can make out sheer rockface surrounding you in the half-light, high, high as you can see and higher, nothing but smooth, sharp rock, shining gray-gold in her witch-light.

"Zella?" you whisper. The last, angry words you exchanged hang in the air between you and you don't know what to say. It has been so long since you have visited this place. "Zella, what happened? Where are we?"

"Shall I tell you a story?" she repeats. Your heart is thud-thudding in the quiet and you nod.

"It happened so quickly. It was night and we were not sleeping. We were up waiting for you, in fact. That's when we heard him. The King. His voice echoed across the whole of Xaymaca. He sang one of our songs, the song of our survival. We ran out into the street, trying to see what was going on. And then the screaming started. I have never heard a sound like it, like these unearthly screams, as though the soul of every witch, everyone I knew, was in terrible, terrible pain. It went on and on and I watched as Kam and my mothers clutched their heads and howled as though their hair was on fire. Until their curls hung straight, their kinks ironed away. But not mine.

"I wanted to help, wanted to do something, but a mist came, so thick and fast, a dark green-gray fog and I could not see my mothers in front of me, could not see Kam beside me, could not feel anything. I did not know where to turn or go. I kept walking around and around in the mist, reaching out, trying to find them, to reach them, crying out for them. Eventually the screams stopped and the silence was almost as bad. So I began to sing. *Brown girl in the ring.* Mama always says the Brown girl song is not to be sung alone. I thought she'd be able to find me that way, but it wasn't her who found me. It was him.

"He smiled. And he spoke so nicely. He asked me how old I was and I said, ten. But then he asked me my name and I told him, 'Just Zella,' because—"

"—there is power in naming things," you finish her sentence and she nods, swallows, continues.

"So here I am. Carrion Ridge. East of Kingstown. He put me here and now I can't leave. And while I'm here, without the Great Forest to protect me, you must not call me anything other than Zella."

"What has he done to the others?" you ask.

"He subdued them by straightening their hair." Her voice is calm, but her hands are shaking. "But it didn't work on me. My hair is different. That's why he had to put me here, away from everyone else."

You reach for her, wrap arms around her, as tightly as your dream state will allow.

"Oh, Zella!" you burst out. "I'm so sorry! It's all my fault. I knew Baker might come and I didn't tell you."

"The damage is done," she sighs. "*Magic is not exact, but it is always intentional.* We used to parrot that without knowing what it meant but I understand now. I am meant to have the power that I have. Your Baker was meant to be taken by the King's darkness. Maybe you should have told us. Maybe not. It does not matter now."

This new, sanguine Zella strikes more fear into your heart than the eerie desolation of your surroundings. "You sound like Kam," you say. "Where is she?"

"I do not know. Maybe they are still in Persea. Maybe they are cast far away like me. I do know that something must be wrong. Otherwise they would have come for me by now. They would have . . . have come to take me home." Her voice wobbles, breaks, and more tears track down her smooth brown cheeks. You hug her tighter.

"Can't you get out?" you say.

"Do you not think I have tried?" She gestures to the rocky outcrop above. "Every time I climb out, something drags me back in."

"Then what will you do?"

She swallows, drags her hand across her eyes. "He wants my name. Because of the prophecy. Then he can have all of my power." She scowls. "All of this so-called power, that I was so proud of—and I cannot do anything with it!"

She gulps. Pulls herself together. "I just have to keep practicing. Master my magic. Sleep. Wait. Will you help me? I do not want to be alone."

And you nod. "Yes."

*

You return again and again. As the weeks pass, Zella spends every waking hour focusing on developing her magic. As she does so, her thick curls continue to spiral upwards and outwards. With each visit the dense cloud expands, dancing ever higher and wider. Her hair colonizes the space above, forming a willow tree-like, protective shade. She once told you, back when your nights were spent in the heaving peace of her garden, that her people gave birth under the willow tree. This is what you think of, now her Afro reaches up to greet the sky, now she is willow and sequoia, now she is Raphia regalis and then some.

"I am not really in control of it any more," she confesses. Each time you appear on the mountainside the place where you wake is more overgrown until you wake in an enchanted forest of hair. Each

105

emotional outburst grows a new curling dark flower, an errant thought sends a shimmering vine twisting through the air.

Mostly she is strong, but sometimes she is sad.

"Sing with me," you say. "The Brown girl song. Zella. We are most powerful when we use our voices."

She glares at you for a moment. And then closes her eyes and sings a different song:

Swing low,
Sweet Chariot,
Coming forth to carry me home.
Swing low,
Sweet Chariot,
Coming forth to carry me home.

As she sings and her voice rises, you feel something brush against you in the mountain clearing. Like a warm breath, a sweet-scented spring breeze. She looks up at you through her eyelashes, but she's not looking at you, she's looking beyond you and her eyes are on fire. The song vibrates inside you and flowers begin to grow around her shelter. Her hair grows to fill the gaps in the air around you. It becomes a ceiling, it covers the sky, taking on new shapes and forms. Life around you crackles and shimmers with magic, and for a second you breathe in and can almost taste the garden in Persea, can almost see Kam, sitting on the white swing beside you both. Instead you find yourself padding barefoot through soft dark patches of rampion spun from her coils, and swinging on long rope twists.

*

In those early days of seclusion, Zella turns her fear into your playground. The dark caves she creates out of her kinks and curls are

106

the worlds of your nighttime in her banished glade. And so her hair grows and expands, creating shelter and life and dense, protective forest. Whether she is controlling it or it is dominating her, you are no longer sure. Birds flock and new plants take root, so that the jagged mountain face around her all but vanishes from sight.

And in those semi-lucid moments between sleeping and waking, in the seconds before the panic caused by paralysis, you sometimes feel her reach out to you, you can smell the summer garden and warm oil smell of her hair around you, her fingers ghosting against your arm.

"Promise me to keep singing," you drowsily whisper, as the fog of another dreamland closes in, claiming you for its own.

"One day they'll hear you.

Don't give up.

You're not alone."

Part Two
Sprout

Part Two

Spring

Five Years After The Curse

The King had some magic, true,
darkness leaves a residue,
but he still grayed, decayed,
could not reach the burning fire,
at the heart of their power
and restore his empire.
In Persea the witches lived without a spark of their craft,
their hair no longer at gravity laughed.
It was said the King to the forest would travel,
off to play a dangerous game,
he would return to his mirror and his hair would unravel,
ranting and raving, "I must have her name!"

FIFTEEN

The queen catches your eye and you look away with a quick, embarrassed smile. You're not sure where this new self-consciousness has come from, around Val of all people.

Val is strong and soft. She is hips and bum and boobs. You have fifteen-year-old bee-stings—that's what your grandma calls them. They were early to arrive and slow to develop. You wonder if you'll ever grow up. Val is grown up and grown again, she is loud curves and cherry drops and her laugh is rare but clear like a bell when it comes.

You sweep up shorn hair. Pale plastic Barbie limbs lie in the corner. They belong to the toddler daughters of some of the customers. They're white ones. The dolls. With the silky hair that matts easily yet yields readily to the dimpled fists and edible rolls of flesh and vacant, painted stares.

And there are mirrors. There are mirrors everywhere, so many that you are reflected and refracted, diamond-like and separate, pieces for examination. You catch a glimpse of yourself, of shapes weaving and bustling, merging and warping with your own in the many mirrors' gaze. Just like your disappointingly small boobs, the rest of you grew quickly and then stopped. You are all limbs, lanky without the excuse of height and while your dance teacher maintains that you are graceful, you feel awkward and gangling and wrong.

You never feel right in the clothes you wear. You resent your short torso, button a cardigan over your bare tummy, pull, pause, fidget, trying to get it to sit flat like Monica French's at school. Ill-attempted panda eyes, goosebumps on your stomach, it's an unseasonably cold summer. You don't look like the girls on TV, you don't want to. Not much, anyway.

You like your brown skin, the night space in your eyes. But you have always hated your name. Awkward to say—and so much pressure, to be named after such a *Strong Black Woman*.

You have not yet learned to love the tight wool of your hair, the heavy macramé of the braids your mum wove this morning.

The endless row of aunties sitting in the salon, day-wearied and commuter battle-torn. Loyal, like you. Waiting, like you. Pondering patience, like you. There in the glass. Recognizing, judging, assessing.

What does it mean to be here, you wonder? Sitting in a salon on a summer's afternoon. Sadness? Hope? Joyful self-care? A boss's respect, a partner's renewed passion, a compliment from the coolest girl in the class.

Your English teacher, Mrs. Cobain, says, "All the world's a stage." It's Shakespeare. She would lean against her desk, clasp her hands and say, "They have their exits and their entrances." You think of all the millions of plays being acted out around you.

Stand and watch a while.

The eyes in the mirrors bob as their heads sway up and down, out of sync with the music, its usual gaudy mix of top forty hits, eighties classics, and gospel. The evangelizing vowels of a preacher interrupts the Boney M. song your grandma used to sing to you, and you look around your little church. You contemplate the ritual.

When you were about thirteen, you sat here, in a chair in front of Val, and sullenly told her that your mum is the "most beautiful."

"She says the same about you, yuh knuh," Val said, and your frown dissolved into a laugh as you shook your head.

"All the boys Baker boxes with are sad Mum's left the rec center because they think she's really peng."

Mum left the rec center when you got into the private girls' school.

She had to; even with your scholarship her salary wasn't enough. She now works doing something called "compliance," for a fancy law firm, and even in that first year you could tell she hated it. The late nights, her heavy dark eyes. She never complained, though. Put one shiny black-heeled foot in front of another. At least you repaid her with good grades.

You miss the rec center. Miss the teachers who wear leotards and shoes of all colors, miss the safe warm cocoon of the familiar rooms with the vending machines flanking the doorways like silent sugary sentinels. You miss all the different music you would move against the barre to and all the different languages of all of your different friends and all the different genders of those bending whirling bodies, you just miss all the difference really. Now you can only wear black and pink, all your new teachers only wear black and pink, and you have so many classes and recitals that you don't have time to take your hip-hop class at the rec center.

The first time you'd picked up Saffy from arts and crafts, awkward in your new uniform, you gazed longingly at the old halls of your past life.

Someone called out to you and you turned to see Baker's boys from boxing. Their loud laughter, their roughhousing, their flashing teeth racing into one-upmanship—this is all familiar, moves to a dance you'd replaced in your memory with passing notes and sleepovers but they were still there, somewhere in your muscle memory.

"Whoa, whoa, whoa." Baker had not needed to shout. He had stood slowly, a lean panther, a sweet-juiced dark berry. Even at twelve he was taller than the other boys, broader across the chest and shoulders than even some of the boys in the years above him at the grammar school. He had first been stopped and searched by the police when he was twelve years old.

Baker's friends had instantly backed off, scurrying away, muttering,

"Safe, Baker, was only a joke." No one ever messed with you when Baker was around.

"You scared them off!" you had crowed gleefully, but Baker had looked sad. Baker often looked sad. He smiled often, would laugh with you quietly, but ever since that summer, the summer before Baker started secondary school, something sparkling had died in his eyes.

"Yeah," he'd mumbled. "I know. They're my mates. Don't know why they take me so serious."

"Well, it's a good thing. No one ever troubles me or Saffy because they know you're looking out for us!"

Baker had kissed his teeth and looked over at Saffy, who was, as always, the last to come out of her arts-and-crafts club. She was wearing a pink wig today, with a heavy fringe. "Saffy doesn't need looking after."

"So it's just me, then?" You felt a thrill in the pit of your stomach.

He had looked at you. "Yes. It's just you."

Baker doesn't meet you at the school gate any more. He crosses the road if he is ever about to walk past a little old lady alone. And the boys from the grammar school tease all the girls' school girls, but not you.

Never you.

LONG SUMMERS

"You know, Mush, I wouldn't be fifteen again for any money."

You grunt your agreement. Mum's nails drum sympathy into the steering wheel as you idle in traffic. You feel this way already, trapped between the heady swoon of the adolescence you yearn for and the one you're actually experiencing. You sit on Instagram, scrolling, scrolling, scrolling, stop and like, scroll, absorb without processing, swallow without tasting body after body that looks nothing like yours.

Saffy sings loudly to Jocelyn Brown. Her wig today is a long, jet-black number. You resent her, sometimes. Her insouciance. Her main-character energy. Val once said, "It's Saffy's world, we're all just living in it." You hope she grows out of it before she embarrasses herself. You also hope she stays like this forever.

"Mum, quick, quick, turn it up this is the bit—OH, YEAH!"

"Saffy, it's not a duet," you snap.

Saffy ignores you and sings louder. Mum tuts. "Don't take your PMS out on Saffy."

"I'm not." You sigh, frustrated. "I'm just hot, I don't know why the heater is on."

"Saffy gets cold in the car in the morning."

"It's August. She's going to be eleven soon; she needs to toughen up and not be such a baby."

You're spoiling for an argument. Saffy sings louder still.

"Saffy, god, shut up."

"You're hungry, that's what it is," Mum says. "I always tell you to eat breakfast, it's the most important meal of the day."

"I've eaten, Mum."

"Chocolate digestives are not breakfast."

You scowl. You wouldn't dare ever tell your mum to shut up. You don't have a death wish. You content yourself with thinking it very loudly.

She glances at you. "And just because you're getting your hair relaxed today, don't think you can start asking Val to straighten it every time you're in the salon. We owe her enough money as it is."

"Val doesn't mind."

"That's not the point. She looks after you and Saffy all the time, I don't want to be an ass—" Your mum clears her throat and stops. Her careful avoidance of even the mildest swear word annoys you even more.

"Val doesn't always look after me. Sometimes I go to Melly's!" You are defensive now. You have a social life. You're not a baby! "Sometimes I go to Cat's!"

"Well, I would prefer it if you would go home, where it's quiet, and do your homework."

This really is too far. "Mum. Are my grades not good? Seriously?"

"There are one or two that could be better," she says. "The next couple of years are important. Dance isn't the only thing that matters, you know. Math is important."

You stare furiously out of the window.

"So I'll what? Become an accountant?"

"That's a very respectable career!"

The bitter-tasting words of self-sabotage creep across your tongue. "Maybe I'll get into the ballet instead."

Mum sighs. "You know I think you're very talented. But it's good to have a plan B." Her tone is placating but you don't fall for it. You know she's thinking about last term's dance show. And your Grade Seven exam. You'd excelled at neither. Your stage fright only seems to get worse and worse.

"Saffy, do you mind just not. Singing. All. The. Time?" Saffy falters slightly, blinks at you, and then picks right back up again.

Blue lights flash in the rear-view mirror and Mum sighs and pulls over. She rolls down the window as the officers approach. Saffy stops singing.

You know what they're going to say before they say it.

"Does this car belong to you, license and registration? Oh, nothing, just a car like this is wanted in a local robbery. Sorry, what does your husband do? No husband? Lucky girl to afford a new model like this."

Silence after they walk back to their car. You feel an end-of-braid knot snarl in your stomach at the name she calls them as she drives away.

AUGUST

You are waiting for your appointment. Val makes you sort the rollers, makes you sort the hair clips, makes you sort the post. Everything is categorized and color coded. It should be boring and monotonous but you find it strangely satisfying. Mum is slowly but surely helping Val organize and declutter.

"It needs titivating," Mum had told Val.

"It needs *what?*" Val had asked Mum, eyebrows raising.

"Titivating!" Mum had said, starting to laugh. "It means, you know . . . sexying it up a bit!"

You had rolled your eyes at Baker.

"I've never heard that word before." Val isn't a giggler like Mum but she was grinning and her eyes were dancing with amusement.

You are quite content in your task, sorting rollers, the afternoon wearing on, sometimes listening to music or watching a video, with your headphones in until Val waves at you to get your attention. She is brandishing a red missed-delivery slip.

"Me uh nuh how me keep missing the post, man! Can you go? It says the package is at that new burger place across the street."

"It's cold," you whine. "It's going to rain."

The truth is, any social interaction makes you nervous these days. And you're scared of the cool waitress who works at the burger place, with all the scarves and jewelery—you've seen her, on her lunch break, drinking coffee, laughing into her phone.

Val's other customers, a familiar pair of aunties, tut. "Respect your elders," they say.

"You and Baker used to love going into all the different shops and restaurants on the street. I thought you were a 'patron of small businesses'?" Val asks wryly.

"Bing's Burgers is not a small business, Val, it's a massive chain!" Val doesn't say anything, just gives you a long look that is really an order. You take your coat off the stand, and head out into the barely summer day.

You drag your feet as you cross. Bing's Burgers has replaced not only Mrs. Goss's community garden, where you and Saffy and Baker used to play, but also the old park as well. There is just a small, scrubby patch of green and brown grass now, and a tiny pond.

You head inside. The bright fluorescent lighting, neon signs, and fried food smells intensify your headache. The cool waitress is there. She is wearing a bright-yellow headscarf today and her jewelery catches the light, bouncing tiny gold shards across her cheeks and neck.

Your mind goes blank. You look into the broad, smiling face, the deep-set eyes full of secrets that you know you won't understand even if she tells you.

"I—um. I think you've got a package for the salon." You stare at the counter.

The waitress laughs. "Why you so shy? I see you around all the time, you and your cute friend."

You swallow. "I'm not shy. Nice to meet you," you say.

Nice to meet you?

The waitress laughs and hands you the package. "You're so cute," she says. Your face burns.

"By the way," she says, "my name is—"

But you are already scurrying through the door and the noise of the street is loud and you don't hear.

You survive the pelican crossing and get back to the salon. It's nearly your turn. The *tinkle tinkle* door sounds again almost immediately after you enter and you turn to see Baker behind you. It's a mark of how distracted you are after your awkward encounter with the waitress that

120

you didn't notice him at first. Because you always notice Baker.

"Hi, Mum," he calls, drops a kiss on her cheek. She turns her lips to the side to reciprocate but doesn't look up from an auntie's head bobbing to a top forty hymn and one hundred and fifty pounds sterling of Brazilian virgin hair.

"Baker, have you eaten?"

"No, didn't fancy fries at the rec center caf."

She looks up at him then. Sighs. "Not eating, nor sleeping." Her eyes scan his face seriously. She points to her handbag. "What d'you want? Miss Annie's?"

"Yeah, okay." Baker turns and catches your eye. Your stomach swoops as you scan his face, track the muscles in his jaw, linger on his lips his eyes his lips his eyes his eyes; his lips are moving but you don't hear the words. One of the aunties nudges you gently. "Yuh turn deaf?"

"Sorry, what did you say?" Baker is grinning at you. He looks tired as usual, but his eyes light up with laughter, darken with something you don't yet have a name for.

"I said, do you want to come and get food with me?"

"Oh. Yeah. Sure." Your face feels as though it is on fire; the aunties are snickering, but Val just says, "Don't be long, my belly's talking."

The two of you head out of the salon, and back into the street, strolling up the high road.

"Heard you did good in your practice exams," says Baker. Your face is still hot and you enjoy the cool drizzle from the rain outside.

"Did my mum—"

"Yeah, she's bare proud of you."

"Not of my math grade."

"Yeah, well, you can't be perfect at *everything*."

"I'm not perfect."

Baker grins at you. "I know."

You elbow him in the ribs and catch him off-balance so he stumbles. He huffs a laugh of surprise and grabs your wrist. "You're getting strong. Didn't know a little ballet-dancer princess could swing like that."

"Ballet is a very physically demanding sport."

"Show me the toe thing. Like in that boat film we watched."

"Don't pretend you can't remember the name, Baker. It's *Titanic*. Literally the most famous film about the most famous boat. You're just embarrassed you watched a romantic film, which is stupid."

He holds his hands up in defeat, laughing. "Aight, I get you."

"It's called 'pointe,' and, no, I will not do the toe thing. It's bad for my feet if I don't have the right shoes on."

He grins. "So what's good?"

You shrug. "Not much. It's summer. I'm either at the salon, at home, or at a friend's house. Sometimes my grandma's. Sometimes in the park. Nothing new to report." You eye him carefully. The dark dreams of your childhood brush the edge of your memory. But he never brings it up, and you pretend to ignore the shadows that occasionally cloud his eyes. "You?"

"Same, really. With my boys. Boxing a bit. Helping Mum at the salon to pay for boxing. Don't always tell my mates that."

"That's stupid. You shouldn't care what they think."

"Uh, look who's talking." You feel a thrill at the irritation in his voice. It's been ages since you've properly wound Baker up. You miss that place under his skin; you would crawl there to prove that your opinion mattered, would find safety in his frustration. You used to hide there often, but as you grew Baker changed, became brooding, too mature to argue.

"You get your hair done more than literally any other girl I know."

You try not to think about all the other girls Baker knows. "That's called self-care. And *anyway* give your friends some credit."

You both glance over the road to the burger place.

"It's a shame about the garden. I liked Mrs. Goss. She always gave us blue ice pops, remember?"

"She's still around. Mr. Feeney finally got round to cutting down all that mess in the back. Mrs. Goss is turning it into a beer garden, or something, says if the pub doesn't go gastro it'll die."

"Really?" You are intrigued, as ever, by local gossip. "Does Miss Annie mind her hanging around him, do you think?"

"Well," says Baker, "when Mum was in the thrift store, Ife said that she'd been in the pub and had heard Mrs. Goss telling Mr. Feeney that it looks bad that he doesn't even eat his own food. So now he doesn't go to Miss Annie's as much and I think she's pissed."

You reach the busy corner of the street, where the pub stands next to Miss Annie's West Indian takeaway. Mrs. Goss clearly has nothing to worry about, the place is heaving.

"Maybe she's trying to get between Miss Annie and Mr. Feeney." Beat. "Which she really has no right to do, Mr. Feeney liked Miss Annie first."

"Do you know what happened to Mrs. Goss's husband?" he asks. You shake your head. "It was back when they first moved over here from Ireland. Apparently he collapsed while he was out running. Just dropped down dead. Got rushed into hospital, but it was no good. And Ife says a homeless man saw it all and asked around till he found out who the dead man's wife was and went and found Mrs. Goss, who was working in a cafe at the time. Got some flowers for her after. Went to check on her."

Something is lodged solid in your throat. "Was that Giles?"

Baker nods.

"I wonder where he is now," you muse, thinking about the crinkled-eyed gift bearer, ghosting in and out of your memory. "I hope he's all right."

Baker shrugs. "Mrs. Goss filed a missing persons for him years ago. The police have never been in touch. Which is probably a good sign, right? Maybe it was just time for him to move on."

You think of Mary Poppins, drifting away on her umbrella whenever the wind changed. Giles was like the garden—seasonal but perennial. You hope he is blooming somewhere still.

You head inside the shop. Miss Annie is bustling behind the counter, serving customers ahead of you. You wonder which ones are like you, locals raised on Miss Annie's ackee and saltfish and festival dumplings, and which ones have heard tell of her spiced banana cake and come from further afield.

You and Baker reach the counter and she gives her usual wry smile. "Me hear yuh did good in yuh practice exams?"

You feel your face warm. "Was my mum in here embarrassing me again?"

Miss Annie kisses her teeth as she begins to heap food into yellow Styrofoam containers, without even asking what it is you want—she assumes a bit of everything and she's right. "Whyuh push up yuh face fuh? She proud! All a mother ever wants is tuh be proud!"

"And fair enuf," Baker interjects. "You gonna run the country someday, yeah, just remember us lickle people and hook me up with them sexy girls with trust funds, yeah?"

He is joking, you know he's joking, but you suddenly imagine Baker on the arm of Monica or Aimee or one of the other beautiful rich girls who laugh behind their hands at you at school and are infinitely grateful for Miss Annie, kissing her teeth again and instructing Baker, in no uncertain terms, to pick a drink from the fridge and stop chatting rubbish.

*

Back at Val's, you and Baker unwrap the food and set it out.

"Why didn't you tell me?" he asks. "About the exams. I went on and on about my results the other day and had to hear about yours from your mum."

"Well, they were only practice exams. They weren't the real thing like yours," you say. He got top grades across the board, because of course he did.

"Still, we'll have to celebrate," he says. "Guess we're both geniuses."

You laugh not even because it was funny but because you like how he tastes the word "both" as he says it, like how the implication of you and he together sits on his tongue.

You hand out wings and rice and dumplings, spoon oxtail stew, warm and comforting into your mouth, sit and pick at your jerk chicken wing with the wooden fork. You are ravenously hungry but you don't want to wolf and gulp and swallow, suddenly self-conscious with Baker so close. Mum always said it's not ladylike.

Like he knows, Baker lifts a wing to his mouth with his bare hands. Chews. Crunches the bone. Sucks out the marrow. You feel that tingle and swoop in your belly again. You pull bravado over yourself like a warm sweater and take a dumpling off his plate. Dip it in the gravy, chew, swallow. His eyes are appreciative. You steal another. He reaches towards you. He wipes a smear of gravy from the side of your face. Your eyes meet.

Val is moving the aunties around, a musical chairs of clacking mules and shuffling handbags, acrylic nails marking places in books and magazines as someone leaves, and they all shift right and over—wash to dry, dry to blow out, blow out to style, and so on, in an assembly line, leaving behind a cape billowing and black like a superhero for you to slip into.

Baker has settled at the empty chair and mirror. He flicks through the book he's reading, something from the Year Twelve biology syllabus on plant life. Then he puts it down and picks up the practice head to neaten his cane rows.

He is focused, ignoring the new *tinkle tinkle* door and draft colder than before, only looking up at the strange silence. You look too then.

Wary eyes.

Work paused. Straightened spines. There is a pale-faced man, in a suit, by the door.

125

IN THE CHAIR

The man is neat and tidy and he smiles too much. You never trust people who smile too much. He smells expensive.

Val meets his gaze, holds it, doesn't flinch. "Richardson," she says. You would have quailed under a kinder look but the man is uptight and upright, clean and polished like the baby grand in the music room at school.

"Hey, man," he says to Baker, ignoring Val almost completely.

Baker's bland expression is vanilla-neutral but a powerfully complex flavor. A muscle in his jaw begins to thrum a steady beat at this immediate disrespect.

The man sees you and smiles at you. The kind of smile he's been told is charming, makes him a people person. You look away and at the floor.

"Hello, Val." You wince at the informality, the blatant lack of respect; the aunties tut. "Could we have a chat, in private, maybe?"

"You can say what you want right here," she says.

"No secrets among friends, hey?" He laughs but no one else does. "Thing is, Val," he says, "we need to discuss the rent. The rates in this area are very competitive. . . ."

You tune out because it's dull, grown-up money talk. Instead you watch the quick two-step of a pulse in Baker's jaw, the way his fingers flex open and closed as he works, like a butterfly's wing, like flowers in spring.

You only come to when you feel the rough scratch of Velcro round your neck and you spin dizzy and tense, suddenly confronted with your own reflection in the mirror. Val is ready to do your hair. You had almost forgotten why you had come to the salon today in the first place.

The man is still talking—"I hate to do this to you, I really do" and "the pressures of being a landlord, I don't expect you to get it" and, peppered throughout it all, the word "reasonable." Val is listening, but she is also working. You look at her face in the spotted glass and see a frown and serious brows. Something that looks like irritation to you burns her face like lye. You won't recognize it as shame until you're older.

Val says to you quietly, "You sure about this?"

Relaxer is expensive, so is the upkeep, and returning to your natural state is harder than leaving it. But you nod and then she is silently parting your hair, beginning to paint the thick white relaxer onto your roots, and you are past the point of no return.

You tune out the man, and focus on your hair. The thick forest of kinks and curls being tamed under Val's hand. You wish that you could learn to love the wilderness. Wish the thought of wide-toothed combs and bristle brushes they don't sell in Boots Pharmacy didn't exhaust you so much. The familiar avocado oil smells like apricity, like warm sun in winter, like a magic potion protecting your scalp from the chemical havoc you are about wreak on it.

You imagine what would happen if your hair was too strong to manage this way. Too dense and untameable. Made too resilient by the years of jojoba, cacao, and coconut hair masks, of castor oils, almond oils, olive oils. Healthy and rich and so alive, a thick grown and dark landscape that no matter how hard anyone tried would grow upwards and outwards, become trees and leaves, birds and butterflies and all the secret magic creatures that belong in such a forest. The image tugs on something deep inside you, but the pale-faced man is still talking, and the magic forest in your mind's eye vanishes in your reflection as Val continues to brush white paste into your roots.

Still the man is talking and still Val is silent. Val is not defending herself. She is quiet. So are the aunties.

You worry that the good guys don't win in the end.

*

"The pickney grow suh!" Val is smiling. Val is reluctantly proud and admiring her handiwork. Admiring you.

You look at Mum and Val and you in the mirror. For the first time, you consider yourself to be someone people might find beautiful.

The sleek, shiny, shoulder-length ribbons bounce above your collarbone. You feel like you're dreaming. You experimentally *toss toss* shoulder to shoulder.

The aunties crow their approval. You laugh and become aware of yourself at once head ducking, hair tucking behind your ear, coy and delicate and feminine like the girls with blonde curls in the movies.

Mum arrived while Val was curling your hair, Saffy in tow, face and hands smudged with rainbows after her summer art camp. Mum beams at your beauty and you glow under her gaze. She says, "We look so alike now!" Saffy eyes you warily, head cocked slightly, as she wanders over to her favorite corner and begins to lovingly unwrap and brush out Val's new wigs.

"Aren't you going to say thank you to Val?" your mum says.

"Thank you," you mutter. "I—I really like it."

She nods.

"What do you think, Saffy? Doesn't your big sister look so grown-up?"

Saffy looks at you and says, "It's not a wig, is it?"

"Obviously not." You fight the snap in your tone.

"It looks nice," Saffy concedes. "I just think wigs are better. I'd get bored with always straight hair."

"Well, she can still wear wigs if she wants, baby." Mum's tone is placating, attempting to diffuse the tension.

Saffy shrugs and you ignore her. She won't burst your shiny gold bubble.

You can feel Baker's gaze on you but he doesn't say anything so you stand and wait awkwardly in the doorway for Mum as she pays. You hug your arms tight around yourself, feel the wind blow through your new hair, lift it light as a feather for the first time. Mum said you look like her now. You smile slightly to yourself.

A group of teenage boys pass, calling out to Baker. They notice you then, clock you, zero in on you like a camera switching to a close zoom.

"Yo, Baker, it's like that, is it?"

"You're always spending free time at your ma's salon."

And then to you: "Ay, beautiful, you know Baker ain't even all that?"

"He thinks he's the best boxer, got the biggest brain, but it's not true, swear down!"

"You're actually hot, you know!"

You're a feminist, obviously, you don't want to be objectified, obviously, but you do want to be . . . well . . . hot. So you laugh, awkward, embarrassed. Val emerges to chase them away then, loudly cussing, "Coming inna me salon and hasslin' me customers!! Yuh think me uh won't call yuh mothers!"

One of the aunties' young sons, a little seven-year-old called Esmonde, slips his palm into yours and yanks you down to his height, whispers in your ear, as though afraid someone will hear. "You look like a princess," he says and your throat tightens like his arms around you. You squeeze his compact little body solid and close until he shouts that you're hurting him.

You look like a princess.

Esmonde tears himself free and runs away to hide behind his mother. Your mother is still paying; everything she does with Val takes twice as long because they chat. Still, you avoid Baker's gaze.

He is standing right there.

You bend to fix your shoelace. When you stand, he's looking at you strangely and you wonder if this is going to be it. The moment. Where he tells you that he sees you differently now, really sees you.

"I think I preferred the way you were before. Well, the way your hair was before."

"Oh."

"No offense or anything."

"Right."

"Are you offended?"

"No."

"You sound offended."

"Do you want me to be offended?"

"Of course not!"

"Okay, then, I'm not offended."

"I don't mean that it doesn't look nice. I just mean that you don't really look like you."

"Well, then, good, I don't want to look like me."

"Why not?"

"I don't know! I look too young, I guess. Or something."

"I think you look fifteen."

"I am fifteen."

"Yeah, I know."

"So you don't like it, then. My hair."

"That's not what I said. Come on, allow it."

You don't say anything because you can't think of anything to say. You want to curl up and be nothing, you feel so small. The balloon popped and the bubble burst. You didn't think you were expecting anything, but you were.

"I just think now you look a bit like everyone else."

You look at him. You are oceans apart. You are islands and cities and streets apart. Because looking like everyone else is exactly what you want.

"Well, I didn't ask your opinion anyway, Baker. But thanks. All the same."

You push past and through the door, knowing you'd prefer to wait in the chilly dying light by the car for Mum than have to go through the usual round of goodbyes, and pretend the tears aren't pricking your eyes.

Two-Faced

You sense her before you even close your eyes. Your being drifts and floats away from your body until you sense the familiar cloudy shift, a distinct Crossing, and then you are there. On a craggy mountainside in a land of an evil king, of witches and a magic girl imprisoned in a forest of hair.

You haven't dreamed one of these dreams for years now. You have a faint recollection of a nighttime otherness, of a lingering in between morphing into a pressure that you'd turned away from. Maybe your unconscious self was more determined than you gave her credit for.

"Tell me about Monica again!" she'd say, and you would put a hand on your hip and swish your head so your bonnet fell off, and say, "Of course I'm taking French, babe, I go to Verbier twice a year!" in your best Monica drawl and even though she could not know its accuracy, and you had to tell her what *skiing* was, she would roll with laughter all the same.

"And then Melly said, 'Monica, *babe*, you're the reason God created the middle finger!'"

"What is the middle finger?"

You'd explained and she'd giggled delightedly.

But soon, the differences between you became chasms.

"Isn't it grim, though?" you'd said, watching as a silvery spider navigated a tendril of hair. "All of those scuttling things rustling through your hair? Don't they get it dirty?"

She'd looked at you coldly. "These are not normal animals, obviously. We are all of Xaymaca's magic, of the earth's magic. We are united. They bring me fruit and vegetables to eat, water and nectar to drink. And they keep me company," she'd added sadly.

You stopped dreaming, after a while.

But now you're back. And after five years, you fear the reception.

Now you step forward cautiously, your years of absence stretching between you. Her back is to you as you slip your bonnet off and hold it in your hands. She is wearing a dress spun of real red and purple flowers brought to her by her forest-dwelling friends and is lying cross-legged on the ground, eating some berries and staring at the sky through the gaps in her hair, which has grown to become so dense that you can't see the rugged, jagged peaks of Carrion Ridge. She has grown, is taller, fuller, more beautiful, but time has started to creep at the softness of her features. She turns and notices you, and her world grows still as she does. The rustling and scuttling stops. The wind on the craggy mountainside dies and the sunlike halo of light created by her magic dims, almost dies completely. There is total and complete quiet.

"Oh, great goddess! What have you done to yourself?"

You stiffen. "Hello to you too."

"Why on earth would you . . . would you *debase* yourself like this?"

And now you're angry. "Zella, I'm not debasing myself! I just fancied a change. I changed my hair, it's not that deep!"

You shiver with rage, right where you stand in your silky pink camisole and shorts. They are a far cry from the holey pajamas of your childhood and she is a far cry from the precocious performer friend and you are as sorrowful as you are scared as you are argumentative. You can't believe that after all this time, this is how she welcomes you.

"It *is* that deep! My mothers and their mothers and their mothers fought the King for generations. He came and straightened their hair against their will!"

"Exactly!" you cry. "But this wasn't against my will! It was my choice! It's not like here, no evil king forced me or anything. I did it because I wanted to! It's up to me!"

"Is it? Is it really up to you?"

You let out a roar-howl of frustration and Zella's magic flares around you at the challenge.

"You told me the stories of your world," she says. "On the . . . the internet"—a smug flicker across her face at her remembering of the word—"and the girls on TVs and in the magazines and in your school. The way they look and dress and sit and act."

"So what?"

"So! You say no evil king forced you to do this. But you have evil kings in your world too. And you are foolish to think they are less dangerous!"

There is a silence. Then she says, "Look. You can do what you want, of course. But ask yourself why. That is all."

You sigh. "I wouldn't expect you to understand the petty troubles of us mortals, when you're so busy dealing with the likes of King Charming!"

At the sound of his name, her eyes widen.

"Just go! Go home!" she orders and you feel your mind respond, fighting to wake your body, to pull you away. Zella turns from you and begins to sing:

> *Swing low,*
> *Sweet Chariot,*
> *Coming forth to carry me home.*
> *Swing low,*
> *Sweet Chariot,*
> *Coming forth to carry me home.*

Her hair glows brighter, the forest around you crackles with magic like electricity, and the descent of the dark falters. You can still see her, hear her singing, but when you reach out to touch the soft fronds of the willow, they whisper between your fingers, insubstantial imaginings, the spirit of something fading quickly away.

You can still feel the heavy-limbed weight of yourself, somewhere, against soft sheets in your own bed, but you're not waking up just yet.

Another face flickers into view, an entity, barely an impression, behind a mist—

"Kam? Kam?" you call to the face that overlays her sister's. Her cheeks have narrowed into sharp edges in the intervening half decade, her eyes have condensed into button bright pinpricks of dark light. Her hair hangs straight to her shoulders, like yours. She gasps when she sees you.

"I'll come back!" you promise, even though you don't know how, even though you'd been sure that after Zella had been torn from Persea the first time, that you'd never see Kam again. "I promise I'll come back, Kam!"

You can feel your eyes struggling to open. The clouds descend, reality intercepts your dream state, and you forget your promise.

The Lost Boy

The lost boy returned to the King every night,
held captive by the promise of truths untold.
The King's darkness fed on the boy's misery and fright
and he ruled Xaymaca as he had of old.
But still he pursued the heart of Persea,
the girl with their magic locked in her name.
"You're looking old, Your Highness," she would sneer
whenever he returned to play their game—
and she was right.
He could not rule forever if she continued to fight.
He could not maintain his ageless beauty
without the full force of the source, of the land,
and she knew it was her duty
to continue to stand
strong against his shadows' dark whispers.
She would close her eyes and think of her sister—
and as the smell of death and despair consumed,
she would conjure flowers with her hair,
inhale their perfume,
and think of three truths:
one, she was strong, stronger than she knew;
two, the King was becoming mortal, he sensed it too;
three, there was nothing he could do, nothing he could tell her,
to make her say aloud, that her name was Rapunzella.

SEPTEMBER

First day back at school, gray skies fading to petrol blue by four p.m., and the taste of fries for a pound on your tongue. You douse them in salt and vinegar, stinging your gums deliciously, but put ketchup on the side because Melly doesn't like it. You and Cat squirt red into careful corners, dip, and enjoy. You walk arm in arm to the bus stop under shortening evenings, clouds brush-blending the dark to nearly night under streetlights and the looming threat of homework.

You gossip about the long not-dramas of your summers, the non-romances, Melly's trip to Spain. Cat mirrors your envious gaze, scanning images of her smooth latte limbs golden from beaches.

"And all the boys there are so peng and no one really cares if you drink underage, and you know my parents are so chill about that stuff so I basically had sexy Spanish boys bringing me cocktails all day," Melly is saying, managing somehow to simultaneously speak, scroll on Instagram, and cycle through the five ballet positions, her muscle memory remembering what ten days spent lounging in Spanish sun had almost eradicated.

"But what about Palma?" Cat asks. "Did you see the Catedral-Basilica? Did you go to the old town? Or the Calvari steps in Pollensa?" You smile slightly as you dip and eat. Melly's family goes to nice resorts and spends their time getting wasted. Cat, history lover, polyglot, and the cleverest person you know, would bemoan Melly's good fortune and call her a "philistine" (a word you'd had to look up the first time she'd used it) and quiz her on all of the fascinating landmarks she almost certainly hadn't seen.

Cat is a scholarship kid, like you. Her single mother is a dentist and you had smiled at her at the open house, bonded with her in your first ballet class at big school because the old dance teacher, Mrs. Johnstone, had said, "Some of you need to go to the greengrocer more and the fry shop less," and thrown a long glance at you, then at Cat. That kind of trauma ties you to a person.

Melly had tied herself to the both of you, firstly by wearing a Hawaiian shirt and cycling shorts to the first ten classes (she had gone to some expensive hippy dance school where they "hadn't believed in uniforms"), and secondly by snorting loudly at Mrs. Johnstone's comment and saying scathingly, "I don't know what's more out of touch, your fat-shaming or the fact that you think anyone still shops at a greengrocer."

Mrs. Johnstone hadn't returned after that term, and though she'd been due to retire that Christmas anyway, you often joke that Melly sent her early. Her replacement, Mrs. Fitzsimons, was a rich hippy friend of Melly's rich hippy parents. You adore her. She actively encourages Hawaiian shirts and cycling shorts, and choreographs dances to her favorite jazz numbers on vinyls from her holidays in Vegas.

Mum had once said Cat and Melly were like chalk and cheese, but you had disagreed. "They're more like cheese and tomato," you'd explained. "Like, so different but so good together on a pizza." Mum had laughed and said, "So what does that make you?" Your smile had faded and you'd shrugged and changed the subject. You didn't exactly want to be the plain, doughy base, even though it was essential. But then any other topping was so . . . secondary. Inessential. Still. So what if you're pepperoni? Or basil. People like those things.

"Cat, I really love that you're so into all of this stuff, I really do," Melly is saying. "You give me great documentary recommendations for Netflix and you're literally a human encyclopedia. But, babe, when I'm on holiday, I just want to take a good bikini pic and check out sexy boys, okay?"

Cat turns to you, expression outraged. "Can you even believe we're friends with someone this basic?"

Melly laughs with you because she's the most impervious person you know, her green eyes dancing. "I know, it's the most English thing ever, isn't it? At least my parents both speak some Spanish. Not that we needed it, in the bloody resort the whole time."

You laugh. "When we go on holiday," you say, "my mum carries her French phrase book with her everywhere and looks up every. Single. Sentence." You give an exaggerated roll of your eyes. "Most of the people we ask for directions speak better English than any of us!"

Your friends laugh with you and you are grateful. For a moment you feel like pepperoni—no, you feel like chorizo, you feel like garlic and salt and pepper. And the base. You haven't been abroad much. Melly and Cat know this but it doesn't really matter. Lazy days in a sunny haze isn't your mum's style. She favors a quick march and two-step around historical sites with cheap flights, fox-trotting from museum to old church, a street dance from the textbooks that she never got to study but buys secondhand from the British Heart Foundation on the high street. You are always reminded on these occasions that Mum is wasted in her dull office. What an amazing teacher she would have been.

She wants more for you. It's nice.

You scroll, scroll, scroll, stop, and like through Melly's SPAIN BISHES PHOTO DUMP, endless versions of the same photo. They sit above a targeted ad about "curves in the right places." Like Melly needs help—she's already gorgeous enough, thanks very much. Cat shakes her head. "I hate those stupid ads, curves in the right places! Like there are WRONG places to have curves, it's actually wild to me that those things are allowed to stay up."

"I know," says Melly. "Maybe we should start some kind of campaign? Start a hashtag against those ads . . ."

"That's such a sick idea!" Cat bounces excitedly. "I can draw up some bullet points. Show the statistical correlation between ads that promote an unhealthy body image and dysmorphia in teenage girls and young women. . . ."

Melly nods. "With my social media skills and your whole being a human encyclopedia thing, I bet we could really come up with something!"

They turn to you, four eyes alight with the fervor of a new project and you feel irritated and frustrated but can't explain why. You only know that cynicism is rising in your throat like bile, you're going to vomit negativity all over them. You are a mushroom or a pineapple or another topping that no one likes.

You shrug. "Yeah, maybe." They sense your reluctance and don't push it. The silence is awkward. You all return to scrolling.

You think about every fold and crevice of your body every day, but you are small details not big picture and herein lies the problem. Monica French did say she liked your new hair today, so did everyone actually. That's something.

Cat's beauty and Melly's beauty are both very real and very different. Melly's beauty is all symmetry and contradictions—big boobs, small waist, big eyes, small nose, big lips, small hips. Her complexion is a warm, rosy ivory all year round which she says is because of an Italian grandmother on her dad's side, but you suspect is actually because she and her family go on holiday about six times a year. She is what every magazine ever told you to be.

Cat is taller than both of you, but she would never dream of shrinking herself. Her skin is a rich umber and glows reddish beneath like the kind of sunsets shepherds celebrate. Her dark eyes are deep-set and cat-like, her cheekbones are high and wide, her nose and lips are full and proud, almost haughty. Her hair, curls both looser and denser than your own—or your own how it used to be—starts the day in a puff on top of her head and, by four p.m., would break free, snapping combs and pins and hairbands, as powerfully defiant as Cat herself.

Mrs. Johnstone remarked on its "messiness" but now Cat wears her hair loose in class, a spectacular cloud of life whirling round her as she moves.

"Baker said he didn't like my hair."

They round on you immediately, zero to outraged in an instant.

"Um, who needs his opinion?" Melly says.

Cat is similarly indignant. "Honestly, can we not escape the male gaze for five minutes?!"

"I hope you didn't let him get to you," says Melly. "You're gorgeous, your hair is gorgeous."

You feel like the whole pizza again.

"I don't care anyway," you lie. "Not like I'd go to Baker for fashion advice." They laugh. "If I get bored, I'll just borrow one of Saffy's wigs."

"I've never seen a more impressive wig collection," Cat muses.

Melly is looking back at her phone. "Should I post another red bikini one? Or is it too many bikini pictures; I don't want to look like a ho?"

"Don't slut-shame yourself," Cat says. "It's the twenty-first century, women can wear what they want, when they want."

"Unless you're just doing it for the likes," you interrupt piously. "Don't do it just to get validation from social media, Melly."

"Why not?"

You scowl. You don't know what's wrong with you today. Maybe you're just sick of it—sick of carefully dipping fries in corners; maybe you want to slather the batch in ketchup, create a sea of red-rage, salt, and sugar to consume at top speed, maybe you want to lick your fingers and be messy round your mouth; maybe you're just tired.

"How do you know they're not dirty old men liking your pictures?" you ask.

"My profile is private." Melly is maddeningly patient. "I check everyone who requests to follow me."

"Well. They could have fake profiles."

"Maybe." Melly shrugs, eyes on her phone. You bite your tongue. You look at the screen with the bus times. Twelve minutes.

You glance over Melly's shoulder at her photo dump, carefully curated, artfully indifferent.

"Melly, when did you get your first period?"

She still doesn't look up. "Um, about a year ago. Wait, a year and a half. Why?"

Cat had started about six months before that. You remember because she had solemnly asked you to show her how to use a tampon, scoffing at your squeamishness, calling it a "coming of age" moment.

"What size bra do you both wear?"

Melly finally looks up. "Why? What's all this about?"

"You know that when you start your period has no effect on your bra size, don't you?" Cat reminds you gently.

"I know *that*." You're defensive again. Although it's Cat, and you really don't need to be.

You pretend to examine the timetable. "It doesn't matter," you mutter. "Boobs are just boobs."

The bus arrives.

The screen still says twelve minutes.

The rain begins in earnest and you don't have an umbrella.

You wonder if you got off at Val's, if she would hot-comb your hair again, if Mum would pay.

You can feel the frizz prickling your scalp under the newly straightened, heavy strands.

The windows are steamy. Cat and Melly discuss new teachers.

You stare into the greasy box. The fries are cold and soggy and yellow.

Kamaka

In these stories there often are
riders from afar,
a man, usually.
See one galloping along,
the road is dusty, the horse is strong,
sweating flank heaving,
harmonized heavy breathing.
But now *she* takes off her hat,
she lets down her hair,
it hangs poker-straight,
she tucks it behind her ear, like all the girls in the movies do.
See her there standing, she's sturdy and lean,
she is not yet sixteen.
Lately she had been riding out every day,
getting further and further away,
searching for—well, she's not quite sure.
She pauses. Frown. She stops and looks around.
She's not totally sure but—
No, she definitely heard a sound.
And as she stood frozen,
not understanding how this could be real,
she could feel her chest,
filling like lungs do with smoke;
she thought she might choke on this something
like hope, she heard—

from further away than she should be able to hear—
a voice like a bell, ringing and clear:

> *Swing low,*
> *Sweet Chariot,*
> *Coming forth to carry me home.*
> *Swing low,*
> *Sweet Chariot,*
> *Coming forth to carry me home.*

Persea

School is busy. A merry-go-round of clubs, work, anxiety, Melly and Cat busy with their Instagram campaign, Monica sneering at you while flicking her hair. You don't dream. Don't know anything of Xaymaca except for the clouds that lurk at the edges of your sleep-time vision, which don't move in quick enough to obscure one blinding moment of clarity, a split second where you see a familiar house, a blinking face, a giant curling forest, and a stab of guilt and anxiety, before being whisked away.

Back to normal life.

But then, one evening, after a particularly long dance class, you take a warm bath to soothe your aching muscles. Mum had often warned you of the dangers of falling asleep in the bath, but you can't resist the gentle bobbing of your mind, through the clouds and onwards.

You float towards a shoreline, laden with golden sand and bedecked with trees that look like palms, only not any you've seen—shorter leaves, wider trunks. You are content to let the current take you, the soporific lapping of the waves against your skin is warm and wet but you are still dry, somehow. You sail along the coast towards the point where the sand darkens into soil, its ripe fertile odor mixing with the sharp tang of salt water and a forest erupts from the earth. A river's mouth comes into view, opening out from the dense cover of trees. You try to remember what your geography teacher told you about rivers but know on some level that textbook explanations will not help you in Xaymaca.

A hush descends as you cruise down the river and into the cool shade of the trees. Where the current is taking you, you do not know, but you don't feel afraid. The current knows. Magic is not exact, but it's always intentional.

Giant, sprawling weeping willow trees line the river, their protective arms drooping into the water like fingers reaching out to touch you, hands stretched in blessing. You remember what Kam and Zella once told you about willow trees. About how they know everything that ever was and ever will be, and how they sometimes choose a witch to share that knowledge with, a Seer. As you pass through them you are almost sure you can hear them whispering to each other, almost sure you can hear them sighing your name. You bow your head in respect and, though you don't know why, send up a prayer to their evergreen heavens. *Please, give me what I need to help my friends.*

Eventually the current releases its firm grip and you find that you can stand in this shallower water. You wade towards the eastern bank and clamber out. You are naked but you don't care, somehow. You are warm and dry and almost tempted to lie there, in the dappled half-light filtering through the trees of the great forest, and rest. You feel so peaceful.

You sit up and look around. This *is* the Great Forest. You know it is. The forest you were never allowed to wander through, the forest that holds and protects Persea—the village named for the coven who founded it—in its center. The forest that Kam and Zella's cottage had backed directly on to. You think about the large white cottage, its cluttered, cozy interior, the burned sienna wood of the kitchen spilling into the worn sofas and heaped blankets of the sprawling living room. You can almost smell the roaring coal fire that piped out of the chimney of the thatched roof, mingled with the thousand rich scents of *life* coming from the garden that rivaled any expensive hot house for sheer number and variety. The green trellises climbing the white stone, the vibrant reds and oranges and blues of flowers that made up the maze of flowerbeds, winding round the garden before opening into the lush green lawn with the white wooden swing in the back.

You can see it in front of you, in your mind's eye. See it so clearly that you begin to walk, as if towards it. Something pulls you towards the image, or maybe pulls the image towards you. You tread lightly and carefully, aware of your bare feet against bracken and twigs, although nothing marks you. Gradually the trees thin, the light brightens and shifts from green gold to ocher and you find yourself parting the last of the low hanging vines and stepping out on to a street.

To your left the street wends away down a steep slope into what looks like the center of a small village. There are a few shops that you can see, arranged around a triangle. In the middle of the triangle is what one might call a green, but it's so colorful, with such a vast and impossible range of flowers growing next to each other within it, that perhaps the word meadow is more appropriate. And all around—witches. Chatting in the streets, bustling between shops, and a group gathering in the green moving in graceful arcs, weapons in hand, as though practicing a lethal kind of dance.

The shops sell books and clothes, jewelery and some furniture, metalworks and tools. But nowhere to buy food or medicine—those things, you suppose, come from the forest. The shops are dotted between houses, some around the green triangle and others scattered erratically down streets. From your vantage point, atop your slope, you can see there are less than a hundred in all, and you can see that while the triangle looks definite and intentional, the streets look like they weren't planned or designed, but merely thought into existence on a whim by whomsoever had wanted to live there. Some are cobbled, some are paved, some are dirt tracks, and some, like the one you're standing on now, are laid with the same gold sand you saw gilding the beachy shore as you arrived. The whole place looks so part of the forest, like the witches hadn't wanted to clear too much of the land they loved and so had worked around it, with many of the gardens and ends of streets being claimed by trees and moss and bracken once more.

To your right, the street climbs higher still, following the forest line and curving right again, and out of sight. You follow it under the cover of the trees until you reach the right turn and stop dead because there it is. The house of your dreams.

If they are all here, you think, and they are all safe, then why haven't they come for Zella? You wrap your nakedness in leaves. The cottage looks still and quiet. There is no sound, no movement. Your heart sinks—but, no, Kam at least is still alive and scowling. You saw her only weeks ago, called to her, and she heard you.

You walk forward, grateful for the soft padding of the sand mixed with earth beneath your feet. You realize you'd never seen this side of the house before, had only ever appeared in the garden in the back. The front door is painted dark green and the trellises from the back creep round the front, so that you can't tell where each vine ends and begins. The front garden is smaller than the back and bedecked with more herbs than brightly flowering buds. Some are herbs that you recognize by smell if not sight—rosemary, thyme, basil, mint, the earthy scent of wild garlic the strongest—and others that you don't but whose perfume mingles with their bedmates to make your mouth water.

You stand there a moment. Your hand on the shining dark wood of the gate. You are suspended, savoring a before time, doubt creeping into your mind. This isn't your land; this isn't your family. Why should you help? *Can* you help?

But then you see movement in the windows, a sudden flurry of light material and dark limbs, and the front door is abruptly thrown open.

Boundaries

The last time you saw each other hangs specter-like between you, the last words you said echo through the years. You swallow. Then her face crumples, the thin, angry line of her lip wavers and breaks and before you can blink, you are sobbing in each other's arms.

"Kam! Oh my god, Kam! I can't believe it's you! I didn't know what had happened to you—I thought you might be—"

"I know, I know!"

"I'm so sorry! For everything that happened before, for my part in all of it. I'm so sorry!"

She hiccups. "It was not your fault. We taught you to fear the truth instead of understanding it."

You pull back and look at her as she looks at you. She is now her sister's opposite. Zella reminds you of a large, bright bird of paradise, generous wingspan and enormous feathers, but Kam, Kam, in her close-hugging black leather leggings and loose black silk shirt, is a prowling jungle cat, a panther or jaguar. Her limbs are long and narrow, her dark hair is slick and straight like yours, tied in a low ponytail. Neither of you acknowledge this change. She looks beautiful, but unlike herself. Her face is lined with sadness, and her hands twitch restlessly like an agitated tail, *flick, flick, flick.* You realize then what's missing. There's no spark. No silver gold ember burning at the end of her long fingertips.

"I saw you," you say. "The other night . . ."

She gasps, seizing your wrist. "That was real?" Her eyes widen. "Come inside. We have so much to talk about."

You feel a frisson of excitement as you cross the threshold into the large white cottage. To come within, to be an insider when you've always been an outsider, is thrilling. The front door opens immediately into the large, open downstairs room you'd always gazed at from your perch on the white wooden swing in the garden.

The squashy old sofas in russet and chestnut are still heaped with blankets, the wood of the floor and the kitchen counters is still a warm terracotta, the coal fire isn't burning because the day is mild. The spiraling engraved staircase leading to the upper level is in front of you and now you can see in full detail just how exquisitely detailed the carvings are. Leaves and vines and flowers, tiny little insects, but not insects that you recognize, many legged and many winged, adorn the ridges and whorls of wood. You squat until you're eye level with the banister for a closer look. The tiny creatures have tiny faces and tiny expressions. You've never seen anything like it.

"Are they not beautiful?"

The unfamiliar voice startles you and you jump, spring up, and turn, aware of your semi-nakedness. It was a voice you'd only heard once before, years ago, raised in quarrel. Ama. More and more, Kam is her double. The same high, vicious cheekbones, the same long, willowy frame, the same air of brooding power. Emerging from the back door that leads into the garden, Ama is wearing a thin, sleeveless blue gown, made of a light linen narrowing at her waist and belted with a braid of leather and brass. Her feet are bare and flecked with mud and grass but gone are her long dreadlocks. Instead her hair is pulled into a high ponytail which falls, dead straight, to the center of her back. She wears a simple gold armband around her toned bicep and several small gold hoops adorn her ears. You have never been this close to her before, but you remember the kitchen window exploding with leaves and trees and flying things. You prepare yourself for the taste of metal on your tongue, for the pulse of raw creation magic in the air around her. But it isn't there. She is striking, of course, but in this place ordinariness is strange and you are wrong-footed.

"I know you," she says. "You are the third girl, who comes to us in her dreams. I am glad we are finally able to meet. After that awful day I was sure we never would. But the currents of this world are strong and mysterious." Her voice is low and husky and warm. Her accent reminds you of someone.

"Weighty words, my plum," a light honey-sweet voice trills. "Could you not have offered the poor child a drink first?"

Cynthia, dressed immaculately in a white cotton two-piece, with low billowing sleeves and wide bell bottoms, is standing at the top of the stairs. The belt slung around her middle is leather, woven with golden brass, and you admire the way the bright ivory offsets her smooth, dark skin. Her hair is without wave or curl and hangs in a blunt bob just past her ears. There is an agelessness about her and it occurs to you, suddenly, that you don't know how old they are. Don't know how long they spent enslaved by the King. Up close you see how much shorter than Ama she is. Her curves are soft and generous, her face is broad and delicate, her eyes almond-shaped and the dappled light brown of the shallows of the River Aphra that had brought you here. Yet this soft, generous woman was the leader of the Great Strike that brought the King to his knees.

She walks towards you and pulls you close, embracing you in a fierce hug. "Come," she says. "You have much to tell us."

You follow her into the familiar kitchen, Ama and Kam close behind you. Little has changed. The large round scrubbed wooden table, the piles of books lining the walls into the living space, the giant wrought iron clock hanging on the wall opposite the window and door you'd peered through countless times. Kam brings you a long lilac gown, one of hers you assume as it pools around your ankles.

Questions well on your tongue. Cynthia takes a bottle from where it stands on the dresser and pours four measures of a dark, amber liquid.

"It is honey wine, made from the nectar of the honey rose. It was Zella's favorite. Let us drink it in the memory of your friendship—and of her."

"In memory of her?" you say. It is then you realize. They don't know.

You put down your glass because your hands are shaking. "Zella—she's alive. She's alive and I've seen her and I know where she is!"

They just stare at you. Your pronouncement stuns the very air into quiet. Then Kam yells, half-wild and half-jubilant, "I knew it! I *knew* it! In the Great Forest, just by the Persean border, I was sure I could hear singing. I thought it must be the trees."

Your eyes widen. "The voice . . . does it sing 'Swing Low?'"

Kam smacks your arm hard, then shakes it, then smacks it again, leaping to her feet. "Yes! Yes! It does! It's her!"

"How on earth can you hear her, from so far away?"

"It depends on the direction of the wind, but . . . I do not know. Maybe it is a twin thing?"

"Excuse me," said Cynthia quietly. "You say she is safe—where is she, exactly? Can you explain what you know?"

You take a deep breath. "My hairdresser put avocado oil in my hair. After that, I started coming to this place in my dreams—I met your daughters." They both nod. "One day I told her son about my dreams. He tried some of the oil for himself. His name is—"

You hesitate because there is power in naming things but Kam dismisses it. "Honestly, do not bother. Our names have no power here, not anymore. There is no longer magic in Persea."

"No magic?"

You are aghast but Kam shakes her head. "You first. Then we will share our story. The hairdresser's son—that is Baker, yes?"

You nod. "Yes. One day, while Kam and Zella and I sat in the garden, he appeared to us. Something went wrong in Persea from that moment on. And Baker changed. He is . . . sad, tired. He never talks about what happened, but I can tell, I always can with Baker. After that, I didn't come back for a while." You glance at Kam—remembering that terrible day. "When I did it wasn't Persea I returned to. I was on a mountain and Zella was there. She said she remembers screaming and then you all vanished. That's when the King appeared to her. He tried to get her to tell him her name, but she didn't. He couldn't touch her, her hair—which is amazing now, by the way—protects her. So instead he banished her."

"To where?" Cynthia demands.

"She says it's called Carrion Ridge?"

"He put our baby on the side of that mountaintop to rot?" Ama is shaking with wrath. "He dares? He *dares?*"

"He can't seem to harm her. She's incredibly powerful. But he was able to transport her, somehow. Bind her to the mountain."

"As he binds us to the forest." Kam says bitterly. "We are trapped here. Without a spark of magic between us."

"It all started after that boy came," says Ama. "He must be helping the King somehow. *A son born of witch and might, a thief who will learn to fear the night, if witches' magic he steals and drains, the King will Persea with darkness stain. . . .*"

"Baker would never do something like that!"

"All evidence points to the contrary." You had not missed Kam's sass at all and bite back your waspish response.

Cynthia is gazing at you thoughtfully. "There is hope yet, in what you have told us. He does not have Zella's name. He does not truly hold our power. He may have drained our magic, but as long as Zella remains free, we can yet retrieve what we have lost."

Cynthia glances at you. "You say your hairdresser gave you avocado oil?"

"Yes."

The two women look at each other. Then Cynthia goes quickly to one of the glass cabinets and brings out a jar, thrusts it under your nose. "Familiar?" she asks.

You inhale. The smell whisks you back to the comfort and ease of Val's chair. "Yes," you say. "Yeah, it's the same."

153

"Exactly the same?"

"Yeah. I think so." You are not following. "So what? Surely all avocado oil smells like this?"

"Not exactly. A powerful homing potion. Needs a powerful spell and a powerful witch. Then it is applied to the hair, which is the portal to all magic."

"But I don't have any magic."

"Everyone has some magic," Kam says quietly.

"A homing potion means that wherever you go, whatever world you're in, you will always be able to return to the root of your fruit. You will always be able to go home," says Cynthia, screwing the lid back in place and retaking her seat. "It explains why you would visit us in the garden, as a child. I would assume that the root of the fruit in your oil"—she points outside the large kitchen window to the wide-branched tree, lending its shade to the wooden white swing—"is right there."

You stare.

"How in the name of the goddess does your hairdresser have a homing potion made with one of our avocado pears?" Ama asks,

"I don't know." Your mind is whirring. "But if I'm . . . I'm tethered to this garden, how was I able to see Zella?"

Cynthia stares out into the garden. Her gaze follows the to-ing and fro-ing of the white swing, the swaying of the branches of the avocado tree. "Anyone who uses the fruit of the root is connected in some way. It's imprecise, but if for some reason you cannot access the original root, the magic finds a replacement. The King's curse robbed Persea of magic and placed a magical border around the village, preventing anyone from leaving or entering. By any means. It makes sense that, after the King's curse, Zella, with her powerful hair, became your secondary root."

"And now?" You look around at the strange familiar kitchen. "How am I here now?"

Ama pierces you with her gaze. "Perhaps it's your hair. Maybe the barrier he has placed around Persea lets you in because it believes you are like us." Her tone is disapproving, even as she says, "A useful disguise, I suppose."

"But the King . . . he has your magic, you're trapped here—so why does he need Zella? Why does he want her name?"

"Because she is the heart of Persea," Kam says calmly. "The child named in the prophecy and the most powerful."

Ama flinches and Kam says, "It is okay, Mama. I have always known that Zella is . . . special."

"You're special too!" Ama is hotly insistent. Kam smiles wanly. "You are! You just have different roles to play."

"A long time ago, when the King first arrived here, his mirror whispered to him of the magic of the Persean witches, of the power of our names." Cynthia drags her eyes away from the window, to your face. "The King learned he need only to speak the name of the most powerful Persean witch and—so long as she was past her sixteenth birthday and come into her full power—all of that power would become his. And so he sought out the most powerful witch and when he found her, introduced himself, oh so politely. And when she, charmed by his good manners, returned the favor, Persea was lost. He shaved the witches' hair, probably just to humiliate them further, but found that their hair was a powerful ingredient in his elixir of life. It kept him young and strong. And allowed him to harness their magic, not just possess it." She shrugs. "As has happened now. Zella, the most powerful witch in Persea, will be sixteen on the Sankofa, in less than two months. She will have reached her full power. And if he gets her name . . . nothing will stop him then."

They look tired and helpless. It is cold, colder than you realized, and you begin to shiver.

"Zella is still free, though," you say. "Still out there." Your teeth are chattering. "I can visit Zella and now I can visit you too. I can pass messages between you, reassure her that you are well, perhaps find some way out of this, together. . . ."

155

You watch as the faintest flicker of hope crosses their faces. Kam reaches out to touch you, starts, recoils. "You're freezing!" she cries with alarm. "Your arm, it's wet."

No! You think, *I'm in the bath!* As soon as you think it, you feel the pull, a swifter tug than usual and you are rising towards wakefulness, almost against your own control.

"I'm waking up!"

"Listen!" Cynthia cries. "You need to know how dangerous this is—"

"It's all right," you gurgle. "I'm not really here, remember!"

Kam reaches for your hand, you try to speak but—

Your words are choked by freezing bathwater. You splutter. Spit it out. Remember, remember, remember you plead with yourself as you emerge, wrinkled and icy cold. The memory recedes as you warm yourself dry, but leaves the faintest trace of determination, that tastes like honey wine.

OCTOBER

"You know, schools in this country are an absolute joke. And we *pay* for this one."

It is an afternoon in late October and Melly is complaining loudly as you head down the grand spiral staircase in the center of the school building. You hush her—girls aren't meant to use these stairs. All the noise might be "off-putting to visitors," you were told when you started. It might send the wrong message.

What message? you wonder. The message that girls go to school here? Vibrant, laughing, loud. Not hushed and quiet, keeping to the back stairs.

There are many things here that confuse you. You'd always assumed that the date, carved into the stone pillars that flank the driveway, was the founding date of the school. But you'd learned that actually those pillars belonged to an old boys' school, the site of which had been round the corner, and that your school had been founded about a hundred years later, amid a post-war rebuild, a great boom, a fanfare of Rosie Riveter ribbon cutting. This sat with you for some reason. The uncertain identity of the place—blazers and iPads and brochures that boast diversity, even as they plaster the same handful of Black and Brown girls across their marketing every year.

"I don't disagree," is Cat's measured response, "but are you talking about anything in particular?"

"This!" Melly explodes, dropping her heavy stack of folders on the stair with a loud *THWACK*. They immediately start sliding downwards and you scramble to catch them before all of Melly's notes on the Third Reich can litter the reception and land the three of you in detention. "It's like they pick this crucial time in our social and emotional development to dump all of this work on us!"

Cat laughs. "Bit early in the term for the dramatics, isn't it? You normally save your 'life isn't about exams, it's about interpersonal relationships so let us party' speech at least until the Easter holidays."

You're in the corridor now and wending your way between heaving throngs of girls towards your common room for break.

Monica French is ahead of you, stowing her books in her locker, tossing her hair so fiercely you wonder she doesn't get whiplash. You try to avoid her gaze, but you're not quick enough. Cat and Melly have headed inside the common room and Monica is approaching you with a terrifying expression of martyrdom. Behind her are Aimee and Amy. Your heart sinks.

In history that afternoon, a lesson about Kristallnacht had segued into a debate about state-sanctioned violence, which in turn had led to a long debate about police brutality (because the school "prides itself on debate") and Monica, rolling her eyes and flip flipping her hair flippantly said, "God, is everything about racism these days?"

The room had echoed and your history teacher, Mrs. Reubens, eyes narrowed, had let it.

You understood why she did this, understood the unwritten laws by which she was bound. The week before, arrogant Aimee, who is disdainful of everyone (unlike adulating Amy who adores everyone) had said, "Mrs. Reubens, can you explain what you mean by the power of capital?"

Mrs. Reubens had looked delighted; Aimee had probably never asked a question of any teacher before, other than, "Can I go to the toilet?" She had given a concise explanation. And Aimee, her eyes flint-like, had said, "So what you're saying is, the person who pays, has power?"

"Well, that's rather crudely put, but I suppose."

"So if that's the case why do we have to do what you tell us to? Our parents pay your salary, right?"

The room had echoed then just like it had this afternoon and Mrs. Reubens had sent Aimee to the headmaster's office. Ten minutes later, a secretary had come to fetch Mrs. Reubens herself and sat with the class while you read from the textbook. When you saw Aimee next, at lunchtime, she had smug expression on her face and you thought of the gluttonous, idiomatic cat who got the cream, licking its lips and belching.

You hadn't meant to respond to Monica that afternoon; normally you left this sort of thing to Cat, who has read more anti-racist theory in her short life than you can imagine. But for some reason, you spoke before giving yourself permission to do so.

"It's always been about racism, actually, Monica." You felt the glare intensify, multiplied as the class's eyes turn on you. "It's about power and who has it. It's about health and life and powerful people choosing whose life gets to matter."

Monica's eyes had gone wide, her mouth slightly open, you didn't think you'd ever said that many words to her in one go. She had hastily swallowed her surprise, painted the familiar, superior girl school mask back on her face—she's disinterested, even amused, and you are a joke and an embarrassment—actually, she's embarrassed *for* you because she's a nice person, really.

"Babe"—the hypocorism nauseated you—"of course I think that everyone should be treated the same."

"I guess you would say that, wouldn't you?" You think of Miss Annie, of Mum, of Giles. Of Val. Of Richardson. The words keep coming. "But the fact is that not everyone *does* get treated the same. I know someone, a friend of mine, who physically couldn't work any harder than they do and they're probably going to lose their business because their landlord wants to raise the rent of their store. If they lose their business, they lose their income so they can't pay the rent on their flat and then they get evicted and then . . . then where do they go?"

Silence, and then Mrs. Ruebens had suggested you move on to the next source.

*

Now they're standing in front of you, Aimee sneering, Amy simpering, and Monica in front, head tilted in concern.

"Babe," she says, "do you really know someone who might lose their business? They'll be out on the streets? Like, that's so sad."

You swallow. Sweat glues your shirt to your back, prickles your armpits; you're almost convinced you see Aimee delicately sniff the air, scenting your fear. "Um, I don't know if they'll end up out on the streets. They'll probably just stay with us for a while."

"No, but even so, it's just, like, devastating."

"Yeah, devastating," Aimee and Amy chorus on cue, like they've rehearsed their empathy.

"They own a business, you said?"

"Yeah. A hairdresser's."

"Oh my god! So cool! Did they do your new hair?" Monica gestures at your head. "Seriously, they're totally talented. I've really noticed the change in you since."

"Yeah. Val is . . . Val is the best." You don't mention Baker. You haven't spoken to Baker since the fight about your hair and there's no way you're saying his name in front of Monica.

You smile tentatively at Monica. She beams back.

"Be such a shame if she went out of business," says Monica. "Listen, so my dad, he does loads of local business investment. Money and consultations and development and stuff. I bet I can get him to invest in Val's salon or something? Or talk to her landlord and make him see that raising her rent isn't actually a good strategy, you know?"

Your first instinct is skepticism. Everyone knows Monica's father—he's a local developer and loaded. Like he's going to bother with Val's business. But then you think—it can't hurt, can it? It wasn't like you'd heard of any better ideas. Mum and Saffy had been chatting about some kind of fundraising event over breakfast, but their idea had started caffeinated and energized like Mum's sugary black coffee and then congealed into gray mush at the bottom of Saffy's bowl of shredded wheat.

"Okay. That would actually be really great. Thanks, Monica."

She trills a laugh. "You're so formal, babe! It's no stress!" Then, "You know, I'm actually having one of my sick parties tonight for Halloween and seeing as how you're literally like a bad bitch now, you should defs come!"

Amy nods with enthusiasm, Aimee nods with the promise of murder in her eyes.

"I can't," you say. "Other plans."

It's not a lie—you're going to Melly's like you always do. But along with the relief, you feel the faintest tinge of regret.

＊

You think about it all through dance class, as you stretch and pointe your body, relish its strength and discipline. The rain beats against the windows of the hall, and as you dance you think of birds arcing towards the clouds, a swell crashing against salt-spot rocks, a verdant forest teeming with strange insects. You can hear singing, somewhere. Somewhere lush and sweet-smelling, somewhere familiar yet strange, somewhere you haven't been for a while. Somewhere you are needed.

But then you blink your eyes open. It is Halloween and the veil is

161

thin and you don't settle back into yourself until the cold air bites your face and Melly and Cat's bickering about scary movie choices drowns out the sounds of singing.

*

At Melly's house, in her large, brightly lit, white marble and gold bathroom, you post a selfie with your new hair. You make sure that your mum is blocked and then unbutton your shirt so that pink lace peeps through, a sliver of skin. Monica is the first to like it.

Interloper

The next few weeks of dreams are fractured and restless.

Often, you return to the cottage. You are all sure you are being spied on.

"The land is always listening," Ama said one night, as you sat in their kitchen.

"Wish it could speak as well," Kam had replied waspishly. "Or do something to help when it sees bad things happening."

"The land has done plenty—we would not have had our magic without it," Ama reminded her sagely. Kam had shrugged but let it go. She is a permanently prowling figure, stalking cat-like up and down the back of the garden, restless and waiting.

Cynthia and Ama reluctantly agree you should act as go-between—taking messages and spells between the cottage and Zella. They hope to teach her how to use her magic this way. Despite forgetting everything in your waking world, your memory of Xaymaca in Xaymaca had always remained intact. Cynthia and Ama drill you on magical mind practice until you can recite their lessons perfectly. Dreams and reality begin to blur and merge like bright ink in water. You fall asleep in class and wake in the night, confused—but you are not the main character and this is not about you.

Eventually, one night, you find yourself in Carrion Ridge. Zella is there, hair crackling purple and gold with energy.

Your last, bitter words hang between you, and you rush in with an apology.

"Look, I'm sorry for everything. I messed up. But the important thing is, I've seen your family in Persea."

163

Zella's mouth opens.

"I've seen them," you say again. "Your mothers, Kam. Persea is still there, it's just hidden by the King's spell. I told them I'd seen you and they're so happy you're okay. Kam thought she'd heard you singing sometimes—depending on the wind."

Zella swallows. "Maybe it's a twin thing."

"That's exactly what she said." The humming magic in the air seems to shift frequencies; you can almost hear the ringing in your head, like a dull pressure against your ears.

"Well, then, why haven't they come and got me?"

"They're trapped in Persea, the same way you're trapped here. They have no magic. Because of that arsehole of a king."

Zella stares at you for a moment and then begins to laugh, mirthlessly. "I don't believe it," she wheezes, almost hysterical. "I don't believe this is real."

"It is, though." You reach out a hand to her, only to pull it away as a sharp pain, like an electric shock, whips through your arm. You look down, expecting to see your hand smoking, but of course there is nothing. Nothing can hurt you in your dreams. "They've given me messages for you, to help you with your magic. . . ."

"They want *you* to help me with my magic?" Zella hiccups and then starts laughing again.

"Zella, please," you say. "I know this is a lot to take in and I know I'm not the ideal teacher. But I don't know how long I have here and I don't know when I'll be back and right now I'm all you've got."

She swallows, composes herself; the air around you tightens, like she's drawing on every force she can summon to hold herself together. "All right. Tell me what they've told you."

And so the pattern begins. Breathing exercises, endless counting, and meditating, all to help Zella harness and control her wild, volatile magic before she comes into her full power. You visit Persea and memorize passages of notes in Ama's narrow cursive, in Cynthia's broad, flowery hand, notes copied from one of the many books in the giant trunk that seems to have no bottom.

One night you arrive at the edge of the mountain and Zella isn't there. You push your way through the foliage that is her forest and find her, pacing up and down, reminding you of Kam. Her eyes are closed and she is breathing rapidly.

"Zella?"

Her eyes fly open and she scowls. "I was concentrating! You distracted me!"

"Sorry! What were you concentrating on?"

"Trying to quiet my mind," she snaps.

Now this is something you can help with; Mrs. Fitzsimons is a believer in combining yogic practices with ballet.

You walk over to her and force her into a sitting position on the moss-like carpet of her hair.

"Close your eyes," you order. Perhaps surprised by your unusual assertiveness, she obeys. "Take a deep breath," you say, sitting down beside her. "And another. And another."

When she is breathing calmly, you repeat the phrases drilled into you by Ama and Cynthia.

Intentionality. Purpose. What are you asking of yourself, of your power? How do you make it work for you? What does power feel like? Smell like? Taste like? Only once you have these answers will you achieve anything corporeal.

Zella opens her eyes. "I cannot do it," she whispers. "I cannot control my magic."

"Of course you can," you say soothingly.

"It is too hard. I will be sixteen soon and there is so much of it already. I am afraid that on the Sankofa, on my birthday—"

"What does your magic look like?" you interrupt her stream of anxiety.

165

"Um . . . I suppose it looks like a willow tree. One of the great old ones on the bank of the Aphra. But when I can feel it getting out of my control, it is like bush fire, a huge flame."

"Okay. Well." You hesitate, suddenly feeling self-conscious. But Zella needs you, so you choke that down and continue. "Imagine all of the energy in you, all of the energy that makes magic. See it as a sort of humming elec—" You realize *electric* will make no sense to her. "A humming, shining light. Imagine it rising up through your body, through your feet, all the way up to the roots of your hair. But you can feel each tiny pulse of it. Are totally aware of each beam."

You watch her take a few deep breaths and begin to focus. It takes her a couple of minutes and a few expletives, but gradually you see a stillness descend and the air around you begins to crackle and thrum. A gold shining light fills her body from toe to crown, a blazing magnificent thing—*she* is a blazing magnificent thing. The gold ball of magic expands until it is overflowing, pouring out of her hair like a shower, like the weeping of a willow tree. Within the glowing umbrella, the world is still and peaceful and safe, and you know nothing, no king and no army, could penetrate this barrier. It shimmers brightly for a long moment, and then dies.

You turn to find her eyes are open wide. Then she turns to you and grins. "Better than butterflies, right?"

You laugh. "Definitely better than butterflies."

NOVEMBER

You hop and skip, the world is your oyster, you are so excited because it's Self-Care Saturday, Saturday-Soup Saturday, maybe Miss Annie will give you extra dumplings.

You've avoided Val's since your fight with Baker, but you need your roots done and, besides, you miss them. You wait for the bus, hop on, say hi to the grumpy driver, beam at the grumpy driver, and watch the dawning sun of your smile warm his own face with a grin, wonder if it's weird that the sour stale smell of hours-old chicken is making you hungry. *Think of wings, think of hot wings, think of three hot wings and fries and a strawberry fizz, strawberry blonde, can Black girls with textured hair pull off a pixie cut, google Black girls textured hair pixie cut, kiss your teeth and taste disappointment fading like plaque lingering in new resentments and boredom of wherever you go there you are.*

You're busy scrolling again and nearly miss the stop. You press the bell just in time. Someone alights beside you, says, "Excuse me, which way is the tube station?"

You stop. It takes you longer than normal to answer. Everything is so different now. You gather your bearings, direct the bemused stranger, begin treading the familiar unfamiliar path down the high street to Val's. You have always been a details person, staring at things up close. Now you step back and behold the full picture.

Your nose senses the absence of the usual assault: spices from the myriad curry houses, tumbleweeds at your feet from the multitude of hairdressers, fish from the mongers wafting strong on the smoggy air, and the *caw* of lost seagulls. Now there is only one curry house, a chain owned by a chef who you doubt has ever set foot on the Asian continent, let alone visited the specific countries and cities his various dishes are named after. Your GP's office is still there but Dr. Pillai, your favorite doctor, has long moved out of the city. Mr. Patel's grocer's is now a supermarket, Mrs. Jaswal's sneering face has been replaced by a chalkboard with artful white calligraphy, a road sign pointing in the direction of change. Smashed avocado with chorizo, flat white. Twenty-somethings with beards and piercings.

You keep walking. Another branded coffee shop, Bing's Burgers where Mrs. Goss's garden used to be, a juice shop. A memory stirs, of shiny signs and quick Hindi chatter and bright fabrics. Where are they now?

As you stand in front of Bing's, waiting for the vertigo to settle, you see the staff clock on, see other Brown faces, and you feel something like relief that you're not entirely a tourist in your own home.

A woman stands in the doorway, blonde bobbed with a severe fringe and condescending expression. She is clocking in staff like a shiny, manicured Cerberus. She looks like a Camilla, you think, flat in "one of the safer parts of the city," parents in the country, riding lessons as a child, and you aren't surprised when you notice the Barbour jacket poking out of her Longchamp bag. Hell is a popular burger chain, you think. You wonder how your cool crush-idol is, whether Camilla winds her up too.

You walk on. You can't deny that the burgers smell really good.

You see barely eight-year-old Baker running ahead of you, sweat glistening on his forehead as he jabs elated, triumphant at the air in front of him, reenacting a particular floating butterfly stinging bee moment from his boxing class.

Next door is the juice shop. You never inspected it too closely. Now you examine the menu.

BABY PINK THINK DRINK
GOODNIGHT, SWEETHEART
MEAN GREEN FIGHTING MACHINE! (NOT REALLY WE'RE TOO CUTE FOR THAT.)

The ingredients include spirulina, saffron, cultured milk, a choice of nut butters.

A loud shout of laughter, working man's club turned old man's pub turned something like a gastropub, suede brown shoes and colorful chinos and yells about the "LIONS, COME ON, BOYS!" and cheers and a song breaks out, loudly, proudly, words that are somehow precious to you although you're not sure why.

Swing low,

> *Sweet Chariot,*

>> *Coming forth to*

>>> *carry me home.*

You stumble and sway slightly. *Swing low—*
You shake your head. You keep walking.
All around you, your home is changing.

Your feet beat the familiar path towards Val and Baker and the others, the pavement unchanged, the same cracks and bumps where the roots of the trees have warped and disfigured the slabs of concrete, you dodge these easily, easy as breathing and rooted deep in your muscle memory. This at least is reassuring; you want to lay your palm against the pavement, but the thought of touching chewing gum and litter and encrusted food is too gross.

You stop at the last pillar of the before time, Miss Annie's Caribbean takeaway shop covered in scaffolding. Looks like it's getting a fresh lick of paint. You decide on the spot to go in, more for the familiar conversation than the food, though of course you ask for your usual and she puts oxtails and fried fish and "jus' a lickle slice a pound cyek" into boxes and bags. You notice the droop of her shoulders and the sides of her mouth, the emptiness of the shop, the lack of her usual staff of chattering nieces and nephews.

"Quiet, is it, Annie?"

She scowls and launches into a reply about "the boss man Richardson" and "the rent haffi go up" and him "buying up-a the whole street!" and how she "nah nuh why the yuppi dem musti haf a Caffè Nero when they have a Starbuck na t'ree doors down?"

Richardson. Again. Miss Annie doesn't droop and scowl. She is belly laughter and a ready cuss word, she would proudly tell the whole street about her boob job at sixty. You take your bag of food, turn from her despondency, see the sign you'd walked right past on your way in, swinging in the late autumnal wind. *For Sale.*

You think of Monica's offer to speak to her dad. You should tell Baker about it. You need to make up with him first.

The doorbell goes off loudly behind you, a siren as you exit.

At last you step into the sticky salon, breath frosting the window before trickling down, condensation like backwash filming the pane. You tune into the hot-haired heat and top forty gospel, a pastor interrupting a song that really shouldn't be played in conjunction with good Christian radio.

You pull up a seat next to where Saffy is sitting, already busy and content. She kicks you by way of greeting.

"Ow!" It wasn't a hard kick. That's not Saffy's style. But it feels good to yell.

"Sorry." She grins mischievously, lovingly brushing out new lace front wigs to replace the old ones on the mannequin heads on the shelves behind the till. Despite the looming threat of closure, Mum is still insisting on continuing her "titivation" project. "Why's your face push-up?"

"My face isn't push-up."

"'My face isn't push-up,'" she says. The imitation is upsettingly accurate, the higher octaves of your superior tone, the one that accompanies your schoolgirl mask, trying on some posh girl passive aggression like artfully scuffed Chelsea boots, when everyone knows you're shiny Doc Martens, really.

"You wondering where Baker is?"

170

"Shut up, Saffy."

"I heard Val talking to Mum when she dropped me off this morning. Mum said you get a push-up face whenever she mentions Baker and Val said, 'He's been sitting round with push-up face too, ya knuh.' I think it's because you two had beef."

You scowl at her. "You don't know anything, Saffy."

"I do! I know lots and lots of things. I know that talcum powder stops a wig looking cheap! I know that a haiku has seventeen syllables. I know that Baker's eyes go all funny when he looks at you and his voice is different when he talks to you AND he basically ignored the pretty girl in Bing's when he went in to get a package for Val earlier even though all of his friends fancy her. But I don't think Baker does. Because"—a pause for effect—"I think Baker likes you."

You keep your face carefully neutral.

Baker likes you.

Sure, it's just your ten-year-old sister's speculation. But you'd half-known it for years, half-wondered.

Baker.

Likes.

You.

Likes you likes you.

And you like him, of course you do, you always have. You know it now. That deep down nagging longing for the long, curled eyelashes, straight white teeth, the dark brown velvet of his skin, Baker's eyes, Baker's lips, Baker's nose, Baker's lips, Baker's lips, Baker's lips.

You shrug. "Whatever." Look back at your phone. Saffy has returned to her brushing but you know she is still peeking at you, nervous she's gone too far.

You bring up Baker's profile, hesitate, open up your chat.

Type: *Hi.*

Then delete it.

Been a while, you try again, and again delete.

171

"Cha, jus' text my boy and tell him to come here after boxing instead of going home if you want to see him so bad."

You jump and start. Val is peering over your shoulder, completely shameless, queenly and entitled to know everything that happens in her kingdom. Her bright dress whispers against your back and you get a gust of her familiar coconut-and-avocado smell, the smell of firm hugs, the smell of your childhood.

You shove the phone into your pocket.

"Val, that's a blatant invasion of my privacy."

The aunties howl with laughter. Val scowls right back at you, indifferent to your indignation.

She kisses her teeth. "I feed yuh?"

"Yes."

"I heat yuh?"

"Yes."

"I let you use my wifi?"

"Yes."

"Then hush yuh mout and text my son."

You glare at her. Reluctantly pull out your phone again.

Hi. I'm at your mum's. She said I should text you.

Instant reply.

Swear? Why?

Idk. She said I should tell you to come here after boxing.

Pause. Ellipses. Typing. Not typing. Typing. Not typing. Typing.

I won't come if you don't want to see me.

You don't know what to say to this. You don't like the guilty feeling it brings to your stomach. You wonder if adulthood is just a string of bellyaches.

I have a Richardson development.

Pause. The longest pause.

Cool. Be a min. You want anything from the shop?

I'm fine. I got us food. Your wings are in the microwave here.

Cool x

You stare at the x. He's never sent an x before.

*

Purple-gold, shiny tinfoil plastic drops into your lap obscuring your scrolling and the chocolate bar you instantly bite into is sweeter for the view of the face hovering above it.

"Thanks."

"Not a problem." Pause. "We good?"

"Yeah. We're fine. I'd basically forgotten that there was a problem anyway."

He narrows his eyes at you, long lashes curling messily shielding his gaze so you cannot read the expression behind them. He yawns. Maybe he's been dreaming, you think. That nagging sensation again—*a bad dream, Baker, somewhere you should be.*

"Well, sit down." The request comes out as an order and you try to soften it by patting the sofa next to you. This action is flirtier than you intended and your insides coil pleasingly at the slow spread of his smile. You tell yourself you just ate the chocolate bar too quickly.

"Yes, miss."

"Ha ha."

"So."

"So."

"What's good?"

"Not much. School. The usual."

"How's Year Eleven?"

"Same crap, different year. Plus more exams."

"EH-EH!" Val kisses her teeth, berates you for your language, but you don't hear over the sound of the blood pounding in your ears as Baker laughs, his wide smile splitting his face; he is bright white teeth and dimples—he has dimples, you count his dimples, you'd never noticed dimples, how had you not noticed his dimples, your eyes flick, flick, flick, flick, flick, flick Baker's face, and you understand how his dimples had escaped your notice, Baker's lips, Baker's eyes, Baker's smile, Baker's eyes, Baker's eyes. Baker's eyes are tired. Baker's eyes are hard to look away from.

You take a deep breath. "There's a girl at school whose dad is a property developer—like Richardson. Says she can talk to him about this place. Monica French, her name is."

Baker frowns. "Monica French? Isn't she rude to you?"

"She's all right now. I think."

Just then your phone buzzes and speak of the devil herself, black characters on your bright screen, your nails click quick as you slide to open and see that Monica French has commented three fire emojis under your new picture, nails click quick you like her comment, nails click quick she's slid into your DMs, eyes blur, and quick nails click she's saying something about a *party*.

You're not sure what's caused this sudden interest. First the Halloween invite, now this—and this time you don't have plans.

"I need to call someone," you say.

"Must be important," he teases.

"Yeah." You call Melly, who doesn't pick up. You try again. Nothing. You try a third time and she answers. "You okay? I called you just now and you didn't pick up."

"I'm busy."

"Doing what?"

Melly's voice is muffled by male laughter and you feel an uncomfortable prickling sensation on the back of your neck. "Melly, is there a boy with you?"

"Yes." She is matter of fact. "It's Kwame, you know—in the year above at the boys' school."

"Kwame?"

"Kwame?" Baker's head snaps up across the room and you realize too late that of course they'd know each other.

"Yes, don't overthink it." Melly's reply is soothing like she's talking to her mother.

"Monica French invited me to her party tomorrow."

"Oh, yeah? You gonna go?"

"Yeah I was thinking about stopping by." You doubt your feigned indifference is fooling her.

"Cool, Kwame and me might go. Some of his friends want to."

Melly's indifference isn't feigned. Melly never fakes anything. Melly is one hundred percent authentic in every sharp word and head tilt and you wonder what it must be like to never feel self-conscious.

"Cool. Well, can I go with you? So I don't walk in on my own like a loser."

Pause.

"You're not a loser." Melly's gentle tone catches you off-guard and you are arched back and puffy tailed, catty and defensive.

"I know I'm not, lol, don't worry. I know I'm a bad b. I'm just saying it would be fun to get ready together and whatever, but don't worry I wouldn't want to third wheel or drag you and Kwame away from each other."

Melly's sigh is too patient. "Kwame and I were going to hang out first. Why don't you ask Cat?"

You hesitate—it's your first party and for a reason you don't want to look too closely at, you don't want to bring Cat. "Don't worry, Melly. Maybe see you there, yeah?"

"Yeah." She pauses again and then says, "Why do you want to go, though? Monica's never been very nice to you."

"Do you not want me to go?"

Melly sounds surprised. "No, of course I want you to go if you want to go!" She takes a breath. "This is coming out wrong. If you think it'll be fun, then go, of course. But I can literally think of several thousand ways I'd rather spend my Sunday night than with my head up Monica French's pert bunda."

"What? Are you trying to call me a lickarse?"

"No, love." Same maddeningly calm tone. "I'm just saying, Monica? Bit of a bitch."

"Then why does Kwame want to go?"

"His mates all fancy Monica and so they wanna go and he can't hack the FOMO. Look we'll probably see you there, okay?"

"Okay," you say through gritted teeth.

"Cool! See you, then. Bye, love you!"

You hang up before you have to say it back.

"Val?"

"Mmm?"

"Can I come in for a hot comb tomorrow? I have a party."

"On a Sunday? It's a school night!"

"We have a school trip on Monday so don't have to go in until ten."

Val harrumphs.

"Check with your mother."

"But if she says yes?"

"If she says yes why would I say no? I'm not your mother. I wouldn't tell you what to do."

This is patently untrue; Val tells you what to do as much as she does Baker, more sometimes. You also know she'll probably do your hair for free.

"Thanks, Val!"

You slip over, squeeze between seats, squeeze Val, squeeze little Esmonde, ignoring the jitterbug tremor in your stomach, this is what it should mean to be on the edge of sixteen—

Baker says, "Is this the Monica French thing tomorrow?"

"Yeah!" You imagine you and him there together, in a crowded room, him handing you a drink and leaning in and—"Are you going?"

"Nah." He picks up the mannequin head to practice. "Not to be mean, but I think Monica's a dickhead."

You laugh.

176

Cake

Cynthia and Ama are baking a cake. It will be a showstopper: three tiers of berries, sponge, and cream, a gift from the cows Kam tells you are kept on the other side of Persea.

"Persean witches would never take the life of an animal," Kam had explained when Cynthia had arrived earlier, her arms laden with eggs, butter, and flour. "But there is a witch, Zahrah, who is Mum's cousin. Her life magic means she is friends with the animals. They whisper to her, or they used to. But now, though she cannot speak with them, they still leave gifts for her to sell in return for her care and protection. Eggs, milk, things like that."

Cynthia and Ama roll their sleeves up and scan the recipe book, frowning. You think of Sleeping Beauty's fairy godmothers, attempting domesticity without magic for the first time.

"I was surprised Zahrah even had a non-magic recipe book," Kam says.

"She said someone gifted it to her for a birthday years ago. As a joke."

"Hmm, yes, hilarious. I'm sure they did not anticipate it being used. However, at least we will have a cake for the Sankofa."

The Sankofa, you had once been told, is the holiday celebrated by the Perseans to honor the land as the year draws to a close. The days are uniform in length now, regardless of the season: the King's doing, no doubt. Ordered, structured, almost seasonal.

Cynthia frowns. *"Fold it in?* What does that mean?"

You laugh and get to your feet. "Step aside, ladies. As someone with no magic, this is my time to shine."

177

"Everyone has magic," Ama says automatically, but they obey, Ama slipping gratefully into a chair as Cynthia heats the kettle on the stove.

You begin to measure out ingredients: vanilla extract, baking powder, sugar, mundane in this magic kitchen. "How come you're still celebrating Sankofa?" you ask. "Now that your magic has gone?"

"That is not the fault of the land, girl," Ama says sternly. "We must still be grateful for what we have been given. We must still acknowledge the occasion."

"We Persean witches may have had our magic taken, but it remains in the land," says Cynthia. "You can still hear the spirits of the forest singing their songs of life and love. I think that is worth a cake at least."

Ama smiles a little sadly. "In the old days, on this night, we Persean witches would get dressed up, and as the day moved swiftly into evening, moved by our excitement or the will of the goddess, we could never be sure, we would feel the sting of magic beneath our skin and reach the height of our power. There would be dancing and music and much revelry." She looks at Cynthia with soft eyes and Kam coughs with embarrassment.

"Okay, I shall tell this part because you two can never get through it without making me ill," Kam says. You laugh and she picks up the story like a dropped thread and continues to weave. "The witches of Persea who were deemed worthy by the land that year would burn bright and hot and those who were meant for them, whether other witches or mortal folk from elsewhere in the land, would find them on that night. They would be mated and have their union blessed by the hand of the goddess."

"And that is how you were, um, mated?" you ask. You add wet ingredients to dry. Examine their spice rack. Stir.

They smile at each other again, that soft smile, and Kam rolls her eyes.

"Yes," they say as one.

"So the King allowed you to celebrate the Sankofa?" You take the

178

saffron tea Cynthia hands you.

"No, he did not," she says, "but we held the celebrations in secret. We would sneak out of the castle into the gardens we tended and would be joined by as many of our coven as could get away without detection. All those years and the King never knew. A more powerful union Persea has never seen." Ama stirs her tea. "When the force of our joining life magic created the children, in our bellies, and ripened the avocado tree, we knew our babes would be born on the Sankofa. We knew they must know freedom as we never did. That is why we're attempting to make this cake," she adds wryly, gesturing at the bowl you're stirring. "A symbol of our promise to Xaymaca. As it provides for us, so we honor it."

You take another sip of your saffron tea, the sweet, spicy flavor making you think of warm arms and imagined, gentle kisses. You finish stirring and rub butter around the baking tin that sits on the scrubbed wooden table. You pour in the batter, then flex your wrist, aching from stirring. You relish the ache; you have given something, no matter how small, to Persea.

The cake goes into the oven. You drink more tea. You wait. To your surprise, given how quicksilver-fast time moves in your dreams, the forty minutes it takes to cook feels like forty minutes. With every month of the King's reign, you can feel the vibrant hum of magic slowly dying and the bright colors and smells of this world dulling into mundanity, muted replicas of your home world.

You take the cake out and leave it to cool.

Later, you and Kam do the washing up. You glance out of the window. You haven't been in the garden since things have changed—you are afraid to, afraid to approach the avocado tree.

"The day is long today," Kam murmurs. "The King knows the date, knows that the Sankofa is at nightfall. Perhaps he is trying to delay it."

"That's like a fairy story," you say absently, wiping down a wooden spoon. "The wicked King, waiting for sunset."

"Do faeries really write your stories?" Kam says. "Just like in our world?"

"No, of course not. . . ." Realization dawns. "Fairy tales aren't real, not for us. They're just made up. For kids."

"Oh." Kam processes this. "Your fairy tales sound a lot like our histories."

"And your histories sound a lot like my fairy tales." You share a dark laugh and look back towards the garden.

Kam finishes her drying and retrieves the bowl of butter icing you'd stored in the cool, dark pantry.

"But he cannot put off nightfall entirely. Sooner or later, we're going to have to bring the coven this cake." She sighs and rolls up her sleeves again, eyeing the cake for all the world as though it's the bigger threat. "Right. Show me how it is done."

*

Night claims the sky eventually, succumbing to Xaymaca's own magic and laws.

"The King can only do so much," Kam tells you. For the first time, you are climbing the delicately carved spiral staircase to the upper floor. "The day must end eventually. No one has that power. Not yet."

There are piles of books all the way up the stairs, tucked against the banisters and lining the edges of the landing. On the landing, there are four doors made of the same heavy orange-red wood as the rest of the cottage, and you wonder if the forest gifted the wood for this house like the faeries gift the books and the animals gift their produce.

"This is the washing room, should you like to use it," Kam gestures to the door at the end of the hall. "That is my mothers' room. And this room we do not go in."

"Why?" you ask.

Kam shrugs. "We can't. We lost the keys years ago and magic would not open it." She seems uninterested and you are perplexed by her lack of curiosity.

"The house has its reasons," Kam says vaguely, her hand on the shining brass knob of a different room. "I'm not going to pry. And this is our—this is my room."

The door swings inwards and you stare around. The sprawling room is softly lit by a golden candle glow, which flickers soothingly across the ceiling. The ceiling itself is scattered with gold stars that dance across your gaze like phosphenes. The rest of the room feels similarly celestial; two large canopy beds against the same wall as the door, bedecked with soft white linen under an awning of sparkling purple gauze. The floor is the same wood as the rest of the house, scattered with plush white rugs and there are bookshelves lining the wall on the left. Of the remaining walls, one is dominated by large bay windows, which look out into the garden.

The final wall hosts an enormous wardrobe, painted white with green and purple flowers swirling up the sides, and two mirrored dressers on either side, painted to match. One is all chaos—dried flowers, books with the pages turned down, a sprawl of jewelery. Though there is no dust, your heart pangs at the thought of Zella's mess, left untouched all these years. The other is painfully neat: bottles of perfume arranged in height order, two jewelery boxes stacked atop each other, combs, brushes in a line.

Kam strides over to her side of the wardrobe and flings it open. It is impeccably organized. For the first time you wonder how Kam feels as the odd one out among the wild, formless Persean witches. You feel sorry for her suddenly, a cuckoo in the nest. The forest coven had their traditions, you know that from their history books; but order and routine is seen as tantamount to the shackles they'd wrested themselves free of after the Great Strike.

But clearly, for Kam, there is comfort here, in her ordered bedroom.

She pulls out two dresses. "These dresses were a gift to our mothers after our birth. Zella and I were going to wear them tonight."

She lays them on the bed and you run covetous fingers over the fabric. They're both white and glittering. One is an elegant slinking thing, long skirt tumbling over the side of the bed like water. It is a high halter neck with ties made from ivory ribbons that weave and cross at the back. Tiny rose-gold sequins are stitched down each side, forming swirls and flowers, shimmering vines of incredible detail. It is simple and stunning. But it's the second dress that makes you catch your breath. It has a full skirt of billowing, rustling, silvery gossamer below a cinched waist and barely there straps. The bodice is bedecked with dazzling clear crystals, catching rainbows in the warm candlelight, amid tiny white pearls, while the straps are twisted with strands of silver, wrought into the shapes of tiny leaves and flowers. It's like Cinderella's dress, only better. A fairy tale, only real.

"Zella and I were always meant to be so important—well, Zella really. The most magical girl of all. Our mothers are powerful, so we would be powerful. We were conceived and the pear tree ripened. Our mothers, when they were pregnant with us, ate the fruit. Mum ate first—and then Zella was born and it was clear that she would be the heart of Persea, the most powerful. We were going to come into our full power tonight." She smiles bitterly. "That was back when we thought that Zella being special was a good thing."

You swallow. Here you are, standing in Zella's old bedroom, running a finger over Zella's sixteenth birthday dress, while she spends it alone in her forest on Carrion Ridge. You feel like somewhere, lurking just beyond the edges of your vision, is an idea, something that you can do to help—but when you try to catch it, it's gone.

"So," you say, as Kam begins to sort through drawers of jewelery, "this ceremony tonight . . . will there be any magic at all?"

"Not from us," she says wryly. "Zella will feel it, though. Out there, on the Carrion Ridge, she will experience the surge and come into her full power. The rest of us must content ourselves with the magic of the singing forest."

"The surge . . . that won't hurt Baker, will it?" you ask hesitantly.

Kam meets your eyes in the mirror. "I do not know," she says coolly. "He's under the King's protection, isn't he?"

"Or he's the King's prisoner," you snap.

"Maybe. We don't know—you don't remember enough when you wake to ask him anything useful, and we do not have access to him or the King. So we know nothing." She takes a breath. "I think it's time you got dressed."

"Into what exactly?"

She looks from you to the dress on the bed, the one with the rainbows and crystals. Comprehension dawns and you shake your head. "No, Kam, I couldn't—it's Zella's dress. She's probably imagined this moment her whole life. I can't wear it—not when this is partly my fault."

Kam gets to her feet and pulls you to yours. She lifts the dress and holds it in front of you. "You did what you did in ignorance and youth. It is not unforgiveable. But now you can try and put it right. There are three girls mentioned in that prophecy. Two of those girls were supposed to wear these dresses tonight. And so they shall."

Sankofa Sixteen

You stand barefoot and breathless in front of the mirror in Kam's wardrobe, unable to believe the sight of yourself in this dress. You are aglow, rainbows dancing along your skin. Everyone has some magic, you think. Even you.

Beside you in the mirror, Kam is angelic in the column of white and gold. She radiates strength and beauty like a sun, and seems to breathe magic, to ooze something entirely otherworldly. A wildcat, showing her teeth.

"Two girls will in dazzling white be dressed. . . ." Kam murmurs.

"Someone made you these dresses, even after knowing what the prophecy said?" you ask.

"Who knows whether our actions affect the prophecy, or the prophecy affects our actions?" Kam gazes at you both.

You imagine meeting all the other powerful witches tonight, and telling them the part you have played in this disaster. Sweat beads on your upper lip.

"Relax." Kam is stern. "You will ruin my masterpiece." You breathe and hold your head high, copying Kam. She has spent some time coloring your face carefully with her makeup, potions, and poultices made of crushed stones and flowers—some imbued with magic from the Before Time, shading and lightening, all with a feather-light touch until you can't tell where the old you ends and the new you begins. *I am Zella's substitute tonight*, you think. *I must do her proud.* You throw back your shoulders, pretend that you too are the daughter of a witch, push aside the image of your mum with her tired eyes, in her pencil skirts with trainers so she can power walk to work, until all you are is the version of you that exists in Xaymaca, and all you can see is an almost-witch girl with wide, dark eyes and sparkles highlighting her face.

You follow Kam downstairs, you hold your skirts like every princess in every fairy tale, you wait for her mothers. When they arrive at the top of the stairs, hand in hand, they seem to float towards you, as if carried by a breath of whatever magic still lurks in the cottage. They are both wearing long heavy gowns, in slightly differing shades of silver and gold, and have exchanged their usual woven leather and brass belts for long elegant chains of gold, encrusted with crystals. Ama's long, full sleeves are almost bell-shaped and mimic the wide flowing of her skirts, while the silk plunges deep to her navel. Cynthia's arms are bare and her dress is high-necked, made of silver-gold velvet, but when she turns, you see that the smooth planes of her back are marred with a patchwork of scars and ridges. You swallow a gasp, look away.

When you look back, she smiles at you grimly. "It was not with magic alone that he kept us powerless," she says.

You tell yourself that she has endured so much; bearing witness to her courage is the least you can do. You raise your chin and this time you do not look away.

*

Your small procession begins the walk through the depths of the Great Forest. Your bare feet struggle to find even footing, and you are impressed by the sure-footed lightness of your companions' steps. Your dresses whisper against the forest floor, the trees whisper to each other, the forest whispers: *The air around you knows things.* You feel the electric crackle and hum of magic around you and you see Ama, Cynthia, and Kam take deep breaths like they've been starved of oxygen, tasting the magic on their tongues, filling their nostrils, sighing like thirsty women drinking at last.

185

Ama and Cynthia walk at the helm, leading you and Kam. You carry the cake you've made and Kam brings up the rear. Her dark eyes sweep the shadows, missing nothing; she is alert and coiled, ready to spring like a jaguar among the trees.

"Kam, you're freaking me out," you hiss. "I thought you guys and the forest were all good? Aren't we safe?"

She doesn't cease her surveillance but hisses back in what can only be considered a patronizing tone, "There are evil spirits who resent the power we have. Or had. The spiteful ones. There's Sasabonsam, the Great Forest Monster, cursed with perpetual hunger, who lurks in the canopy above, waiting to snatch his next meal. . . ." You stare at her and she gives a splutter of laughter. "The real problem is the King. He has spies everywhere. And he knows that tonight is special."

You continue on, at first with nothing but the shimmering silver of the moon to guide you, terrified of the spirits but also of tripping and dropping the cake. As you get deeper into the forest, you feel hundreds, if not thousands, of tiny eyes upon you and a strange music begins to permeate your awareness. It is unlike anything you've ever heard, ethereal but with a weight to it. It drops kisses down your spine, licks your arms and legs with a wildfire, pricks your eyes. It makes you want to dance.

After about ten minutes of walking, the music grows louder, swelling, expanding inside you, you see a flickering orange light and notice torches bracketed to the giant, murmuring trees. Before you can wonder at the wisdom of open fire in a forest, the trees thin and you are standing before a wide clearing.

The Sankofa celebrations are in full swing. About a hundred women and girls are gathered in the clearing, all whirling and dancing. The music swells, the tempo changes, and their feet mark the switch, beating out the subtle pulsing rhythms and your back arches slightly, as though your body is being pulled towards them, aching to join in.

Ama and Cynthia take each other's hands, breathe as one, step clear of the line of trees and into the glade. The music halts for just a fraction of a second, the silence falls through the air before being caught by sound once more. The women bow to Ama and Cynthia and they bow back. Kam drags you down into an ungainly crouch, so swiftly you almost drop the cake.

"They bow to us, in respect and acknowledgement of the powerful gift our family was given by Xaymaca," Kam hisses. "We bow back in honor of the responsibility we have—to guard the avocado tree and to protect Persea."

You straighten by her side as Ama and Cynthia lead you forward, across the glade, to where an enormous table is set in its center, laden with food. The dancing has not resumed and all eyes are on you. Women murmur, "Blessed birthday," and Kam nods, acknowledging but not smiling or speaking. Expressions range from curiosity to wary suspicion to blatant hostility as people consider you. Sweat beads in your armpits, prickles in your lower back. The table itself is an enormous equilateral triangle and is beautifully carved with the same flowers and tiny creatures as the banister in the cottage; Cynthia's handiwork, perhaps. You gently set down the cake and Ama gives you the briefest smile.

"Witches!" Ama calls in a clear, rich voice, and the music quiets around her. "May I wish you a blessed Sankofa! On this night, despite our suffering, despite our loss and hardship, we nevertheless gather in thanks. In the name of Yaa, the great goddess herself"—and the earth seems to sigh as Ama names her deity—"we offer gratitude for the land off which we thrive. We offer gratitude for the River Aphra, the source through which flows our power from She who is mighty unto us. We offer gratitude for the River Mumma, who guards this source. We offer gratitude for the power which, though stolen by darkness and spite and despair, is ours by birthright and ours to reclaim."

She takes Cynthia's hand in one of hers and Kam's in the other, and all around you witches are joining hands, a circle around the triangular feast. Kam takes your left hand and a small, slight girl in a cerulean blue robe, with dimples, gently takes your right hand and squeezes it with a shy smile. "And finally, we offer gratitude for each other. For love, for life, for community. If we stand together, we witches, if we raise our voice as one, we witches, there is nothing that cannot be done."

Cynthia is walking around the circle now, holding a large cup to the lips of first Ama, then Kam, then you, and so on. You hesitate when she reaches you, but she whispers, "It is just *chicha*, a corn drink. If we wanted to poison you, little one, we would have done so by now." You suppress a giggle and take a sip. It is smooth and subtle with a slightly nutty aftertaste. "Yaa blesses you," Cynthia murmurs and continues round the circle.

Until an angry voice calls out, "Cynthia of Life, what can you mean by this? I will not drink from that cup until I know who she is! You go too far!"

"She's right," snaps another voice. "An outsider, at Sankofa!"

You freeze and turn to look at a small, round-faced woman, who is glaring at you.

"We will explain," Cynthia says soothingly. "As soon as the libation is completed. You would not break the ritual practiced by our foremothers for generations, would you, Cassia? Myrtle?" Her voice is still calm and low, but there is something stronger there, an echo of the magic that used to sing beneath her speech.

The witch called Cassia sighs and nods, and Cynthia continues to circle the group. But now you have a sick feeling. The witch called Cassia is looking at you coldly, and so is the witch on your other side, Myrtle. You open your mouth to say something but the music suddenly swells again.

It happens so quickly you miss it, but suddenly they are twisting away from you, as if pulled by the music of the forest spirits. Kam has whirled off to her left and joined the dancing with a ferocious grace that entrances you. Her mothers have been likewise swept up by the music, dancing apart, then together, then apart again. The witches are in formation and then they aren't and each move is inexact but entirely intentional. Fierce and dangerous but achingly beautiful. This is more intense than mirrored walls and pointe shoes; you are barefoot and cannot see yourself at all, only *feel*.

All around you are clouds and mist. You think you are floating in the air, but you're not quite sure where is up and where is down.

Hello, interloper, intones a strange musical voice.

You don't reply because you don't need to, simply smile your acknowledgement and drift downwards. You come back to yourself, shift from being more mind than body to feeling the lush grass beneath your feet, the whispering gauze skirts of your dress against your skin, the wary eyes on your face.

The music has quieted. The witches have stopped dancing.

"Who is *she* to answer the call?" The witch called Cassia is pointing an accusatory finger at you and you remember where you are and why you are there and feel stupid and embarrassed for getting so carried away.

"I think it's about time to answer some questions," the witch called Myrtle sneers. "Not that it wasn't a very pretty display."

Kam appears by your side and takes your hand. You are grateful for the support but, to your surprise, she kisses it and whispers. "That was Yaa who spoke to you just now. She blesses you. You are welcome here."

You are bewildered but before you can speak, Cynthia is stepping forward.

"Sisters. After we lost Zella, and with her our magic, I told you a story. You will forgive me for refreshing your memories."

You realize right away that it is your story. Yours and Kam's and Zella's—only told from Cynthia and Ama's perspective. How she and Ama watched you emerge in their garden night after night; how they watched the three of you grow up together, watched your friendship blossom and fade and blossom again. Until that one night, when Baker

189

had appeared.

She turns to you and Kam then, and says, "But now our interloper, as she has been so named this night by Yaa herself, has returned." She inclines her head in a clear indication that it is your turn to speak.

You swallow. Take a breath. And begin.

"I first met Baker when I was six," you say. "His mother gave me avocado oil. And that night, I had my first dream."

You tell how you kept the garden and your dreams a secret from him, tell of the strange waking forgetfulness. Until one day the truth escaped you and suddenly your inability to speak up would prove cataclysmic. You tell them of his curiosity, his jealousy. Your fear that one day he would indeed try the avocado oil for himself.

"I didn't know," you say, stumbling over your words. "I didn't know it would be so dangerous. He came and he was so scared. Darkness covered him and I couldn't help him—"

"No," says Kam quietly. "I stopped you from helping him. Because I thought he was dangerous. But maybe you could have saved him that night and saved all of us. If you could have helped him, he wouldn't have gone to the King. Can you forgive me?"

You feel a lump in your throat and squeeze her hand back. "You don't need my forgiveness."

"Let me get this straight," says Cassia. "The mortal girl's boyfriend shows up and everything goes to hell. He helps the King abduct your daughter—" she points at Ama and Cynthia "—and trap us here with our own magic."

"He doesn't *want* to be helping the King," you say, and the witch called Myrtle laughs.

"Then tell him to stop!"

"It's not that simple," you say weakly. "When I'm awake, I don't remember my dreams. Neither does Baker. We just know that something bad is happening."

Cassia is unconvinced. "And what about this Val? We don't know

190

any such witch. She is not one of us. And yet she knows our potions, has somehow used one of our avocados, and sends her son to wreak havoc, in league with the King. . . ."

"No," you whisper. But they aren't listening to you anymore. The angry faces swim around you, beautiful and ferocious, and for a moment you are tugged towards your sleeping body, restful in bed, and contemplate returning, forcing yourself awake.

You look down at the spangled dream dress and think: *What would Zella do?*

We are most powerful when we use our voice.

> *There's a Brown girl in the ring*
> *Tralalalala*
> *There's a Brown girl in the ring*
> *Tralalalalala*
> *Brown girl in the ring*
> *Tralalalala*
> *She looks like the sugar in the plum*

You only realize it is you singing when the witches fall quiet. They are staring at you. So you sing again. This time, after a moment's pained hesitation, Kam joins in. Then Ama and Cynthia. Then many of the others. When more than half of the Persean witches are singing with you, the pure and shining spirits of the forest join in.

When the song ends you feel stronger. You say, "I have seen Zella. She is strong. She has magic still. She is resisting the King. And she's trying to harness her power to free you all."

There are cries of shock, gasps. The small, round, dimpled witch has tears in her eyes.

"Mortal girl," cries another witch. She is tall and muscular and wears her straight hair cropped short. She should be intimidating, but her eyes are surprisingly gentle and her broad mouth looks prone to

191

laughter. "I think it's time that we asked some *practical* questions, if we may." She throws a look of deep disdain towards Cassia and Myrtle.

"Speak, Bedia of Protection," Ama says calmly. You remember that Zella had once told you that while Persean witches only have one name, their given one, their full titles are that of whatever power Yaa had blessed them with. Cynthia and Ama of Life. Kamaka of Roots. And, whisper it, Rapunzella, the Heart of Persea.

"You say you have seen Zella? How is this possible?"

"I don't know," you say helplessly. "The avocado oil, I think. It's how I get here too. I never know where I am going to end up."

"Did the King change your hair too?" asks Bedia, eyeing your sleek hair, tied now in a knot atop your head.

You shake your head.

"I had it straightened."

Bedia flinches and the witches begin to murmur among themselves. "You chose to do that?"

Cynthia frowns and steps forward. "Choice is a precious gift, is it not?" The murmurs quieten.

Quiet. The spirits sing softly. The grass and flowers sway along, their dance continues on without you; they are parts of the Great Forest, home to the source and blessed by the goddess and you are tiny specs in their infinite cycle of life and magic.

"Well," says Bedia bracingly, "at least we know where Zella is. The most powerful witch of us all—no wonder that sniveling worm wants to keep her locked away. We find Zella, bring her back, and then I'll personally run a spear through the King's pampered chest."

The sweet, dimpled witch dressed in blue, who looks to be about your age, wipes their still damp eyes and says, "Bedia, it will not be that simple. Zella is trapped on Carrion Ridge. She cannot get out and I doubt very much that we can get in."

Ama and Cynthia nod and Kam smiles at them gently. "Zuri of Water. And a dear, dear friend." They smile back tremulously.

At that moment, a clap of thunder echoes around the forest. And then another. And another. And then, from far in the east, further away than even Kingstown, a golden glowing light appears.

You would have assumed it was the sun rising, but the sun could never scorch the skies like this, could never set the forest ablaze with its beam. You all turn towards it and you see white eyes and white teeth glowing orange in the dark-light of the glade. Ama and Cynthia are on their knees, tears tracking down their cheeks. Kam's nails are digging into the back of your hand.

"Yaa help her, Yaa help her, Yaa help her. . . ."

You understand. The surge of magic that occurs every Sankofa has happened and Zella, far away on Carrion Ridge in the east, has just stepped into her full power for the first time. Unimaginable power—and she is trapped and alone, without guidance, with the King more desperate for her name than ever.

Bedia turns to you, a new urgency in her now. "Mortal child! You are the one who can travel beyond our border. You alone can breach the King's tower and free this boy."

Your face slackens and you stumble back, looking incredulously at Cynthia and Ama, but they are frowning in thought.

"I can't get involved in that way," you say at last. "I'm just having a dream. I'm . . . observing, that's all."

"It may be time for you to do more than just observe, child."

You turn quickly, looking for the owner of that voice, a soft, high, slightly reedy voice, the voice of the wind through the branches of a willow trees. An elderly witch is walking across the glade to you. Her eyes are somewhere between gray and gold, offset by the long black hooded cloak she is wearing, which covers her hair. She ghosts across the grass towards you, and Kam murmurs, "Yvane of Sight."

"I am glad that I am able to see you again," the Seer says, taking your hand.

"I don't think we've met," you say, eyeing her warily.

"That is not what I said." There is music in Yvane's voice; she almost sings. Her brilliant light eyes stare deep into yours. She smiles and seems to sag with relief. "Yes. Yes. *One of us, and yet not of this land.* Yes." She kisses your hand, just like Kam did, in exactly the same spot, and whispers, "Yaa blessed indeed." And then, to your utter horror, all of the witches around you sink into an approximation of their earlier bow. Even Kam and her mothers. You look at them, bewildered, and tug on Kam's dress.

"What are you doing? Get up, stop it!"

"You are being acknowledged by the coven," she whispers. "It is our way of saying you are part of us, part of this."

"I am not part of this!" You take a step away, looking in panic around at the circle. "I'm sorry, but I'm not."

"Yvane has the gift of sight," Kam explains, as though that changes anything. She gets to her feet. "She is the Seer who saw the prophecy."

"No, no, no," you say firmly. "I . . . I don't want it. Any of it. I don't want to be part of your prophecy. And neither does Baker. He's just the son of a hairdresser. And I'm—"

"Yes?" The Seer raises one eyebrow. "Yes, child? Who are you?"

You falter. Stutter. You look around wildly at the circle of faces—Ama, concerned; Cynthia, sympathetic; Kam, frustrated. You take in the lopsided cake and realize that you won't get to eat it and think, *Well, that's probably for the best, I bet it tastes like shit anyway.* You only realize you've been moving away from them when your back hits a rough tree trunk.

"I've done enough," you whisper. You turn and run. As you're moving, weighed down by the heavy skirts of your dress, you feel the familiar pull towards waking, feel the weight of your dress meld seamlessly into the weight of your body as you return to it. You look back and see Kam and her coven, exactly where you'd left them, staring into the trees after you. You push down your guilt, like vomit, turn away, and awaken. And emerge into the waking world.

Coming of Age

The twilight was purple,
the shadows were long,
the girl in the forest
sang a solo song.

There's a Brown girl in the ring
Tralalalala
There's a Brown girl in the ring
Tralalalalala
Brown girl in the ring
Tralalalala
She looks like the sugar in the plum

The rushing tide of adulthood
catches her unawares.
It burns her from her fingers
to the roots of her hairs.
It is pouring in and pouring out,
it can't be contained.
She is wild, she is verdant,
she will not be restrained.
Her magic curls upwards and outwards,
snapping combs and breaking rules.
Laughing at your conformity tools.
It is vast, it has grown,
it has a life, it has a soul,

it has a voice of its own.
She forgets who she is,
she forgets where she's from,
and while she fears her very core
her magic rages on.

PARTY

"What are you doing?"

"Getting ready to go out."

"Go out where?"

"To a party, Saffy. God, what do you want?"

Saffy looks down at the floor. In her hands, she is holding a battered DVD case.

"I thought you might want to watch this. . . ." Her voice trails off and you remember, too late, that you'd promised to watch Roger and Hammerstein's *Cinderella* with her. November movie nights are a long held tradition, ever since Saffy had complained that "nothing happens in November."

You can feel the guilt morphing into a sneer twisting your mouth, the poison pouring out. "Watch a stupid baby film with my stupid baby sister? No, thank you."

She doesn't say anything, just blinks, then turns and leaves. Your indomitable sister rendered silent.

Your head hurts and you are tired. You think you had a bad dream, although you can't remember it now.

Your room is the pink of a previous person that you no longer want to be associated with, even though you've covered most of the dusty fuchsia with slick-haired, clear-skinned, bare-chested actors.

You have nothing to wear. Staring at the crowded rails you miss playing dress-up like you used to. The image of Monica French in PE last week is burned into your memory, the sly peek of a lacy blue thong under her basketball skirt, shorter than everyone else's. You are wearing white M&S shorts.

You try to channel a different version of yourself, light-hearted, funny, pocket money from Daddy to go shopping with. You find a strapless fitted bodycon dress, too old for you, and trainers that you would never pair, tie your hair with unfamiliar ease, and try her on. This new you. Paint your face in smoky sultry difference, change your voice to long vowels and blurred consonants; you remember how hard you'd worked to twist the sounds your mouth made when you were younger, Mum persuading you that it was better that way, a code that switches one way and gets stuck. You can be a chameleon. You take the costume for a test, strut, strut, strut about your room, and laugh at the transformation. How easy it is, you realize, to be someone else.

The confidence on the bus half an hour later isn't yours but you like it. It tastes heady and sweet like excitement, like the bottle of cheap white wine you swing and swig, like the lip gloss you are wearing. You sit on the bus and listen to Monica's playlist and feel not like yourself in the best way.

Her street is wide and tree-lined and picket-fenced and every house has two cars in the driveway. Hers isn't the biggest, but it has the nicest exterior with gravel and trees in pots and twinkly lights and a festive wreath. You smack your lips and strawberry lace gloss answers with a snap like elastic, rubbery plastic like a Barbie doll, and you savor it. You agonize for a moment between the door knocker and the doorbell. The music is already blaring inside and you opt for both.

Monica answers in low denier everything and you don't know where to look. She is tanned and toned with boobs that bounce, bounce, bounce in her demi-cup bra and you suddenly feel self-conscious in your strapless fitted monochrome.

"YOU LOOK GREAT!" she shrieks, and you flinch at the volume. "I LOVE THIS HAIR LOOK FOR YOU. IT'S SO SLEEK, IT'S SO CHIC! COME ON UPSTAIRS. WE'RE ALL GETTING READY!"

You brave the shiny hallway after her. You remember the Zora

Neale Hurston essay you'd read for Mrs. Cobain's homework, glimpse a big room, wide white spaces, sharp white edges, a sharp white background, and you feel so strange as you head up the many stairs, past the many floors of the big house.

Monica has a dressing room. You didn't know people your age had dressing rooms. Girls are sprawled on the floor; Paris and Maddie and Aimee and Amy and the others who you know more by their sidelong glances than their names. There are red plastic cups like in American movies. You finished your wine on the bus but Monica fills you up a red plastic cup with red plastic liquid to match your red plastic lips. You worry about spilling it on the pale gold carpet.

Sit, chit chat chit shit, sweet liquid passes your lips and heats you from the outside in, taking you from wine-warm to something more specific and pronounced; everyone is telling you how hot you look. "You're just Hugo's type," Amy says—but this is Amy, not Aimee, and she is nice to everyone.

"I'm not here for boys," you say and the consonants have become a struggle. "I'm just here to have fun."

"Oh, bullshit!" says Paris, a girl in your year who you know plays field hockey with Monica. "Everyone's here for boys. You didn't get dressed up for us, right?"

"Unless you did?" chimes in Maddie, Amy to Paris's Aimee. "It's totally okay if you're into girls, you know. I mean, it's the twenty-first century after all and there's bound to be at least one lesbian in our year."

You shake your head. "No, that's not—who is Hugo, anyway?"

"I can't believe you don't know him!"

"Year older, so peng."

"He'd definitely think you are too. You look like a snack in that dress!" Aimee—who isn't normally nice but has moved on to shots—says it *schnack* and you giggle and decide to stop thinking and warm up even more. You sip gratefully, you hadn't realized you were so thirsty; you pass the cup round, staining their lips with shiny pink, shiny red.

The doorbell starts to ring and doesn't stop ringing all evening and you sip the sugary drink and dance and dance, arms round various necks of various brand-new friends. You see Melly over in the corner, laughing and you stumble over.

"Steady on, love, you're having fun, then?"

Maybe there's something in her tone that makes you uneasy, that makes you double down.

"YES, YES, yes, yes, yes. The most, most, most fun!"

She laughs and says, "Babe, this is Kwame."

"KWAME, hi!" You are too enthusiastic, trying too hard to be fun but chilled but warm but cool. "You know Baker. I know Baker REALLY WELL!"

"Yeah." He smiles gently, and you have the faintest impression of angular wide features and full lips. He glances at Melly. "Yeah, he talks about you all the time!"

Melly lowers you into a chair. "Have some water," she advises you kindly. She's ruining your fun.

"MELLY, PLEASE, YOU'RE BEING BARE BORING!" You're up and off and stagger trip fall into the crowd of sweaty bodies, ignore the laughs and swears as you career around because you're young and wild and free and you love this song you LOVE this song YOU LOVE THIS SONG.

"I LOVE THIS SONG!" Your new friends cheer as you twerk and dagger stagger tumble stumble trip fall ignore the bruises bones blue purple flesh of sharp edges, sharp white background; your toxic mix in the red cup tastes like strange fruit swaying like your vision, like your hips have never before. You want to be her, the girl from your bedroom, you want to be her you don't want to be yourself you want to be whatever they want you to be.

Blurry blurry hazy laughter. Shot after shot that you don't taste but know that each one is leaving a bullet in your brain, you won't feel it until the next morning and you laugh because you're immortal and indestructible and this is stupid and delicious.

Blurry blurry hazy pause. A pair of eyes from across the room. The eyes are part of a face, a nice face, a face ripe for kissing. Stumble tumble trip and fall into his lap but you like it, it's the most charming thing you've ever done and you laugh because you're so charming, and he seems to think so too. His eyes are sleepy, lazy, entitled, and it's not your usual cup of tea, but tonight you want something stronger so you stroke his cheek and hair and laugh again as he squeezes your bum very gently, as though testing the limit, maybe you're both enjoying the attention. He's saying something that you don't quite understand you what? WHAT? And he says something about ten pounds and splitting the winnings but you're too busy watching his mouth move and feeling his hands on you, you're the girl at the party in the lap of the boy with the nice mouth and light eyes and you're surprised because no white boy has ever looked twice at you.

There's a hand on your wrist. It's Melly, angry, Kwame by her side. Melly is trying to tell you something.

"You posh white kids are all the same," Kwame is saying, looking at Hugo in disgust. "Melly, let's go."

"I don't understand," you slur. "You're being ridiculous. I can have my arse felt up if I want to."

Melly says something else that you can't hear so she has to yell your humiliation in your face. "YOU. WERE. A. BET."

"What?"

"A bet, babe," she says. "I heard Maddie and Paris telling Monica. They were laughing, the fucking bitches. They're not fucking laughing now."

Behind Kwame's shoulder, you see blotched faces and mascara running. You have no idea what Melly said to them.

All you can think right now is that this might get you uninvited to Monica's next party.

You look at Hugo—*you were just a bet, this is so embarrassing, so painful*—but the vodka and tequila soften the blow and you rally— smile, hair, flick, flick, flick. "A tenner?" you cry. "Is that all I'm worth?" You stare down Paris and Maddie, watch them watch you grab the light-eyed boy's ripe face, too ripe now, too sweet and pigmented and soft under your decisive grip, and kiss him.

Cheers and laughter, whooping and applause, and a strawberry laces smack smack he's kissing you back, his tongue is an overenthusiastic puppy's, your eyes are open the whole time, seeing far too much, so you retreat into a small dark spot inside yourself and let the hot liquid of hours fill the vacuum, you grin, you cry, "Ten each, yeah?!" And they cough up, because it's all just banter, and they can't say fairer than that.

Melly and Kwame fade into the crowd of your new fans, warm bodies shielding you against their shared disapproval. That's fine by you.

Because Melly knows that that's the first time you've ever kissed anyone.

DECEMBER

Last day of school and you're in the classroom exchanging your Not-So-Secret Santas. Paris gives you a bracelet you know she found at the lost and found. It actually turns out to be Amy's that she'd lost last term so you give it back, and she feels bad, lets you choose one of her chocolates; you watch the talent show, Year Eights singing acoustic R&B covers; you wait for term to end.

Cat is next to you, talking, and you tune in, hear the quiet reproach as she asks, "We never talked about Monica's party?"

"Yes we did. I said it was fine."

"Just fine?"

Beat. You wonder why she is bringing this up now. It's been a couple of weeks, heavy head and a mouthful of sawdust vanishing faster than the fear-of-foolish feeling in your stomach that had lingered after that night. Maybe the FOMO had silenced her. Maybe she is aware that the looming separation of the Christmas break presents you with ample opportunity for avoiding her questions.

"Melly said you had your first kiss?"

You feel sick. "Barely."

"Well . . . how was it?"

"Fine, Cat. It was fine. It like . . . wasn't a big deal."

You ignore Cat and watch the Year Eights. You tune back in when Aimee's nasal tone grinds its way through your reverie. "I way prefer it now," she's saying. "You know?"

"Oh, yeah, I guess," Amy replies. She sounds uncomfortable, you think vaguely.

"Otherwise it's a bit like Cat's, isn't it? Like Velcro."

You and Cat both turn, see Aimee/Amy, etc., sitting with the rest, see Aimee drawing her hand back and realize she'd just fingered the end of Cat's cane row. You feel a phantom shudder down your spine, like it's your personal space that has just been violated. The tiny violent act reverberates through the air.

"I just mean, the texture. I'm not being rude," Aimee says.

You speak up. "Like Velcro? What is?"

"Well, her hair." Aimee gestures at Cat.

"Cat's beautiful Afro hair is not like Velcro." You say it quietly, looking her dead in the eyes.

"That's not what she was saying—" Amy says quickly.

"I wasn't talking to you, Amy." Amy falls quiet.

"Aimee. Do you want to try and explain yourself a little bit better?"

You eyeball her and she says, "I was just saying your hair used to be like Cat's hair, but now yours is smooth and neat. Cat's feels a bit like Velcro, but, like, not in a bad way. That's just the example I used."

"Wow." You and Cat look at each other. "What the fuck?"

"Seriously, Aimee?" Melly is shrill, a row in front of you, craning to hear. "What the fuck did you just say?"

"Year Elevens! Quiet! At the back!"

You all turn forward, straight-faced, quiet, wait for the teachers to return to watching the show—don't want to risk last-day-of-term detention—then you all spin quick, head flick back, to see Aimee's angry, embarrassed face.

Melly says, "If I ever hear you say that or anything like that again, I will bang you in the face. Cool?"

Aimee is torn between panic and pride, girls' school number one rule is never show weakness—but then she says, sarcastically, "Yeah," and drops Melly's gaze.

You look ahead, jaw tense. In the corner of your eye, Cat's head is bowed slightly. Her face is in shadow, but it looks like her eyes are closed.

"Can I come into Val's with you?" Cat asks. "Please?"

You hesitate under the streetlights. You're going to Val's to get your hair straightened for another of Monica's parties and Cat isn't invited.

"If you like. Won't your mum expect you back?"

"No, she's working late today. I think she wanted to give us the place. I forgot to tell her there had been a change of plans."

Guilt is a hole in the pit of your stomach. You had said you'd hang out with Cat before Monica gave you a better offer. You think of Cat going home to an empty house.

"Yeah, of course," you say. "Come in." Because you're outside now, and you know Val will invite Cat in anyway. Val's always liked Cat.

Loud, steamy hot, and chatter over the sounds of blow dryers and music, Cat eyes the room she's only been in a few times, slips carefully into a seat next to you and whispers, "Is HE here?" You shush her as Val greets you.

"Your skirt is so short, lahd gahd, did your mudda let you out like that, yuh wan' cetch col'?" She kisses her teeth long and low, something like patois and somewhere like your home in an irritated melting pot baked with a pinch of, "Dem tights are transpuhrent yuh nekid suh, yuh nah have a lickle more material pon yuh body suh?" It pours off her tongue in a mixture like her slow-cooker chicken, warm with a kick.

She wraps the robe around you, leads you to the basin, begins the routine of cussing you for not looking after your hair properly.

You leave your body in her capable hands, blissing out completely. You are back in this chair that you've been sitting in for years, in this room that you've been visiting for years, with Val, who rubbed your scalp like this when you first came to have your hair braided, no more than six years old. It's one of your earliest memories now that you think about it, and in that moment you remember something—*another world, a girl in a forest, the taste of honey wine in a cottage kitchen, voices raised in song—they want you to help them—but—ah, it's gone!*

As you doze, you hear Val say, "Cat, who normally does your hair?"

"My auntie."

An auntie chuckles from across the room. "There's always an auntie stealing your future customers, Val!"

"I guess that makes me everyone's auntie," says Val. "Cat, I can do your hair after if you like? Would you like something fun for this party?"

Your breathing catches. You keep your eyes closed.

"Oh, I'm not going. But thanks, Val."

"Why not, love?"

"I wasn't invited."

Pause.

"But you two could go together, no?"

"I really don't want to go. I don't get on with Monica that well. Or her friends. That's whose party it is. Not that she invited me."

A pause. When Val speaks to Cat again, her voice is gentle. "I can do your hair," she says. "I've got a free evening."

"Thank you!" Cat sounds mortified now. "But I really just wanted to hang out here for a bit, I feel like I barely see her these days, unless we're in lessons."

Cat laughs awkwardly. You feel both of their eyes on your face and you keep your eyes shut. "I'm sorry to hear that," Val says quietly.

Val shakes you and you make a show of waking up. Cat says, "I hope you have enough energy for tonight."

"I'm sure I'll be fine with a few vod—I mean, a few Red Bulls in me!"

You and Cat chat in the mirror. She sits behind you as Val blow-dries and styles your hair, all the while complimenting Cat's curls and kinks and twirls, eventually persuading her to wrestle it free of its pineapple, so she can "get her hands on it." You watch in awe as Cat's Afro expands and lifts, the vast crown of an empress.

It reminds you of something, of a girl in a forest, except she is the forest. A forest you can sometimes feel yourself floating towards as you drift off to sleep. But before you sink entirely into unconsciousness, you turn away, guilt coloring your dreams. Somewhere you should be. Something you are afraid of.

Cat averts her eyes from her own reflection, catches yours instead and you see there an expression of self-loathing so familiar it takes your breath away. You realize again: maybe you're not the main character. Maybe Cat pokes herself and prods herself and pulls herself apart like the frog you dissected in biology last week.

Val cane rows Cat's hair. You sort through the outfit options in the bag Mum left at Val's for you, discuss makeup with Val, Cat, and the last few aunties of the day. This should be so much fun, this moment, so fun and carefree and fifteen but your stomach hurts, you can't eat anything, not even the wings Baker arrives with, musky in the best way after boxing.

You're glad he can see you like this. Sleek and shiny and soft with dark lined eyes and a sense of your own prettiness, standing beside your coarser friend and you hate yourself as soon as the thought forms. Baker is lovely to Cat. You see her light up from the inside under his kind, warm glow, his infrared winter heater eyes. Even tired, even with dark smudges under his eyes, Baker makes people beautiful, you realize.

Baker is laughing at something Cat has said and you feel jealous. That laugh—that thrilling laugh—that's *yours*. Isn't it?

"I'm not sure what else to do with my face," you say loudly and they both turn back to you.

"Your face looks fine to me." You don't want Baker to think your face is "fine."

You ignore him and ask, "Cat, what do you think? Sorry, no offense, Baker, just Cat's a little more cosmetologically experienced." You are smug because that was a good line.

"Well"—Cat is digging in her bag—"I was going to give you this at school, but . . ." *But you were talking to your other friends.* "Maybe this?"

She's handing you a small wrapped present. You, Cat, and Melly always exchange Christmas gifts on the last day of term. But this year you had to buy all the drinks and new outfits for the parties and Monica had expected a Christmas present and then Amy. And in the midst of all of this, you'd forgotten to budget for Cat's.

"Oh, Cat! Wow, thanks, I didn't expect this."

She doesn't say anything because of course you did, you've been doing this every year since Year Seven.

"I mean, I'm obviously going to get you a gift, I just have to do it with next week's pocket money. But I know exactly what I'm getting you and I'm bringing it to our movie night when we reschedule." You add, in a very small voice, "Sorry."

"It's fine, oh my god, don't be silly!" Cat's voice is slightly too high and her eyes too bright and she isn't looking right at you. You can feel everyone's attention on you, even though Val is in the corner tidying combs and Baker is on the floor with little Esmonde who is murmuring "Nee-naw" to his fire engines.

You open the gift. It's the highlighter and lipstick that you told Cat months ago that you wanted. She'd remembered. You know that was more expensive than her pocket money could afford and so you know how long she would have saved to get it for you.

"It's perfect," you say. The hug between you is awkward for the first time ever and as you paint your face with Cat's gifts, your skin feels sticky and grubby with shame.

You say goodbye to Val and to Baker who is seemingly struggling to stay awake. He becomes more alert as he looks at you, though, eyes scanning your new face, new hair, new clothes, a once-over that makes you shiver, ever so slightly. "You look nice," he says. His smile is a little sad.

As you head out into the evening, off to Monica's street with the big houses and the big gardens full of twinkling lights, you look back. Val is braiding Cat's hair. She is telling her a story, one you have heard before, one that starts,

"There was once a witch,
on the run . . ."

The Weaver's Crossing

There was once a witch,
    on the run
    from a terrible darkness and
a danger to her son.
She clasped the boy to her breast,
like she had done once before,
her family and her home she left,
waving farewell upon the shore.
They crossed the vast expanse of sky and seas
in a ship made from willow trees,
until, after many minutes or weeks,
they came to heavy, dense, gray clouds.
On and on and on they plowed.
By her sister she had been given a gift,
an avocado from the rebellion tree,
saying, "With this fruit did we quell a king,
and by this fruit we shall all be free.
We of life and roots and earth,
can use this fruit and make it strong.
And though your life is different now,
to Persea you will always belong."
And, yes, she was alone and far from home,
her only talismans a brush and a comb,
but she knew three things for certain:
one, there was magic in her blood that had quieted a king;
two, the future of her child remained her choice;
three, she was most powerful when she used her voice.

CHRISTMAS BREAK

Tinsel lights, foggy windows, tinny carols blow out to greet you from shop fronts with gusts of warm air. You are huddled between Monica and Amy. Aimee sweet-talks the vendor into giving you all boozy hot chocolates. You warm from the inside out as you sip from the non-eco-friendly cup.

The boys are at the market too, Hugo and his hangers-on, new friends with cash to splash. You're nervous about money—you're all going out for dinner later.

Monica nudges you. "He really fancies you, you know, babe?"

"Does he?"

"OMG, yeah, like the bet was totally just a dumb boy tactic to kiss you!"

You say you're not the betting kind and Monica laughs again.

Monica is always laughing, until she's not. Paris and Maddie are coming over with the boys. You nod with your chin at the boy with the sweet, ripe face.

"Hi, Hugo."

"Hey, you. Can I buy you a drink?"

Hey, you. He doesn't remember your name, you think. "No, thanks, I have a hot chocolate."

"Oh, yeah." His lopsided flirty smile. "I like chocolate too."

The others laugh, Monica crows, "Ew, Hugo!" You smile.

He steps closer and you smell the mulled wine and back away, grab Monica's elbow and tug her over to look at some baubles. Their glimmering gold reflective surfaces refract your reflection back at you, a thousand twinkling *yous*. A pair of eyes appear above yours, dancing in the gold light

210

and for a split second the gold light marring your vision and the eyes, those eyes, remind you of someone—

A cold hand brushes your neck and you jump and shriek.

Baker is laughing behind you, his laugh is your port in a storm, you grab his hand and feign violence but really you just want to hold his hand.

"Hi."

"Hey! Who are you here with?"

"Kwame and Melly. You?"

"Monica and the others." You gesture towards her and notice that her gaze is locked on Baker.

"Well, hey there," she says. You've never heard this voice before. Without looking at you, she says, "Why don't you introduce us?"

"This is Baker." You shift uncomfortably. "His mum is my hairdresser. Baker, this is Monica, from school."

"Your hairdresser?" She takes a step closer to Baker. "OMG! The one with the money problems?"

You say quickly, "I didn't say she had money problems, Monica, I said her landlord was—"

Monica cuts you off. "Sorry, I'm so tactless with this stuff." Her eyes are fixed on Baker. "I've heard all about it, honestly it's outrageous. My dad works with a lot of small businesses so I'm sure I can get your mum some good advice!"

Baker is clearly torn between deep embarrassment and hope. "Well, if you can help . . ."

"Not at all! Maybe Val could do my hair sometime."

Baker blinks. You turn a laugh into a cough.

"Why don't I buy you a drink?" says Monica. "They do amazing boozy hot chocolate here. With vanilla." Her tongue lingers on the last word, as though it has more Ls than usual. Her gaze flicks to me. "I think Hugo was looking for you, babe."

"He's a bit drunk," you say.

"Oh, don't be like that, he said you're a really good kisser!"

Monica pouts at you, as if to say, *Don't ruin my fun*, when suddenly Melly, marvelous magical Melly, is there beside you. She says, "Was Hugo that weedy little shit that made that bet about you?"

Now you wish the ground would open; you wish for a steaming chasm, a sinkhole, a hidden well, anything to swallow you into its dark gaping maw.

"What bet?" Baker asks.

"It's nothing. Leave it. A joke." You feel your heart beat in line with the two-step in his jaw.

"HEY!" It's Hugo, voice loud as he pushes through the crowd. "I thought I'd lost you!"

"Nope. Not lost."

Your voice is cold but he reaches for your waist, laughing, "You're so sassy!"

You are not remotely sassy.

Your eyes on Baker's face, flick, flick, flick, watching his expression freeze between humor and something dangerous; his other hand is twitch, twitch, twitch, years of boxing and butterflies' wings before your eyes and you know it's so unlike him but this is so unlike you.

"Baker, no! It's fine! It's not worth it!"

But Baker has swung you behind him, is in Hugo's face, his pulse racing in his neck.

"Baker, it's okay! Leave it!" Melly is pulling him away, Kwame on his other side. "She can fight her own battles!"

You realize you're the *she* whose battle Baker is fighting, even though you never asked him to. Hugo is backing away, hands up, saying, "Calm down, my brother."

Aimee/Amy are laughing awkwardly, Paris and Maddie are threatening to get security "if you're going to be so aggressive."

Kwame and Melly haul Baker away. He looks back at you and the set of his mouth, the total absence of dimples, the expression in Baker's eyes, Baker's eyes, Baker's eyes, well, it damn near kills you. He looks at you like you've picked a side. Maybe you have.

"Well, that was uncivilized." Monica is laughing again and Kwame turns and snaps,

"It's sexy till it's not, but we move."

Monica doesn't understand, but you do. She looks at you and laughs again.

It dawns on you how much you hate her laugh.

WHAT CAN I GIVE HIM, POOR AS I AM?

"Nothing extravagant this year, I'm afraid, girlies!"

Mum loves Christmas. This morning she is resplendent in Christmas pajamas that match yours and Saffy's, and she is wearing giant Rudolph slippers with red noses the size of golf balls and a white-trimmed red Christmas hat. Her usual cooking apron has been traded in for her festive one, an unusually racy choice for Mum, bearing the slogan: *It's Christmas time, Screw the Mistletoe, Bring on the Wine.*

Mum's Christmas cheer is an unstoppable force and even your sullen teenage mood can't dampen it. She has transformed your three-bedroom house into a winter wonderland, all on a shoestring budget. When you stepped out of your room on December 1st and saw tinsel coating the banister, paper snowflakes hanging from every shelf in the living room, and piles of gingerbread cookies filling the biscuit tins in the kitchen, Grinch-like you felt your heart swell.

And so, on the morning of the 25th you put on holly-sprigged pajamas and pull your elf slippers onto your feet. Saffy has the same pair but yours are red and hers are green. Saffy has spent days, under Val's watchful eye, carefully dying one of her old and well-loved blunt blonde bobs until she'd achieved a shade that wouldn't have looked out of place in the Emerald City. Instead of a Santa hat, she is wearing a glittery headband with two light-up Christmas trees attached to it by springs. When pressed each tree plays a tinny, yet still haunting, version of "In the Bleak Midwinter."

Your own glittery headband has a jaunty *Ho Ho Ho!* written in red cursive. Melly would make a joke about that, you think. Another kind of "ho."

You wonder if your regular Christmas movie night with Cat and Melly went ahead without you. The WhatsApp had lit up this morning with Merry Christmas messages and a funny little dancing elf video, but you think you're being given the cold shoulder. It suits you to think that at any rate. You send a curt *Merry Christmas*, then leave your phone upstairs.

Downstairs a *Happy Birthday* banner is hung by the door—"For Baker, not Jesus," Saffy says. She makes that joke every year. Your stocking is overflowing with little trinkets: clementines and lip gloss, sweets and chocolate, novelty socks and the kinds of hairbands and hairclips that would never have contained your hair before.

"Santa must know you got your hair relaxed!" Saffy is delighted. You and Mum exchange a look. This is probably the last Christmas you and Mum can continue the deception. You hope Saffy isn't too furious at the thought of a large, bearded white man taking the credit for your mum's hard work. Saffy had once been thoroughly scolded by Grandma for saying that she didn't believe that God was white, like he was in all the pictures in your children's Bible, and if they were lying about that then what else were they lying about? Mum had then scolded Grandma for scolding Saffy and told Saffy it was okay to ask questions.

Saffy has bought you a new bag for dance and some leg warmers and a foot roller for your aching tendons and arches after hours in pointe shoes. You know she must have saved her pocket money for months.

"Thanks, Saffy-baby! They're perfect!"

"You're welcome! Mummy, open yours next!"

You and Saffy have bought Mum a deal for a spa for her and a friend. You hope she takes Val. Her eyes fill when she opens the gold envelope.

"Oh, girls! My girls! Thank you so much!" She wraps you both in a giant hug and she smells warm and spicy—like perfume and turkey seasoning and coffee. For a minute you're eight years old again.

Then Mum pulls away, patting at her eyes, and Saffy delightedly opens your gift to her—a miniature hairdressing kit, complete with miniature straighteners, miniature tongs, and a miniature comb and brush. "It's so CUTE!" she exclaims and smothers you with wet stocking chocolate kisses before solemnly handing out the last few gifts under the tree.

Grandma, who this year is with the sister your mother doesn't speak to, has sent massive Christmas cards and money. You wonder briefly if you should give it to Val, a contribution for all the free haircare over the years, but you know she wouldn't take it. Saffy passes around your main gifts from Mum, identically wrapped in glittery purple paper with a gold ribbon.

You both open the careful wrapping with careful fingers, peel smooth, peel smooth, gentle tug, don't rip because you can iron and fold and save for later, caress the ribbon, spool it softly, place under a book on the low wooden coffee table before focusing on what lies beneath.

"Mummy!" shrieks Saffy delightedly. "I don't believe it!" It's her own mannequin head for hairdressing, like the one Baker has, except Saffy's doll's head has a bubblegum-pink Afro and her skin is warm sepia. Saffy is enraptured.

"You're welcome, Saffy-baby." Mum is glowing with the balmy gold of her own generosity and turns to you. "Your turn, Mush!"

You pull back the last of the wrapping with a flourish like a magician revealing something marvelous. You are not disappointed. Bound in dark purple wrapping and embossed with gold stars, a glorious journal falls into your lap. It has *Dream Diary* stamped across it in foil lettering and a gold pen tied to it with a black ribbon. It's perfect. You didn't even know it's what you wanted, but it's perfect. "Thanks, Mum. I love it."

She says, "Well, now you can write down your magic dreams."

She winks at Saffy.

Magic dreams. The nagging sensation of forgetfulness, reaching and slipping, like trying to catch clouds.

You hug Mum again. It's brief and you sense her wanting to cling, feel her long pine-green manicured hand press against the back of your head, but she lets you go.

The rest of the morning passes as it usually does, a breakfast of oven-cooked festive canapés and boxes of chocolates while Mum prepares dinner. You and Saffy clear the table, tidy the perpetually tidy house, sing along to the radio and festive playlists, you as loudly as her for a change. When everything is in the oven Mum pours herself a mimosa, pours Saffy an orange juice, pours you a shrewd look before handing you a mimosa as well. The bubbles, the effervescent tingle of almost-adulthood shoots carbon and excitement up your nose, and you stick on *The Wizard of Oz* while you wait for Val and Baker to arrive.

The doorbell chimes at a quarter to one and there they are. Val's reddish-brown hair is adorned with a holly hair piece and her customary bright loose dress exchanged for a sequinned red and green onesie. Your gaze performs its usual rotation around Baker's eyes, Baker's face, Baker's lips, Baker's eyes, Baker's eyes, Baker's eyes, Baker's broad shoulders and long legs and gleaming teeth, and Baker's body. The tension that you felt when the door first opened, the heavy cloud of your last exchange and all the things you didn't say melts away as he stands there. Looking sheepish and faintly ridiculous in an elf onesie.

Maybe it's the mimosa, maybe it's because it's Christmas, or maybe it's because your mum insisted everyone wear a Christmas onesie, but an enormous balloon of laughter erupts from inside you, softens the edges of your swollen heart, loosens it from your throat, and erupts from your mouth.

The five of you stand in the doorway gasping for air, howling with laughter, tears running down your faces. You don't think you've ever

217

seen Val lose control like this, you've never seen her heave and shriek, clutching your mum for support, but it's the happiest and fullest you've felt in a while. You exchange Merry Christmases and then you turn to Baker. "I am sorry my mum made you wear this on your birthday."

"I don't know," says Baker, still grinning. "It's an improvement on last year. Those pom-pom sweaters were *ugly*."

You laugh again. Laugh more quietly. You say, "Happy birthday, Baker."

When you'd learned that Baker was born on Christmas Day, you'd initially felt sorry for him. Now, though, it was just something that made the day more special.

Mum and Val go into the kitchen to finish the food—or gossip—and the three of you sit on the sofa watching Judy Garland's magical journey into a technicolor dreamscape, watch her ruby slippers shine ("I want a pair!" Saffy declares), watch her decide that, *There's no place like home*.

"That's true," Saffy observes sagely as the film draws to a close.

"You reckon?" you ask, thoughtful. "I don't know. Oz is pretty cool. Magic and adventure and ruby slippers, Saffy, come on!"

"Would you pick nice shoes over your home, though?" Baker asks.

"I think I'd pick magic and technicolor dreams over . . . over pretty much anything." You sound suddenly somber and you're not sure where that came from. You nudge Saffy, to lighten the mood. "You're the one with the big imagination!"

"Dreams and imagination are different," Baker says quietly.

Saffy says, "Yeah! Oz is fun and cool and magical and everything, but there's also scary stuff like the witches and the flying monkeys!"

You tug gently on Saffy's green hair. "You're right, Saffy! I'm only joking! Obviously there's no place like home, silly!"

Mum and Val walk in at that moment and announce, "Presents before dinner!" You move next to Saffy in your rehearsed seats around the tree. Val and Mum never give gifts to each other and instead save their money for their annual Big Night Out. You're never really sure where they go or what they get up to, but you and Saffy will stay with Grandma or a friend and when Mum collects you the next day she is almost always looking seriously hungover, hiding behind dark glasses.

This year, you and Val seem to be on the same wavelength as she's bought Saffy overalls—"to protect your clothes when you're practicing with hair dye"—made of a glittery sunset orange along with a pair of matching rubber gloves. Baker has bought her a blanket shaped like a mermaid tail and a set of face glitter. "When you were little you smacked a girl who said you couldn't be a mermaid," he tells her. "Do you remember?"

Saffy shakes her head, running her hands over the sequins. "I don't know." She grins. "I can be one now, though."

Baker gets boxing gloves and cologne from Mum, for Christmas and birthday combined, and from Saffy, a packet of seeds and a book on gardening. Your turn. He hands you a shiny pink envelope. "Mum and I went in on something for you together this year." You raise your eyebrows, open the envelope, and shake out the contents. It's tickets to the ballet. Your face slackens at the unexpected, at the generosity, at the hours of braiding two pairs of hands completed to afford this.

"Thank you," you whisper. "Thank you."

Val barks a laugh when she opens her gift from you and Saffy. She's impossible to shop for and claims to need nothing, so you and Saffy had compiled a gift box, on which you'd stuck in silver letter stickers: VAL'S LOST THINGS. An assortment of things Val could never seem to find in the humid chaos of her salon. Scissors and Scotch tape, safety pins and hair pins, different colored pens, empty jars for all of her homemade hair oils, and a pot to keep her keys, which she was always losing. She kisses you both, grinning. "Nothing me love more than what is useful!"

Your heart starts a bass-like thrumming in your chest as you hand Baker the silver-wrapped packet. You should have got him more. This was stupid. "It's not much," you say. "Not exactly ballet tickets."

He unwraps it and something white and shiny falls out.

"It's a dreamcatcher." You can't read his face and you can't read his tone. You curse yourself again. "I know you have bad dreams." Your face is hot. Stupid, stupid. Something told you that Baker needed help, needed saving from his dreams, and this was all you could think of.

But Baker isn't looking at you like you're stupid. He's holding the dreamcatcher in his hand, looking at it eyes wide.

"It's perfect," he says quietly.

"Stupid," you mutter.

"Shut up, will you?" He laughs and shakes off whatever had descended. "It's genius. Like you."

You slip on your posh private-schoolgirl mask and say, "I don't need you to tell me I'm a genius." And he laughs and the tension ebbs and flows and then it's time for dinner.

Turkey and perfectly crispy potatoes and honey-roasted veg. A swimming pool of gravy. Christmas crackers pulled by interlinked arms, battles for the pigs in blankets, terrible Christmas jokes, chosen family, blood family chosen still. You and Baker are allowed a glass of wine and a beer. Mum brings out a sugar and chocolate cream monstrosity of a birthday cake, Baker blows out seventeen candles, you sing, Val kisses his cheek softly and looks at him like he is precious because he is.

At around eleven o'clock at night Val calls a cab to take her and Baker home, heaving herself away from one of the many Christmas boxes of chocolates. Saffy has fallen asleep on the sofa, her head in your lap and you are leaning more of your weight against Baker than you would like Val to see. You are both sleepy and full.

"What you doing New Year's?" you ask.

"I'll have a birthday thing with my boys." He frowns. "You going to Monica's New Year party?"

You sigh. "Probably."

"Don't you usually hang with Melly and Cat?"

"Melly's in Thailand and . . . Cat won't want to come to Monica's."

"Yeah, wonder why that is."

"Look." You're annoyed but can't keep the pleading tone out of your voice. "I need to stay on Monica's good side. It helps at school, believe me. Besides, it sounds like her dad might be able to help Val, so—"

"Firstly, yeah," Baker interrupts you, "I don't trust that Monica girl as far as I can spit. Secondly, don't lie and say that you're begging her friendship for me and Mum's sake. All right? Don't lie to yourself. And don't lie to me. Not on my birthday."

You don't know what to say. The word begging echoes in the quiet living room. Saffy snores on gently.

Val calls. You hear the purr of the waiting taxi, see its flash of headlights gold and yellow like baubles outside. Baker is getting to his feet, pulling his coat on over his absurd red and green onesie, stuffing his feet into trainers that look new. You flinch as the backs crease beneath his heels. He reaches over to the coffee table and picks up the white string and brown beads of the dreamcatcher you got him. He folds it back into the wrapping paper with surprising tenderness and when he turns to you again his face has softened.

"Let's not end today like this, okay?" you murmur hopefully.

"Yeah," he sighs. "Merry Christmas."

"Merry Christmas, Baker. Happy seventeenth."

He leans towards you. Your heart swoops, flips, takes flight like a hummingbird behind your ribcage; you are on fire again. He kisses your cheek. The blaze condenses to that one spot. "Sleep well," he says quietly against your skin.

"Sweet dreams," you return.

He chuckles softly, gesturing with the rewrapped dreamcatcher in his hand. "I guess I will now."

JANUARY

New Year's passes in a strobe of flashing fireworks, mince pies, and vodka cranberries shared with people you don't really like. January descends like the rain and wind and in the pre-term days you hit the sales. When you reach the wide maw of the underground, though, you can't find your travelcard.

Melly ("screw the system") and Cat ("an act of anti-capitalism") slip past the barriers all the time, but you're too chicken. Usually. Now, you time it right, wait for the staff to look away, choose the exact moment to slide through the always-unlocked gate for suitcases and strollers. You know the barrier will be open on the other side, it always is. You breathe. Relieved. Step onto the escalator.

A few paces ahead of you, a couple kisses as the escalator falls over its crest and begins its slow cascade. You look down on them and tut and then realize someone just ahead of you is doing the same.

It's a woman, beautiful under the station lights. She glances back up at you. "Can't they keep their hands off each other for five seconds?"

It's her. The Bing's Burgers waitress, who you always admired. Her locs are twisted up in a bright-yellow scarf interweaving and her dark skin glows gold to match. You used to think that boys liked small girls, quiet girls. But the Bing waitress isn't like that and Baker and his friends worship her, so maybe you were wrong. You don't think Hugo would like the Bing waitress.

She glances up at you and rolls her eyes, easy comradery, instant ingratiation.

"I hope they trip at the bottom," she whispers conspiratorially.

Her heavily accented English is hard to place; almost French-sounding but rich vowels, an undiluted cordial.

You nod and kiss your teeth, agreeing, "Innit." You share a smile.

You walk together on to the platform, overtaking the kissing couple and jump onto the empty end of the tube. She sits opposite you reading her book. You covet her outfit and wonder if those trainers are on Depop.

"I'm probably just bitter, you know."

"Sorry?"

She lowers her book.

"I mean, I'm single so I'm probably just bitter. You look young, you shouldn't be bitter. We should be happy for people like them, people in love."

"I guess."

She leans forward. "I'm trying to practice this manifesting positivity thing, New Year's resolution, and bitching to a kid on the tube about someone else's love life ain't it really. Anyway, just trying to put the good stuff out there."

You say, "okay."

You smile at each other again.

"Are you dating?"

"Um." You think of Baker, think of Hugo, say, "No!" a little too quickly. She laughs.

"Don't be shy! I'm not going to tell Val or anything! Do you like anyone?"

Your face heats. You think of Baker. Think of Hugo. Think of her. Your face heats some more. You shrug diffidently.

"Well." She smiles gently now. "If you like someone, here's my advice. Firstly, be okay with them not liking you back. Like be *actually* okay with it because, honey, if they don't, it's their loss, but you need to *know* it's their loss, you know?" You nod even though you're not sure what she means. "And secondly, once you know that you like them, really like them—tell them." You gape at her but she is emphatic. "I'm serious! Own it, honey, it's powerful!"

You get off at the same stop, move autopilot towards the exit, it's only then that you notice the closed doors and remember your tiny act of defiance. You begin to panic. You squeeze in behind her as she goes through, press quick against her back, hold your breath, half-close your eyes. You're through to the other side. No one has seen you, no one was even watching, you keep walking.

Outside, she looks around. "This street, man. It's changed so much since I been here."

You are giddy with relief. "Yeah! I know! I've been coming to Val's for years and years and it's so different. There used to be five Caribbean takeaways and now there's only one, but there are five coffee shops, and, I mean, I wouldn't mind if they were a bit different but—"

As if to make your point, a woman pushes past in Lululemon, holding a resusable coffee cup, talking loudly to her friend. Her gym tote knocks against you. Sunflower Locs kisses her teeth, big earrings swinging, and you overhear, "See, told you this was the ghetto."

You wince but Sunflower Locs swings round, hollers, "IF YOU'RE GONNA SAY IT THEN SAY IT WITH YOUR CHEST!" down the street.

"The audacity." You say it with gusto.

She smiles at you sheepishly. "Sorry, yeah, I just hate all that postcode-lottery shit, man!" She kisses her teeth again. "The ghetto. So when Mr. Tallyman stan' outside countin' out avocados four for a pound issa Third World Country but charging fifteen quid for a plate of avocado on toast is supposed to be what? Civilized?" She laughs. "Trus' me, I come from a so-called 'Third World Country.' Those women have no idea."

"I wonder when it'll stop being the ghetto, then," you say slowly. "There are chains and juice bars and cocktail hours here now. What else can they possibly want to change?"

She smiles at you, shrugs, reaches into her bag and fishes out a two-pound coin, saying, "Here, buy yourself a travelcard home or you'll give yourself a coronary!" before walking off. You choke back your shyness, draw a breath, and, a little too loudly, call, "Happy New Year!"

She laughs.

"Bonne année."

One Day My Prince Will Come

The sixteen-year-old girl with her magic would wrestle,
trying to get a grip on all she would become,
but the enchanted forest of her hair was a vessel
for a power burning brighter than the noonday sun.
The more afraid and alone she felt,
the fiercer the gold and the life and the light,
and without her mother and sister's help,
the less she believed she could continue to fight.
And in the dark of every night,
a rotting stench, a whispered blight,
"Come, pretty witch girl,
let me touch your hair,
let me run my hands through it.
Oh, it isn't fair!
I've tried every spell and enchantment I know,
I've begged and bribed but even though
you burn with your magic's flame
you still will not tell me your pretty witch name."

FEBRUARY

You've always told you were born in the spring—you like the sound of that: new life and fresh chances. But really February isn't spring. February is definitely winter.

You wonder if that's more fitting. An uncertain month. Feeble attempts at sunshine, and predatory gray clouds quick on their tail.

Cat is only half-speaking to you, Melly is only half-speaking to you, Baker is only half-speaking to you, Monica runs hot and cold like the bathwater at home, your mum is too busy to call the plumber.

Monica is desperate for you to throw a birthday party and won't let up.

"Come on, babe," she wheedles. "I've thrown loads of parties and, like, I love it obviously, but it's not fair that it should always fall to me."

"I don't really have the setup for parties the way you do." What you mean is your house isn't big enough. She knows this, she must.

"There's nothing to it," she says, eyes wide. "I ask my parents to get some alcohol, make a playlist, and that's it."

"My mum wouldn't get me alcohol."

"What about your dad?" pipes up Amy.

"Stupid, she doesn't have a dad!" says Monica. "God, you're so insensitive."

"If you give me the money, I can get it. I always get served and can just use my sister's ID," says Aimee.

You swallow. You pray for an intervention.

Your salvation arrives in the form of Monica's dad, pulling up outside the school gates in the sports car that screams "family man has midlife crisis."

227

"Monica darling! Get in! This is a double yellow, I can't stop!"

Monica grabs your wrist, calls back to the others, "Don't worry, she's having dinner at mine tonight, I'll wear her down!" This is the first you're hearing of dinner at Monica's but your refusal gets stuck in your throat. You feel mounting dread as Monica drags you over to the warmth of the sports car's interior.

You clamber awkwardly into the back seat, ducking under the doors, which open like an aughts flip phone. The interior is red leather and smells of cigars and strong, expensive aftershave. You are already prone to motion sickness and now in the back seat, with the windows of the low-suspension car firmly shut to prevent Monica, who is pale and wraithlike, from catching a chill, you feel the familiar cramping nausea settling in your stomach and throat.

Monica's dad looks nothing like her. Where Monica is willowy with her mother's blonde beach waves and bored expression, her father is short and stocky, dark-haired and red-faced, with such a plummy voice he sounds like he's slurring.

"Well, Monica, how was school, darling?"

"Fine."

"Fine?" He imitates her poorly. He rolls his eyes at you in the rearview mirror and you smile weakly, nausea growing. "How are *your* grades, dear?" he asks you.

"Oh." You flounder, unsure of what the right answer is. "Okay?"

Firmly in her own territory now, Monica is her most Monica. "Don't be modest, babe. You're top of every class."

"Well! That's very impressive!" Monica's father guffaws. "You could learn a thing or two, Monica darling!"

Monica's pale blue eyes narrow and you sense the permanently thin ice beneath your feet begin to crack. "Well, I mean, you have to be top of our class, don't you?" she says. "If your grades slipped, you'd lose your scholarship place."

"Oh, scholarship girl, are you?" says the father. "Well."

Don't be sick, don't be sick, don't be sick. You look out of the window. Try and tune out, try and focus on the world whizzing by.

"Daddy, her hairdresser is the one I was telling you about. Her landlord wants to evict her and turn the salon into some Starbucks or something, I said you might have some advice."

He smiles benignly. "Well, it depends on her lease but ultimately, you know, the landlord owns the property, darling. He's the boss. Private ownership is the foundation of our economy. Do you know who the landlord is?"

You open your mouth wide enough to say, "Richardson," before returning to the battle with your esophagus.

"Richardson, Richardson . . . Oh, yes, young chap. No, I'm afraid if it's that boy there's not much chance he won't get his way. Knows every trick in the book."

Don't be sick, don't be sick, don't be sick, don't be sick.

Monica's watching you in the side mirror. She pulls an "oh, well, I tried" face. It's just a game to her.

And suddenly, you're not in the mood. You stop fighting. You give in. You open your mouth.

And vomit all over the back seat.

Monica shrieks, her father swears, and, even though you're crawling in traffic, riding the clutch, he slams dramatically on his breaks, flings open the doors.

The beige and pink of ham sandwiches spray the red leather and the carpeted floors, the stench of stomach erases the cigars and aftershave odor.

"I'm so sorry," you mutter.

"For heaven's sake, girl! If you were feeling sick you should have just said!"

As her father scrambles frantically in the glove compartment for a tissue, for a wipe, for anything that can begin to clean up the spectacular Jackson Pollock-style splatter on the back seat, you meet

Monica's gaze. Sick is trickling down your chin, spooling on your good school coat. But you don't care. You wipe your arm across your face. You grin at her.

For once she looks genuinely unsettled.

Then before you can think any better of it, you're off. You grab your bag, leap out of the car, turn, and run, darting through the traffic, horns blaring behind you, Monica's dad bellowing, but you, you're laughing the whole way.

*

You barrel in through the door of Val's salon just over ten minutes later, flop down, your bare legs getting goosebumps in the cold, sticking to the leather seats. You rang your mum as soon as you were out of the car.

"Mum, it was so bad, Monica's dad was driving us back to hers in his sports car and I got carsick and I threw up everywhere!"

"Oh, Mush, no! You poor thing! You know you can't go in low-slung cars! What happened?"

"I ran for it!"

"Oh, baby," she said, and that's when you knew the sympathy card was working because Saffy is the baby now. "Well, you need your roots done anyway, so see if Val can fit you in and I'll pick you up later?"

Now, though, as you wait for Val, the adrenaline of your projectile protest has worn off, and fear about what Monica will say the next day has sunk in, and as the February rain begins to descend, so does your bad mood.

A message pings up on your screen.

Hugo, who has been tepidly texting you since Christmas. He usually suggests you get a drink, get a coffee, go for a walk. Sometimes, though, the tone changes: HEY B, WHAT R U WEARING/UR UGLY/I WANT U IN MY BED. Hugo's mates messing around on his phone. These are always followed by Hugo's hasty apologies but the whole thing makes you uneasy, like you're the butt of some joke that you don't quite understand.

"Hey." Baker's shoes appear in front of you. You freeze.

"Hey." You take a breath. "Listen. Monica's dad can't help your mum after all." And then, just because you really needed to say it out loud: "She's such a bitch."

He snorts. "True. She is. I'm going shopping, you want anything?" His lack of gloating makes you feel, if possible, even worse.

"No, thanks."

The door swings behind him. You slump lower.

A foot pushes against yours. "Sit up," Val instructs. You sigh and comply.

"Yuh healthy?"

"Yes." You look at the vomit stain on your coat and pick up a packet of wipes behind the till. "Mostly."

"Yuh alive?"

"Yes."

"Yuh got dinner tonight?"

"Yes . . ."

You know where this is going and feel your eyes preparing to roll at the People Have It Harder Than You speech, but Val stops. "Jus' eat whatever Baker bring yuh, okay? Then he'll smile and you will smile and yuh can sit down and come get yuh hair done all nice and pretty pretty?"

You are annoyed at how accurately she knows what will cheer you up. "He's only half-talking to me."

"Well, he can't ignore you. You know that."

The Hershey's Kisses that he places in your hand five minutes later brings a lump to your throat.

"Thanks," you mumble. "And sorry. About Christmas. And the market before that."

Baker says, "It's cool. You want to talk about it?"

You're tempted, but then the door opens and you both turn. It's Richardson and he's brought a friend.

She is wearing a shiny suit skirt and is carrying a clipboard. "Hi all," he says cheerfully. "This is Karen."

Her name is actually Karen? Your eyes meet Baker's and you both giggle.

"She's just here to take some measurements," Richardson says. "For when the space becomes vacant in April."

"Ah, okay." Val hesitates and you hate it, hate what it means to see intrepid, sure-footed Val hesitate, are thrown by her strange Queen's English. "Only we hadn't actually reached a conclusion, Mr. Richardson. You said I have until April to come up with the money so . . ."

"Well, I'm sure you can understand, Val, that I have to hedge my bets." He lowers his voice confidentially although you can all hear every word. "The money due at the beginning of April includes the rent increase. Anyway, Karen will be managing this place when"—cough, awkward tickle, cough—"*if* you decide to vacate."

"Well, we haven't decided."

It's Baker. Everyone looks at him because this tone in his voice—clipped, assured—is new. Even Esmonde looks up from his cars.

"You know she doesn't want to *vacate*," he goes on. "Say it how it is. Rent goes up nearly ten percent in as many months. That's madness but okay. You're the landlord, bossman, I guess it's on you if you want to be the dickhead that evicts the locals from their home and turns it into a Starbucks. But if that's the case then at least say it with your chest."

Richardson holds up his hands. "Community matters to me, believe it or not. It won't be a Starbucks here."

"No, no! I'm a hairdresser too," says Karen. "So we'll be keeping a lot of the key elements actually."

You think about Karen using the basins Val had fitted, the

hairdryers that had cost her a fortune, the shelves in the exposed brick wall on which Mum had artfully arranged displays of products for sale.

Baker kisses his teeth. "You wouldn't know community if you ran it over with your Lambo!"

You reach out to take his hand. Baker turns to face you. "THIS IS BULLSHIT!" he yells. There are tears in his eyes, but you will not let him cry here in front of this stranger.

You grab your bag. You say, "Val, be back in a minute," and pull him out into the cold street with you.

Streetlights flickering on. Commuters never looking up.

It's raining properly now, as you knew it would. He gives you his hoodie to keep your hair dry. You squeeze his hand. He squeezes yours back. He breathes.

You go to sit in the Starbucks a few doors down and sip on too hot, too bitter coffees neither of you have actually developed a taste for yet but you pretend you have.

"Why is everything pink in here?" he asks in a hoarse voice.

"Because it's Valentine's Day this weekend."

"Oh yeah. 'Course." His distracted indifference has you scrambling to tease, to lighten his heaviness.

"Yeah." You smile wanly. "Got any valentines?"

He laughs. "A few." This wipes the smile off your face. "Not from anyone I really like."

"Oh?" you say, raising your eyebrows. He looks you right in the eyes and words fail you. So instead you say, "Hey, how's my dreamcatcher working?"

He says, "Mmm, like, it's nice to look at. But in terms of stopping bad dreams, I think it's a dud." A beat. He fiddles with a packet of sugar. "Actually, if anything, I think I've been having them more since Christmas."

You hesitate. In the last few years you've barely discussed your nighttime dreamland with Baker. That's something you both grew out of. That's what you told yourself every night before you went to bed.

"I'm sorry to hear that," you murmur. "I've been trying to write in my dream diary but as soon as I try . . . I forget everything." Creeping shadows sit at the corner of your vision. *A dark cloud, a girl trapped on a mountain, a forest of curling mahogany . . .*

And then it's gone.

*

A few days later, running some errands for Val, you see the Bing's Burgers waitress walking to work. She has a scarf with flamingos on it today and even though you prefer the sunflowers, the pink looks lovely on her and you wish you could be like her, or at least tell her so. Easy breezy unaltered in her twenties and so independent going to edgy bars on the weekends, bars you only go to if you already know about them and you can't know without knowing someone who knows—and she'd know.

She catches sight of you across the street and waves, says "Hi!" then "You're up early!"

You say, "So are you!" and she rolls her eyes about an early morning training session. You want to chat more, but she's outside work and you're outside Val's and you smile wave to each other again.

You watch through Val's steamy windows as she goes inside, is one of only a few there, puts on her apron. Camilla is there, wearing a shirt patterned with dogs, and you wonder what an early morning burger joint training session could entail. You are waiting for the stationary shop to open and you bounce on your heels and watch as the cool waitress makes a tea, yawns. You're just picking up a spare hairdryer for Mum but you make the task last so you can linger there, watching her covertly.

You are idly watching as the white van doors open and men, dressed black and blue like bruises, pour out. You sprint down the street, as do lots of people in shops around you, some stand silently sad, some silently smug, and some not silent at all, Ife from the thrift store hurling abuse at the black and blue men. "Evil cowardly SCUM."

They stream into Bing's Burgers and, within seconds, people are bundled into the street. One of them is her. The waitress. They are led out into the street and into the van and you now notice HOME OFFICE emblazoned on it.

You walk closer. You want to do something. You have never felt younger, smaller. She is asking to use the toilet, she is uncharacteristically quiet and calm and polite, but they tell her no and someone grips her arm to make sure she won't slip away.

You want to help her, but what can you do? You think of all her things, imagine her collection of colorful scarves lying abandoned somewhere. Would she be allowed to go home? Who would tell her family or her flatmates? The cool, collected Camilla-type is watching from the doorway, arms folded.

You find the bright pink flamingos again, meet the gaze beneath the twisted rim of the wrap. She doesn't look afraid. Embarrassed, maybe. You don't look away.

You will witness.

The Source

You are thinking about birthdays as you drift off tonight. You are thinking about the party you do not want; you are thinking about friends you're not sure you have, and of vomit and red leather seats. And then you're thinking of a cake you didn't get to eat and a birthday that you ruined.

After the Sankofa, you had exhausted yourself with dance and late nights, dreading sleep without really knowing why. For three months you had drifted off after midnight, lingering in an in-between place where a glowing canopy of hair flashes with dark and gold, a sense of malevolence swirls with darkness amidst a perpetually burning forest fire. In that place beside the clouds you have rare moments of clarity, a flash of understanding where you fully see both your worlds. In those moments you know that the King seeks Zella still. You turn away regardless and drift off into dreamless sleep, forgetting everything when you wake.

But then, that night, you dream.

The Great Forest forms around you, coming into focus. Vast. You begin to walk, feeling a pull and following the instinct until you realize you can hear the laughing River Aphra, bubbling through the forest.

You reach the banks and look around. You know that the source of Xaymaca's magic is in the river and you imagine the great goddess Yaa pouring power into the frothy teal currents, pushing and pulling the pieces of this world like flotsam and jetsam. You sit on the bank and watch the river for a while.

Then, you slide off the bank and into the water. You slip beneath the surface until the water pools over your head and you feel the slime of river plants coating the pebbles that exfoliate the soles of your feet. You hold your breath. You stay there, avoiding all reality. *Can I drown in my dreams?* you wonder.

A current forces you back to the bank. A shadow falls across you as you lie there, cool and dry and panting. Black robes drift across your vision like curtains and you look into brilliant gray-gold eyes.

It is Yvane the Seer. "Ah, mortal girl. I am glad you answered my call."

You stand, slowly. She hands you something—a belt, woven with leather and brass, like the one Kam and her mothers wear.

"You have come back to fight for us."

"I don't . . . I don't think I can," you say tremulously.

"I once heard," says Yvane, her eyes never leaving the water, "that the smallest pebble can change the way the river flows. The tiniest change, a shift in resistance, and the current shifts, adapts, and the world twists after it." She clears her throat. "I have made terrible mistakes, child. I have behaved more like a gossiping old crone than a seer. I should have listened to the prophecy.

"The prophecy told me of a son of witches who would aid the King. So we sent all the sons of witches away. As if I thought we could outrun a prophecy! But I have learned my lesson. I will listen to it now. And what it told us is:

"*Three girls will fight, two will stand, the other of us, and yet not of this land.*

"*You* are not of this land, child. You have much to do here. But I am done. It is a terrible thing—to be a seer who cannot see." Yvane the Seer smiles. "We have a saying." She presses her lips to your forehead and murmurs, "Out of many, one people."

Then she is gliding away, slow but upright, taking care not to shake or wobble. For a moment you think she is going to leap across the river, as she approaches its bank with an assuredness you don't understand, but she slips down the bank and into the teaming, foaming blue green. She begins to wade towards the center, dark hood slipping off and showing her slick hair to be the brightest silver white. You know what is going to happen next. And yet you cannot look away, will not look away. You will witness. She raises her arms high above her head and over the roaring of the water, you hear her cry, "Yaa! Unto the source I shall return what I was gifted!"

More bubbles appear on the surface of the water and a figure emerges. A thick curling mass, an Afro of dark green, skin that is shining brown like the pebbles on the river's bank, and eyes of a shocking petrol blue, the color of the sea during a hurricane. Her breasts are bare and glistening. The River Mumma rises to meet the Seer, her thick tail the green-gray of seaweed and gently rippling, keeping its owner upright. You take a step back. She is as beautiful as she is terrifying. She is the gaping maw of a river personified, she is the keeper of Xaymaca's source and you know without thinking that she is older than the land, perhaps as old as the great goddess Yaa herself. A mermaid.

"I see you, magicless child. Turn and face the River Mumma." Her voice is like the roar of the tide, a rushing waterfall of power and feeling. It is a voice that none would dare defy.

You realize that Yvane has gone.

"Are you the girl the trees whisper to me of?"

"I, um . . ."

She laughs. It is such a strangely human sound. "Well, Yaa always did have an odd sense of humor."

The River Mumma looks down into the murky depths of the river. "The burden of sight is a great one. I see that she has given you her belt. That is a powerful gesture. Magic is inexact, but always intentional."

"I've heard that a lot, but I've never really understood what it means."

She watches you, her head tilted to one side.

"Before the prophecy, there were no clouds. But one day a Persean witch, a Weaver, paid me a visit. She begged for the benefit of my wisdom. Wanted to know where she should take her son, where he would be safe from his father, the King, who once forced himself upon

238

her as a crude insurance against whatever he feared the Perseans would do with the prophecy. I told her of a faraway land with no magic and suggested she board a boat to there.

"But there was one more thing to do. If any spoke her name, or that of her boy, there was a risk they would be remembered and found. I owed this witch a great debt, one I had been looking to repay for many years. And so I sent my waters into the sky, sea spray and foam all joining to form the mist, clouds which blur the sight and blur the mind too. Fogs the memory, creates the illusion of forgetfulness. I'll bet when *you* wake, girl, you don't remember much of your time here?"

You nod. "I forget nearly everything."

"This witch chose to vanish, to have her friends and family forget her, to have her son forget his home, in order to keep them safe. See? Magic. Inexact, yes. But intentional. Purposeful. Effective."

You close your eyes. Avocado oil and locked, half-forgotten rooms. For once, the thread between this world and the waking world is clear.

"It was Val," you whisper. "She was that witch and Baker is her son. And that means . . ." Baker had never known his father.

"That means Baker is the King's son."

You shudder and the River Mumma nods. "She sent you here. Where you are needed. She knew that you were the girl from the prophecy, even if she couldn't remember everything."

You feel the lush mossy bank beneath your feet. You breathe deep, trying to tether yourself to your reality, but you think this thought and your mind scatters like the pebbles between your toes because you are losing grip on where your reality begins and ends.

The River Mumma begins to fade.

She reaches over and tosses you the belt, the belt that had belonged to Yvane.

"Keep Val's secret, girl. The King's shadows know better than to eavesdrop on me, but they are not always so wary. Good luck, magicless child—and tell Val that we are even now."

MARCH

You have been dreading the next morning and Monica's retribution for the vomit in the car. You sit in the corner of the common room, praying to go unnoticed. Monica flounces in shortly after and wastes no time telling everyone what you've done.

"God knows how much it will cost Daddy to clean," she says. "Red leather seats don't come cheap."

"Don't they?" Melly says, fabulously disdainful. "Red leather sounds pretty cheap to me." You meet her eye from where she sits with Cat on your usual side of the common room.

"Just shut up, Monica," Cat adds. "No one cares about your dad's tacky sports car. It's bad for the planet and he's clearly compensating for something."

The common room erupts into laughter. Monica flushes a blotchy claret.

You gather your things, gather yourself, walk across the room like it's no man's land and you're crossing enemy lines. Except these aren't your enemies at all.

"Hey," you say breathlessly. Cat and Melly survey you in cool silence. You try again. "Thanks for that." You jerk your head towards Monica. More silence and you say all in a rush, "I'm . . . I'm really sorry, okay. I've been a dick. I took you both for granted and lashed out when I was feeling shitty about myself and have been an all-round rubbish friend and cared about all the wrong things and . . . and . . . yeah. I'm really sorry." Silence. "Well, that's all I had to say." You turn away.

Cat sighs. "Wait." You turn back, hopeful. "You *have* been a dick. But you've not exhausted your forgiveness quota yet."

You grin at her tentatively and she grins back.

"So you got literally sick of Monica, then?" Melly is, understandably, a little smug.

"Yeah. I thought she might help Baker and Val, but it turns out she's, you know, a bitch."

They laugh and you slide in next to them. "So what's going on with you and Hugo and you and Baker?" Melly says quietly.

"Baker's just Baker. He's just a friend." You don't even convince yourself.

They both laugh. "Yeah, right."

"And Hugo's super popular and cool and goes to all the parties . . ." you add and they both swat you and you laugh. "Okay, I've learned my lesson. To be honest, he gives me the creeps." You squeeze their wrists, gratitude and relief washing over you. "You know what I really want to do for my birthday next weekend? I want our regular movie night, but with extras."

"Extras?" asks Cat and you nod.

"Yeah, extras. You'll see."

*

Mum is away on the evening of the Saturday after your birthday—she and Val are going on their spa day and staying over. She apologized about twenty times about the timing and said you could have friends over, of course. Which is actually perfect.

"Saffy," you say to your sister as you scroll through movies on the TV. "We've not had a sister secret in a while, have we?"

Her eyes widen. "That's true. Wait. Do you and Cat and Melly want to drink *alcohol* tonight? I know that's what you all do at parties now. But it'll be a sister secret." She extends her pinky to you.

"Thank you." You smile. "Can I ask for one more?" She nods solemnly. "I was thinking, while it would be really fun with you and me and Cat and Melly, maybe it would be even more fun if we ask someone else. Who am I thinking of?"

She thinks and then gasps. "Baker! Is Baker coming?"

You smile wider. "He is if you don't tell Mum. And he's going to bring his really fun friend Kwame! But it's also a sister secret, okay, because Mummy gets worried about girls and boys sleepovers."

She clasps your pinky in hers. "Yes, because she's worried that you might . . ." She giggles and mouths, "S-E-X."

You giggle. "We can talk about that one another day. But she obviously has nothing to worry about. I just want to have my favorite people together on my birthday."

Saffy smiles. "Your favorite people. Melly and Cat and Baker and Kwame and . . . and me?"

"Of course and you!"

"Yeah! Of course me!"

You laugh together, squeeze her to you, and then you say, "Right! Let's order the pizza!"

Saffy springs into action, frenetic excitement, orders, "Alexa, play Jocelyn Brown!" and when the key changes you both scream, "OH, YEAH!" at the top of your lungs.

*

"I know it's three months late," you apologize, picking up the red-and-gold wrapped packages, "but better late than never, right?"

You are sprawled in the living room, comfy clothes and cans of Red Stripe open now that Mum has finally gone. The boys haven't arrived yet.

"It's your birthday, you shouldn't be giving us gifts," Cat protests, and you shush her. Melly and Cat tear at the wrapping paper in a way that would have nauseated your mother.

"I wish we'd ignored you and got you birthday presents now!" wails Melly, opening the eyeshadow pallet.

242

"Treating my friends who deserve it is kind of like giving myself a gift anyway." You grin.

For Cat you've bought a silver pen and notebook, a cheaper version of the one Mum had given you for Christmas, and she is as thrilled as you'd imagined she'd be. "It's beautiful!" she beams. "Ooh, I can write up my film reviews in here!"

The doorbell rings and it's the boys and Saffy is fizzing with excitement. Eventually you all resettle. Melly rests with her back against Kwame's legs, testing out the pigmentation of the various jewel tones against her rosy skin. Kwame is sipping a beer and leaning over the arm of the sofa to flip through your mum's collection of classic R&B vinyls, making various impressed noises,

"Your mum must be so cool, this Marvin Gaye vinyl is mad rare!"

Baker is sitting cross-legged on the floor with Saffy, expression intent, discussing the night's movie picks. It's a serious business.

"I think we should do a Ghibli marathon."

"That sounds sick, Saffy. Have you asked the birthday girl if that's okay?"

"Well, she said I could pick." She glances at you and you nod, smile, drink them all in, all sitting there, your people, your comfy, cozy crew, a warming fire in a grate that had been long boarded over in the interest of practical modernity.

The snacks come out. The drinks are poured. The pizza arrives. You settle in.

Hours later, you are still warm, their soft embers glowing thickly inside you. Melly and Cat are lying on two of your three sofas under heaps of blankets. Melly's hair spills over the arm rest and almost tickles Cat's nose. Cat's matching blood-orange bonnet and pajama set look like a dying sun against the midnight of her blankets. Kwame is on a mattress, his fingers centimetres away from Melly's. Saffy has long ago been sent to bed, after her sugar levels rose then crashed and she began nodding off. You are lying on the third sofa, and Baker on the mattress by your feet; you are turned towards each other, on your sides, drifting away together. Yours is a story of maybes.

"I'm glad you made up with your friends," he murmurs sleepily, softly drunk and sweet.

"Me too."

"You seem happier."

"I am. I wish there was something I could do to help you and Val, though."

He sighs. "It's just one of them things. We're all too small, really."

"Your mum can always get a new salon, right?"

"Maybe."

"What do you mean?"

He's drifting away from you. You grab him. "Baker?"

"Hmmm?"

"Are you still having bad dreams?"

His breathing changes. Then he says, "Yeah."

"How long has it been?"

"Five years, six months, twenty-three days."

Silence.

"Every night?"

"No. A couple a week. I don't remember what happens in them, but I know it's bad."

"I should have bought you a proper dreamcatcher, shouldn't I? Not the cheap, appropriative tat?"

"Do you still dream your magic dreams?"

"Yeah. I don't remember them either, though." You frown. "I think it's important I go back there, for some reason. That there's something I need to do."

He fumbles around in the dark, patting the floor for his bag. He pulls something out. The white thread of the dreamcatcher glows faintly in the chink of light from the streetlamp.

"Maybe it'll work tonight."

You smile to yourself in the darkness and you see his teeth return the favor. "Maybe."

He picks up your hand from where it rests on the floor and presses your fingers to his lips. He closes his eyes.

"Happy birthday," he whispers.

Darkness descends, tiredness closes in, you drift away together. "Sweet dreams, Baker," you reply.

And then your world goes to hell.

Part Three
Flower

Baker, Banished

Baker's hand is warm in your own and the warm veil of darkness is pressing against your lids. You are happy and content and your soul is dancing, pirouetting towards the clouds, the pearly white descending on you. With Baker by your side you feel buoyed, prepared for your return to Persea. You knew there was a reason you had to come back. You don't notice your hand slackening in Baker's and coming to rest atop the black-and-white dreamcatcher. You're vaguely aware of the thread tickling your wrist, the beads uncomfortable, pinching your skin, but you are frozen in sleep paralysis and are focusing on what you have to do, willing yourself towards Carrion Ridge or the forest.

You are coming back to where you are needed. You are ready to help them now, in any way you can.

But as you hover between, floating above that place where the clouds clash and the sea changes color, you can tell that something is wrong. The clouds aren't white but gray, black, dense, and pitch. Your hand, heavy against the black and white beads and thread, isn't pinching but burning, aflame. You try to move but you can't. The pitch mist is rotten and stinking, decay and tar, and you can taste it on your tongue.

The scene changes. You are blinking under bright fluorescent lights and you realize—this is Baker's mind.

"There must be something you can tell me, Mum."

"We came from Jamaica just before you turned seven. What more is there to say?"

"But what was it like there? Did I have friends? Did you have family?"

"Warm. Yes. Yes," Val had replied distractedly.

"And what about my dad?"

"You don't have a dad."

"Everyone has a dad!"

"That's not true. I don't. You don't. You have plenty of friends who don't."

Silence.

Then she said, "When we lived in Jamaica, my family loved gardening. We had the most beautiful gardens in the world. I can tell you about them. . . ."

*

Later, much later.

The house he appeared behind stood at the end of a long winding street, atop a slope, and sat further away from what he assumed was a village green, shaped like a triangle. Some instinct told him not to be seen and so he would creep out into the dense, undisturbed forest that protected the village from undesirable eyes. From there he would move from shadowy tree to dense undergrowth, familiarizing himself with the plants and animals, both strange and familiar, hoping to remain unseen.

He presses his fingertips to the damp terracotta and a bolt of something like truth goes through him. The answers are here. The answers to the endless questions of his childhood. A family, maybe. A father—maybe.

This place is so beautiful, why would his mother leave it? My dad must have been a wicked man, he thinks.

I'm a burden to my mum.

She doesn't trust me, won't be honest with me.

Maybe she thinks I'm wicked too.

Bad, wicked, too wicked to be here.

He lurks in the shadows and the shadows whisper back. The pitch mist, the darkness, alive and heaving, murmuring terrible, vicious things, low into his ear.

But then he comes upon a garden and it is so lovely that he lingers, watching a strange flower open to bloom by the moonlight. The outer petals are red like shining rubies, and its inner petals are so white in the moonlight they are luminescent. The fleshy pink inside looks like a soft tongue, rimmed by the teeth and lips of some strange kissing creature, some hungry monster. He stands, transfixed, and starts, heart pounding in his chest, when he hears his name.

"Baker?"

A voice he knows, calling for him. But two girls are pulling his friend away. He hears the laughter of the shadows around him, as a long-fingered, pale hand reaches inside of him and grips on to something fragile and precious. That hand, those elegant, bejeweled fingers. They have no right being there. No right to take what is not theirs.

*

"I can give you answers, Baker."

He is sprawled on a vast, black marble floor. He is cold and shivering, looking up into blue eyes.

"Who are you?"

"Well, exactly. That's one of the answers I can give you. Though, surely you should be asking the same of yourself?"

Baker shakes his head and you feel the heavy pounding as though it is your own. "I know who I am."

"Do you?" The pale blue eyes are narrowed and framed by golden hair, flecked with silver and gray, that tumbles in waves to the ground. The King regards Baker with an almost indecent interest. "Do you really? Or have you always felt like an outsider? Noticed how nervous you make others? Sensed a humming beneath your skin and fought to quiet it?"

He is so high up. The windows of the vast black marble room show only the night sky, flecked with stars.

"Tell me, Baker, son of Val the Weaver. Where are you really from?"

"How do you know who I am?"

"I know many things. I have a magic mirror. I am old and wise and powerful. I can show you how to be powerful too. Powerful people get answers, are always told the truth. Wouldn't you like the truth, Baker?"

Baker's heart beats in his chest as he looks up at this strange, pale face, this face so undeniably mired in evil, and recognizes something there. A glimmer of familiarity.

"Who are you?" Baker asks again.

The King smiles.

*

An empty room. A small window, high up, but ground level. The room is a basement, a dungeon, is damp and dingy and cold where the stone floor meets your knees. No, not your knees, Baker's knees. But Baker's knees are your knees and Baker's eyes, Baker's eyes, Baker's eyes, are your eyes. And Baker's hair—Baker's locs are roughly shorn and hanging short and limp. You stare around the stone dungeon of the King's castle and understanding dawns at the same moment that your host becomes aware of you.

"You shouldn't be here!" Baker cries. "This is my dream, not yours!"

The sky outside is darkening rapidly, a thunder-like clap splits the air, and you cover your ears.

"Go! Go!" Baker orders. "It's too dangerous for you here! Go home!"

He flings the last word at you like a javelin and you feel the weight of it hit you in the chest, send you careening away, through closed doors that burst open as you launch into the air, through windows flying wide and you see stone and brick walls, halls of a castle and shocked faces before you are sent skywards. You are not flying exactly, you are being pushed, pushed through the skies above Kingstown, pushed over neat and tidy rows of neat and tidy shops and houses, all organized neatly and tidily around the castle you are being driven away from. Away from Baker.

"Mirror, Mirror, on the wall,
what will it take for the witch girl to fall?
I feel my heir, retrieved in vain,
if I cannot take her name."
The mirror interrupts the King's ranting,
"I once sensed a disturbance in our land,
someone lending a helping hand,
and now I see her little face,
eyes like sky between stars and space,
the third girl from lands far away,
has found a way to come and stay.
A rip, a rift, a rent in the magic of our world,
and through this tear I see the girl—
loping between places
and ruining your plans,
restoring faith in family,
guiding tools to hands—
oh! This a challenge she has presented."
"Then this child must be prevented!
What can I do?" the King asked his old friend.
"She travels by use of a curious blend
of magic and avocado pear."
King Charming could only swear,
"That cursed fruit thwarts me once more—
well, I'll raze the tree to the floor!"

The Burning

You are lying in the sand outside the cottage.

The front door bangs open, scattering your thoughts. Kam is striding towards you. "Look what the wind blew in!" and you feel grateful that she is without magic.

"Kamaka! Enough of this!" Her mothers follow her out.

"She abandoned us! She decided that we are not *real* enough for her and she ran away!"

"I am sorry for that!" You scramble to your feet because Kam is towering over you and you don't want her to see your apology as weakness. "Please, I saw something. Let me tell you what I know."

"It's too late," hisses Kam. "Who are you, mortal, magicless girl, to know anything?"

Mortal girl. You press your hand to the brass and leather of your belt and cry out, "I am she who answers the call."

They fall silent and look at the belt.

"That is Yvane's belt," says Cynthia.

"She gave it to me," you say. "I am she who has answered the call again and again and again. I am not *magicless*," you add with some asperity. "Everyone has some magic."

Kam just looks at you, her face unreadable.

Cynthia squeezes your shoulders and murmurs, "Yaa blesses you."

Ama strolls to the front door of the cottage, still flung wide. "Come," she orders. "Let us not stand here squalling like common crones for the whole coven to hear."

Kam strides inside, followed by Cynthia, who gestures to you to follow.

The cottage is the same. Sunlight streams in from the large open window. The fire is out as the day is mild. Ama fetches glasses, pours the honey wine. You slide into your usual seat, aware of Kam burning a hole through the side of your head with her scowl. The others seat themselves around you and turn to you expectantly. The honey wine is sweet and warming and fills you with something like courage, reminds you of the swelling peaceful arching in your soul as you danced barefoot through the sky on the Sankofa. *Everyone has a little magic.*

"Yvane is gone," you tell them. You begin your tale.

*

The sky darkens around you as you talk and the house, that somehow has retained some of its magic, lights the candles, sets the fire kindling as the day cools to night.

"I was right all along, Baker is being held prisoner," you say. "I knew he would never willingly work with the King! We need to save him." You press forward, despite Kam showing every sign of interrupting. "Not just because it's the right thing to do, but because it will restore your magic. The Seer said it was a mistake, to try and prevent the prophecy, to expel all the men and boys. She wanted me to tell you that."

Cynthia and Ama are nodding slowly, but Kam's arms are folded and her expression is stony. "The Seer told me that you have a saying: *Out of many, one people?* To me that means solidarity is what makes us strongest," you finish softly. "If you help Baker, Baker will be able to help you. It's the only way to save Zella before the King can reach her."

"I thought you didn't want to get involved," Kam says coldly. "I thought you didn't believe in the prophecy."

"I do now," you say. "I understand that there's something I'm meant to do here."

"I wonder how you entered Baker's dream," Cynthia muses.

You pour some more honey wine. "Maybe it was the dreamcatcher." You laugh.

No one else laughs. Cynthia grips your arm. "A dreamcatcher?"

"Yes." You're bewildered. "It's just a bit of tat I got in a market. I gave it to Baker."

Ama curses. "A dreamcatcher is never just a bit of tat! Why do mortals mess with things they do not understand?"

More gently, Cynthia says, "You see, dreamcatchers, well, they do what they say. They catch dreams. Catch them and hold them fast. Ordinary dreams, good dreams, bad dreams—this does not matter. What matters is who made them—and how. And why. They're powerful charms after all, and come from a powerful people. Was this dreamcatcher made by those who understand their significance?"

Your eyes are wide, confused. "I . . . I don't know. Like I said, I got it from a market. It came in a packet, I've seen ones like it in shops or on the internet. . . ."

Kam growls, "That damn internet!" but you ignore her. You did not think it possible to feel worse, but worse is brewing. You remember the stall at the Christmas market, the blonde couple with dreadlocks. The man wore a T-shirt that said THE EARTH IS MY SPIRIT ANIMAL. You should have known better.

"Long ago, our goddess Yaa offered an invitation to the Spider Woman of the Ojibwe people. She visited Xaymaca, and we revered and admired her. She befriended the spiders of this land, powerful and wise beings who we call Anansi, and taught them how to weave dreamcatchers, special webs of protection. They taught us in turn, but after she left, it has been rarely attempted by any Xaymacans. Her teaching was thorough, but even still, we lack the knowledge."

You feel sick; you have never felt this kind of sick here before.

"And so . . . if someone weaves a dreamcatcher . . . and isn't Ojibwe . . . or wasn't taught by the Ojibwe . . ."

257

"The result could be catastrophic," says Ama bluntly.

Cynthia's mouth twists in worry. "The sharing of things between people can be beautiful. But the theft—theft by the people who have already stolen so much, have acted with such violence and brutality . . . Do not think that just because we are here without your internet and televisions, that we do not know of the horrors of your world. There are things that we know. We know of the stains left by bloody hands. Baker's dreams are something else. How this dreamcatcher was made, the conditions, the maker . . . there is a darkness there. And that darkness has called out to a similar darkness, held on to it. It sounds like it's not just the dreamcatcher. It's Baker too. His dreams are something else. And this dreamcatcher has been holding on to, will hold on to, something dark and powerful for months now. It sounds like when you fell asleep, in contact with the dreamcatcher, it pulled you inside whatever dark place Baker visits."

"And who else can see Baker's dreams?" Ama says wearily.

"The King . . ." you breathe.

"Basically," snaps Kam, "King Charming knows you're here now."

What happens next happens so fast, so abruptly, it is like Kam's words are the trigger. A *bang*-like a shot fired, a wave of darkness crashing around you all, blinding you, the smell of tar and pitch and damp. Ama is cursing, Kam is yelling, and Cynthia is intoning a prayer to her goddess, the slightest tremor in her honey-wine voice.

Then, your head is on fire.

A scream of pain rips from your throat. You smell acrid smoke.

"It's the avocado tree!" someone calls. Someone is dragging you outside, you can feel cool grass beneath your feet, are dully aware that this is the first time you've felt pain, real pain, in Persea.

You'll wake up in a minute, any minute now, you think.

You collapse on to the ground and look up. Ama and Cynthia and Kam stand beside you. Their faces are slack, hands braced against knees, mouths open in silent cries of horror. The avocado tree that has always stood at the back of their garden, the tree grown from the seed of the pear stolen during the Great Strike, is a mass of ash and embers.

The flames that caress the branches determinedly persist, licking, kissing, embracing until the whole tree, with a great creaking sigh of resignation, collapses into the darkness. You hear screaming. But everything is faded and hazy, you are drifting away and you feel such sweet relief that you are about to wake up, that it'll all be over—when you wake up—

Easter

You don't wake up.

You are stuck here, in Persea.

Your dream world has become your waking one. The days, and then weeks, that follow the burning of the avocado tree are mostly terrible. You try and try to cross back to your body, to reach the clouds, but the harder you try, the further away home feels. Sometimes, when you're drifting off to sleep or just waking, you see Baker. Zella mists in and out of focus in hazy flashes: her forest, her face sad, pensive, determined, and the sparks of gold light that combat the dark shadows lurking at the periphery of her vast, expansive Afro. You can't reach either of them. Your corporeal body is somewhere, out of reach—*white sheets, harsh lights*—but you are rooted in Persea now.

You spend most of your time with Kam, who glares at you at every opportunity.

"Yvane left the belt for me," you snap one morning as you dress for the village council. "And I came back. Doesn't that mean something?"

"I said nothing."

"You think I got exactly what I deserve."

"I think that now you can't cross it's going to be impossible for you to get messages to my sister. You brought the King to our door. Destroyed the tree."

"You can't loathe me more than I loathe myself."

"I'll do my best," she said and slammed her bedroom door dramatically.

All the same, she waits for you at the bottom of the stairs and walks through the village with you. She is on your side still, you think.

In the meadow in the center of the village, the coven has gathered to hear what you learned from Yvane and the River Mumma.

"The Seer has spoken," Cynthia explains, and you look at the belt around your middle. "We must save this boy."

There is a frisson in the air, a sense that as soon as a freedom came, the witches would be ready. Over the last few weeks, the witches have been getting ready. Cynthia and Ama pore over books with renewed vigor looking for . . . anything. Anything at all. A magicless mortal journeying across Xaymaca on foot to confront an immensely powerful king . . . surely it wouldn't be hard to think of something better. But they come up empty. Despite that, throughout Persea, swords are cleaned, arrows carved, armor hammered. Battle training is led by Bedia, naturally. You are joined by a few of the other younger witches, all of whom avoid you, except for little Zuri. They are not as openly cold as Cassia or Myrtle, but they keep a polite distance and stick close together.

They teach you the art of battle and you are surprised by how well you do. You don't match them, not even close, but, "You do not fall on your arse half as much as expected," according to Bedia. After two weeks, you almost find yourself able to disarm Zuri. Your years of dance training keep you light and agile on your feet. But it doesn't cheer you much. Even with all the training in the world, you can't outrun magic.

If you die here, you wonder, will you ever wake up?

*

"Why won't she wake up, Mummy?"

You can make out, behind your lids, indistinct shapes. Bright fluorescent light. An electric hum and dull, consistent beeping.

"Well, sweetheart, they couldn't say exactly, but the doctors are doing their best to find out." The worry in your mother's voice, concealed for Saffy's benefit, sends an agonizing pang through your chest. Your mum, your poor mum, who has been through so much and soldiered on for you, for her children. You hate yourself for what you are putting her through.

"They must know something?" It's Cat. Cat is there with your mum and sister. There are other figures in the room, you can see, indistinguishable from one another but you count six.

"No," says Baker. "No one has any idea."

Baker. You lurch closer to the wall, raise your hand to it.

"She moved!" comes Melly's whispered cry. "I swear she did, she moved!"

"She's done that before," Mum is saying. "Sometimes her body twitches or her lips move and I almost think . . . I almost think she's just sleeping. But she just won't wake up."

"She will wake up." You know that voice. Val, it's Val, and you want to shout at her, scream at her that this is all her fault.

"She's missed so much school," says Cat and you smile.

"She's missed so many good parties," corrects Melly. "We had so many fun plans for this year."

"The year's not over." Baker's voice is low and calm. "She will wake up," he says, echoing his mother.

"Maybe she's just having her magic dreams," Saffy says and you can almost hear Baker smile. The foggy shape that you think belongs to him reaches across your vision and you imagine him bringing in Saffy for a squeeze.

"I bet she is," he murmurs. "I just hope it's a good one."

You feel fingers brush your temple and jolt. You are barely aware of your real body, can just about feel, when you really focus, the crisp clean cotton of the hospital bed sheets, the cooling sheen of something like silk against your skin and half-laugh at the thought of your mum dressing you in your good pajamas. The warm dry fingers that caress your brow are achingly familiar. You hear the heartbeat monitor pick up pace and the murmurs of those in the room.

"Can she feel that?"

"Does she know it's you, Baker?"

"Can she hear us?"

But you can't answer; you are falling back into the body that lies in Zella's bed. As you rise towards wakefulness you hear Saffy's voice, as if from very far away, saying, "Baker, maybe it's like the fairy tales. Maybe you should kiss her and she'll wake up."

And maybe you're still dreaming when you hear him say, "Maybe, Saffy. But I always thought the prince kissing the princess while she was asleep was kind of weird. She can't say yes or no, either way. If I was going to kiss your sister, I'd want her to be able to kiss me back."

End of the Rainbow

The rain that lashes against the kitchen window is distracting. It is unlike any storm you've ever seen. The clouds are thick and dark and flash with silver lightning. It fills the house with the smell of life, of fertile earth, despite the closed windows. Every few minutes a rainbow arcs across the sky like a shooting star, glows faintly for a moment, then vanishes.

The witches at the table ignore it; it is as usual to them as April showers are to you. But you cannot smother the occasional gasp as rainbow after rainbow illuminates the sky. Saffy would love this, you think to yourself, and cling to the sight of the rainbow as the image of your sister's face fades.

Cynthia is studying one of the vast, ancient books. "He burned the tree," she murmurs, "to break the tether. You're trapped here now. You can't travel between us and Zella—she is completely cut off and vulnerable. And I can't figure out how to get you back without it."

"Why didn't I get trapped in the real world?" you say sulkily. "I mean, my world," you amend, as Kam's eyes flash.

"You were here when you became untethered, and so here is where you must remain," Cynthia says absently, turning the page. "Zella has that tree's power . . ."

"So maybe she can get me back?" You bolt upright.

"It's worth a try, isn't it?" Kam pipes up. "She needs to get home."

She gives you a small, hesitant smile and you smile back.

Cynthia shakes her head. "The journey to Carrion Ridge is not possible for you, remember. And Zella as a secondary tether only works if the root source—the original tree—is intact." She is frowning

264

at the small print. "But maybe we can restore the tree. It says here that we need another avocado, from the original pear tree. Then we would use its seed to plant a new tree, and that new tree would serve as a new tether."

Kam's mouth falls open. "You mean the one in the King's garden?"

They nod. Thunder rumbles in the distance and somewhere far away, a flash of lightning.

"In that case, it may as well be gone too." Your eyes fill with angry tears. "You're all still trapped in Persea. Zella is still confined on Carrion Ridge and losing control of her magic by the day. Baker is still in his cell and the King is still using him to leech your power. And I am stuck here, go-between, messenger and interloper and magicless mortal who may never see her family again."

A silence greets your words. Eventually Ama nods her head. "That is about the measure of it."

"Great. Really fantastic!" You push your chair away from the table and get to your feet. Striding to the sink, you deposit your glass, and then fling open the back door. The rain is still coming down hard but you don't care as you splash outside. They don't follow you and you are glad.

"I'll never forgive Val for sending me here!" you say to yourself, to them, to the garden. The flowers and plants flutter in response, and you can almost hear tiny voices tittering. "Oh, shut up!" you snap. You stare at the glistening rainbow, high in the sky, shimmering into view and throwing multicolored light across the garden as though a giant diamond hangs before the sun. *You will find her at the rainbow's end. . . .*

You start across the garden to the forest. The heap of ash and gloom at the back of the garden that was once the tree is sodden. The white wooden swing creaks in the wind. Without the avocado tree behind it, whispering branches telling secrets on the breeze, the swing looks lonely. It rocks as the wild wet wind sweeps a gust forward, but when it drops back, there is no one there to meet it.

*

It doesn't take much time at all for you to get lost. You are better now at identifying certain trees, at marking out their distinct voices, but you are still a stranger to Xaymaca in many ways. You force yourself through the foliage. You feel lost and dull and more human in this world than you ever have. You are louder than before; you crash through the brush, get stung by nettles, and your bare feet are soon bloody and sore. After a few more minutes of hobbling you give up and fling yourself to the ground. The rain has stopped, you think, or maybe it's just the dense awning of leaves providing coverage. Though you are grateful for the shelter, the density makes it nearly impossible for you to see the rainbows that light up the sky, to see where they begin and end. You will never find the River Mumma like this. You step on a rough piece of bark and let out a hot torrent of filthy words your mum would be ashamed to hear you utter.

"I do not know what half of those words mean, but I am fairly sure it is disrespectful to say them in the Great Forest."

You should have known they wouldn't have let you go off on your own. You sigh and stand, wincing at your tender soles touching the ground. You can feel pain in this world now. You face Kam, scowling.

"What do you want, Kam? To gloat? Well, I feel bad enough already so save your breath."

"Why on earth would I gloat?"

"I don't know. Because now I finally have as much at stake as you guys? Because now I've lost everything too? Because now I can't just wake up? Because I've finally admitted how useless I am?"

"You are not useless. You were sent here for a purpose. You are mentioned in the prophecy, remember! Magic is in—"

266

"Shut up!" And then you are crying, properly crying, and Kam watches quietly until you are all cried out. Eventually your howls become hiccups, and you haul yourself to your feet. You are exhausted. Kam wordlessly passes you a waterskin. "Come back to the cottage," she says. "Mum can patch you up."

You begin walking.

"Kam?" you say, your voice barely audible. "If Cynthia and Ama, with all their books and knowledge, can't help me, then who can?"

"*We know,*" whisper the shadows.

You jump, wheeling round. Kam doesn't seem to have heard anything.

"Did you hear that?" You grab her arm and pull her to a halt.

"Hear what?" She is perplexed.

"*Hear us, young Persean.*" You jump again, fear gripping your throat. Something is wrong.

"Something just spoke," you whisper.

"*I'd let go, if I were you,*" the shadows whisper. "*You don't want to bring her where you're going. You don't want to do her more harm than you already have. . . .*"

"Shut up!" you cry.

Now there are faces, twisted mocking faces whispering to you in a voice you've heard before, whispering all the worst truths you've ever known:

Selfish, ugly, cowardly. Just like your father. He ran out on your family and now you have too.

You've lost them all, lost your mother, your sister, Baker. The witch girls will never forgive you, their mothers will never forgive you.

Look at you, stupid, magicless child, trying to fight this. No one can save you.

The shadows descend until you can barely make out the wood from the trees. You tear yourself away from Kam and run, run away, staggering through the dark.

267

You hear her calling out to you, begging you to come back but you ignore her.

That's it, magicless child. Help me and I'll help you. You can ask me many questions, I only need one answer. . . .

Branches whip at your face, snag at Kam's clothes on your back, and still you run, far away, until you can't hurt anyone anymore.

Testing

You are standing in front of Zella, and you are surrounded by dark clouds.

"Why are you here?"

"I don't know," you answer honestly. "I thought I couldn't come here any more." Suspicion flares. "So what brought me here? Or who?"

Dark and rustle, rustle, the bright light, the shining sun, she is the shining sun. You reach out and touch the brush and the brush brushes back and black-brown tendrils twine around your fingers, eye lingers on each strand of branch and curling frond enveloping you in their midst.

Do not be afraid.

That voice again. The air smells hair-hot and heavy like avocado oil on a warm, damp scalp; you run your fingers through the leaves of the trees, the winding rope of your tether, and you know that you are safe because she is at one with this forest, it is part of her, her dense inner jungle conflicting rough loud bark, silky soft and green feelings, rustle, rustle, dark and safe and more intense here than it's been before, but you are not afraid because there is a bright spot at the core.

She needs you, the shadows whisper. *You can save her. Just tell me the name.*

"What is it?" Zella asks. Her eyes widen and you shake your head.

"Run," you whisper. Zella backs away at the exact moment that long, pale fingers curl around your throat.

Of course, he was the one to bring you here. To taunt you, perhaps. To test both of you. The King.

Zella begins to sing.

SWING LOW,
SWEET CHARIOT,
COMING FORTH TO CARRY ME HOME.
SWING LOW,
SWEET CHARIOT,
COMING FORTH TO CARRY ME
HOME.

You're coughing and retching from the force of those fingers around your neck but you hear her, and still manage to rasp, "Just keep singing, okay."

You don't know if she hears you, and the darkness devours you once more.

Galvanized

K am yelled out into the night
  with a fire in her belly that was something like adventure,
  she was not a conformist and the King's spell incensed her;
her chest had tightened, her brow puckered, and
she clenched her
fists, and knew that she must recover what had been stolen and
     forgotten.
How dare he—with his limp, lanky locs,
the coiffurical equivalent of sandals and socks—
out of tune with the rest of the world.
She knew the key of each curl, the note of each plait,
this magic was hers and theirs, and that
was something King Charming, in his fear and haste, had ignored—
he did not understand their hatred of their master
who'd robbed their hands stained with grease and clothes smelling
     of castor.
But she did and at that moment she knew three things for sure:
one, her women knew magic once and could know it once again;
two, the King's throne stood alone—but she had a home,
amongst the leaves and the trees, from willows to canella;
three, she would make her sisters safe; she would find Rapunzella.

Coming Forth To Carry Me Home

The first thing you are aware of is how dry your mouth is. The cough that rattles out of your throat is sharp as knives and you wince, slapping your tongue to your tacky palate. It tastes bad. Your lips are dry too, cracked and sore. You force your eyes open. The candlelight emitting from rickety brackets hanging on the walls is guttering in a breeze that comes from nowhere.

You are a prisoner, evidently.

You take in the four walls of the cell. It reeks of damp and there is not one surface left uncovered by slime, not one crack free of green and brown matter. You wonder how long you've been here.

A wave of panic washes over you and you wrestle with it, struggling to regain control of your body.

It's okay to scream and let it all out, the shadows whisper to you. *Things are bad, things are worse than bad. You abandoned your family and now you've abandoned the coven. The coven will never forgive you; Baker will never forgive you. You'll go the same way as Baker, stupid magicless child, captured by the King. . . .*

No! You stagger away from the corner and the shadows there. You wrap your arms around yourself and stand directly in the middle of the cell, right in the spot where the glow of each flickering candle meets, banishing all shadows.

I am she who answers the call, you say to yourself. *I am the interloper. I am a friend and a daughter and a sister. I am brave, I am strong, I am smart, I am a child of dreams not a child of nightmares,*

I will not give in to shadow and despair, I am most powerful when I use my voice, I will go home. . . .

Again and again you speak your best truths, arms around yourself, thumbs hooked into the leather and brass of Yvane's belt. Slowly you feel your breathing ease. The voice recedes.

The smell is more tolerable now, the cold less biting. You move towards the heavy bolted wooden cell door and peer through the tiny, not quite window. You can't see much. More stone, a hallway, a door at either end, a cell opposite you.

You blink.

You could have sworn you saw—

In the same tiny window, in the same wooden heavy door, across the hallway—

Exactly where yours had just been—

An eye.

You don't have time to register or recognize the depthless onyx stare because you can hear footsteps echoing down the corridor. They are loud and heavy footsteps, shiny boot steps, steel-capped toe, steel-capped sole, steel-capped soul; you scramble away from the sound. A guard in a shiny black and gold uniform.

"Follow me."

"What if I don't?" You straighten, throw back your shoulders and try to pin him with your best Kam death stare, made less impressive by your stained and soiled clothes.

"You can follow me up on two legs, or you follow me as I drag you on your knees. The choice is yours."

You follow him. More stone, more bare slimy walls, until you reach a staircase at the end. You try to memorize the route, but committing the row after row of bare, damp corridors to memory is made harder by how indistinguishable they all are from each other. Left turn, right turn, a staircase, left turn, another left turn, a right turn, or was it a left turn, you're not sure anymore, another staircase, and then another.

273

All are framed with heavy curtains, torn and moth-eaten and molding. The little light able to permeate the darkness is fractured and cloudy and all the doors are heavy and wooden and bolted like those in the floors below. You have no way of knowing what they lead to—outside or more cells or more endless stretches of stone corridors.

If this is the King's castle, then where are the bustling servants, the suits of armor, the fine portraits? Where are the simpering nobles and sycophants? Everywhere you look tells a story of disrepair. Forgotten corners that host shadows and dust, cracked vases with decaying flowers, dead flies fallen on window sills like corpses on a battlefield.

The halls are lit by candles, wax welding each bright bulb to sticks, flecked with rust, gold blurred with dust. The stone floor slaps beneath your bare feet that are now so cold and sore that you have become numb to the discomfort. You follow the guard on towards the next doorway, but you notice as you get close that there is no door. On the threshold you can see a vast, dark stain, like melted tar cooled solid. Your heart starts a rapid staccato against your ribs. A familiar smell invades your nostrils, a pitch and tar smell, the scent of sadness but this time it's laced with other things. Rich, overpowering perfume, sickly sweet incense, the tang of alcohol. You fight the bile rising in your throat.

Higher and higher you go, following the guard. After a couple of flights, you make a turn and see light pouring in ahead of you. There are windows up here, proper ones. Clean and arched and open, sunshine pouring in. You glance out of a window that you pass, look down and see smooth white, solid and weather worn. *A real ivory tower.*

You look out across the landscape and falter for a moment as you take in Xaymaca, properly, for the first time. Zella had once told you that Xaymaca means "The Land of Wood and Water" and you are finally able to see why. To the east, the dark smoldering peaks of Carrion Ridge blight the skyline with shadows and smoke and flashes of bright white-gold. *So Zella battles on.* You feel braver. Beyond the lawns of long grass and weeds, south to the coast, where the petrol sea glitters, and west lies the rest of Kingstown. Slices of green are perfect squares and equilateral triangles, trees stand silent sentinel over slivers of streets, everything evenly spaced and perfectly, viciously ordered. As you gaze further west, Kingstown becomes rolling hills and meadow and then is abruptly cut off by the hairline of the Great Forest, erupting forth from the scalp of the land, thick ancient trees claiming the skies like so many vast porous follicles. You take strength from the sight of it, and follow the guard.

Doors lead off each small landing space between flights of stairs. Most are closed, but some are open, showing bedrooms, dressing rooms, and you begin to put together a picture of what remains of the King's court: those nobles who had returned along with his power or had been bought back into his clutches with riches and promises of influence. They poke their heads out at you, heads adorned with flowing locs above aristocratic clothes—jerkins and doublets and women in tightly corseted dresses. They gape at you as you pass, filthy and reeking.

You reach the tower.

The door opens and you step aside, unwittingly pressed into the shadowy corner of the threshold. The smell of tar and sadness and decay burns your nostrils.

And there he is, standing in front of you.

After ten years of nightmarish mythologization, the reality of the King is somewhat anticlimactic.

He is handsome, exceptionally so, and his azure eyes are empty and cold. Golden hair (he brushes it twice a day, you think). Nobles, elegantly dressed, watch and murmur among themselves.

He holds out a hand to you, still crouched on the dark on the floor. "Charming. Charmed."

The King's chambers spread out, a royal bachelor's penthouse

275

atop the tower. Everything is decorated in dark wood and dark leather, with walls of exposed brick and finished with gold. There are swords and stags' heads and portraits of sneering dead men scattered across the walls.

You look back at his hand. The hand that ripped you away from your friends and family.

The King clicks his tongue impatiently. "Come on, silly mortal. You have seen enough of our world to know that if I wanted to harm you, I would have. You are no threat to me now that you can no longer cross. You are the interloper no longer."

"Then why have you brought me here?"

"Come." He walks across the room to where a vast chair is propped on a dais in the center of the antechamber. It is made of more dark leather and gold, with a golden eye wrought into the top. His hair snakes along the floor behind him and you try not to trip on it as you follow him. He lowers himself on to the throne. "I would like you to take a bath and change. The sight and smell of you offends me. Though, I must say, your hair is lovely," he purrs. The hairs across the back of your neck and arms spring to attention.

"I would rather stay as I am." You can sense the eyes of the court on you, but other eyes too, the eyes of the shadows, watching, waiting.

"I would rather you *changed*," snarls the King and the shadows pounce. They tear the clothes from you, all but the belt. And then you hear a creaking groan, a sloshing sound, and you realize what's happening a split second before four hundred gallons of freezing cold water come crashing down atop your head.

Cold.

Your teeth rattle in your jaw and your skull clangs a dull tintinnabulation as your face smacks the marble floor, the weight of the water bearing down upon you. A thousand icy needles stab at your face, your chest, your legs.

The King throws you a tunic.

"Now that you've calmed down and cleaned up," the King says, digging his hand into the pocket of his doublet and holding something aloft—the room goes completely quiet, "I wonder . . . do you know what this is?"

You don't answer.

"This"—he holds his hand out to you—"this is the stone of an avocado pear." You sit up. "This stone is a seed. A seed from an avocado tree that was grown in my garden. The tree itself I burned long ago. This is all that is left. I happen to know that you need this to get home."

There is no sound save for the dripping of water. "What do you want?" Your throat is raw.

"Now that *is* an interesting question." The King's pale pretty face is alight with malice. "I shall ask you the same. Tell me, mortal girl. What is it that you want? Really."

You know it's a trick, but you're too weary to fight. "I want Baker back," you say. "And I want to go home."

"Ah! I thought so. In which case, you and I can come to an arrangement. You give me what I want, and I'll give you the boy and send you home."

What I want. An image blurs your vision momentarily. Zella, in her forest, fighting the King, holding him back again and again. The King and his shadows, prowling at the periphery, feinting and twisting, testing.

"Do you promise?" You cringe at your childish question.

He tosses the seed lightly in the air and catches it deftly, his polished black boots echoing against the marble as he paces in front of his throne. "You have something I need. I have something you need. If you give me what I need, you and the boy go home. You need never think of this place again. No more bad dreams. But if you don't . . . Well . . ." His eyes narrow contemplatively. "I wonder what will happen to your mortal body if you are never able to return?"

If you give in to the King, what would become of Xaymaca? If you give in to the King, will Baker and Val ever be able to return?

"What do you want?" you ask again. But you already know.

"Just one thing, mortal girl. It's quite simple really. Her name. The name of the heir to the Persean power. The name of the girl with the forest hair. I have offered her much, learned much about her ways, her defenses, the chinks in her armor these last five years. But she denies me. I am ill and ailing. I do not look it, but I am an old, old man and I cannot be well again without her name. Would you have an old man suffer so? That is my price, magicless child. Her name."

He sees the answer in your face before you utter it. He clicks his fingers at a guard. "Get him. It should be night there now." The guard jumps and scurries to the stairs.

You know who is coming before you hear his footsteps.

"You promised!" Baker yells, seemingly unafraid of the roiling shadows that lurk, ready to pounce once more, at the corner of the room. "You promised you wouldn't hurt her if I helped you!"

"The child is willful and refused to do as I asked."

His arms are around you. His face is warm against your cold skin. "I'm sorry, I'm so sorry."

"Your hair has grown back." You don't know why it's the first thought to form on your numb lips, but the sight of his heavy locs hanging to his shoulders once more warms you with relief.

"He makes me cut them every time I come here, he uses them in his elixir." His hands are checking you frantically, feeling out the hurt. "They grow back when I wake up."

"Nothing can hurt you in a dream." Your wild laugh escapes through your chattering teeth. "Nothing lasts if you always wake up."

"Shh, it's okay." He clings to you, soothes you distractedly.

"Take us home. Take me home, please."

There are tears in his eyes. "I can't! I can't leave here. It's not that simple!"

"Why?" You are desperate.

"Because . . . because he's my father!" The words burst from him and conflict rages across his features.

"Tell me her name, girl." The King's clear command rings out through the chamber.

"So what if he's your father?" you say. "Let's go."

"I can't," Baker says simply. "I've tried to fight him, but I can't—I'm weak like he is. Bad like he is. That's why Mum left him and why she never trusted me. She knew what would happen if I came here."

You see it now. See how the King had wielded his knowledge to gain control over his son, his heir, his hair. Darkness and doubt are powerful weapons, just like the witches said.

"Baker," you call, your sudden inspiration tethering you to consciousness. "You are more than his son. Hear me call your name!" His eyes flicker to you. "You are Baker! You are the son of Val of Life, the Weaver and a witch of Persea. She fled this land, Xaymaca, left her sisters and her coven years ago to keep you safe from the King who now holds you. The King you were caught by in ignorance and fear. She has root magic and she passed it on to you. You are Baker of Life! Baker of Life and Roots! You are not lost!"

There is power in names.

The green light that fills the space is the color of sunlit meadows, of scrubby city parks, or gardens with litter and lavender and staining blue ice pops. There is darkness suspended at the corner of your vision amid the screams and yells of the King's court as the world around you shatters. Ornaments blasted into pieces, portraits ripped and torn.

Several things happen at once then. Baker breaks from his bonds as effortlessly as though they were made of sand. The King howls, and in that instant you lunge for the dais, for the round, brown seed there.

The King moves a split-second after you do, but he is bigger, stronger, and infinitely more malicious. His face is twisted in a grimace of fury as he swipes the seed from where it rests and, like a child throwing a temper tantrum, hurls it out of his window.

That was it. Your last chance—to restore the tree. To return home.

You do not know where the rage comes from. You aren't a very angry person.

But you are filled with such a loss that it rips from you in a fury. You lash out blindly and your fingers find something metal and biting cold. You don't know what possesses you, some instinct, but you raise the cold metal something above your head and bring it, smashing, to the ground.

There is an explosion of glass and darkness and the King howls.

"My mirror!"

You barely notice the searing, blinding pain striking you anew, the adrenaline numbing you to a stab of something sharp and dangerous spearing beneath your rib cage.

The King bellows to his guards, "No! Stop them! Stop them!" But it is too late; the stunned guards and nobles are too far away, too dazed by the force of whatever Baker had unleashed, pinning them in place. His arms are around you, his hands are gentle at your waist, your spine, his breath is warm in your ear as he murmurs your name. He lifts you like you weigh nothing at all and maybe, to him, with the strength of every Persean witch running through him, you don't.

"Where are we going?" Your numb lips form the words. The answer is so sweet.

"Home. We're going home."

He carries you on sure, strong, long legs to the wide bow window, and leaps, you in his arms, out into the streaming sunlight.

What's in a Name?

With rage in his heart,
his blue eyes aglare,
King Charming let down,
let down his long hair.
Now he is icy calm,
the pitch in his heart a soothing balm,
without his mirror to tell him to wait,
his actions are rash and driven by hate,
he no longer cares for the rules of the game,
he descends his hair to claim her name.

Stay a While

Someone, somewhere, is calling your name.

"What happened?"

"What did you *do*?"

The voices are familiar, distressed. You are swimming against the current, trying to pull yourself up from the cold darkness of not-sleep, of sleepless unconscious, but it's hard, so, so hard. Baker's arms are still tight around you.

Someone, somewhere, is calling your name. You're not sure if it's here or there or somewhere else.

"Baker," you whisper, forcing your eyes further open so as to take in enough of the scene that you can reassure the coven, whose faces sharpen briefly into focus, that you are alive and Baker is innocent. "Baker . . . tell them . . . Tell them who you are."

"What is she talking about?" Kam's face looms over you. "We know who he is. He is the thief of our power!"

"Give her to me." You hear the command come from somewhere above your head, coloring Cynthia's honey-sweet voice. You are passed from Baker's arms to Cynthia's. The warmth of her breast pressed against you is instantly comforting and even as your body twists to find Baker once more, you think, *I want my mum.*

"Just listen to him," you plead quietly.

Someone, somewhere, is calling your name.

You're not sure who it is.

"I . . . I did not work for the King willingly. I am not a thief." Baker's voice is tremulous but grows in certainty. "I am Baker of Life, Son of Val, a witch of Persea."

The air seems to pulse in recognition. Ama appears next to Cynthia, who is examining you with sure hands. "That's not possible. There is no Val here, there never has been."

"I have magic that I didn't know about. The King . . . the King is my father. I think the King's shadows found me because I was lost and afraid and alone. He used me. Used my power. Put my locs in a cauldron and took their magic." He takes another breath. "He told me I wouldn't be lost any more."

There is power in names. You can feel the truth, spreading through the room, heating it like a body in a warm bath. *Ahhhh.*

They move then. Ama releases her wife and daughter and in two strides has crossed the sandy road between them and embraces him fiercely. You see his shoulders stiffen, relax, shake. His arms wrap around her too. They stand in the strange and the familiar. The moments pass. Tears track down Cynthia's face.

"I am Ama," Ama whispers. "Ama the Liberator. Ama of Life. Ama, sister of Val. And we are your family."

Someone, somewhere, is calling your name. You can hear them clearer now, those voices. The voices of your family, your loved ones. Someone, somewhere, is shouting your name through a cloud bank that is rapidly thinning and disappearing.

"She's hurt," says Baker.

"It's all right," says Ama. "A graze, that's all."

You are sticky and wet with red and close now, close to the crossing but far away from everything, suspended in an in-between where all possibilities are true, all worlds are reality.

You are lowered on to the rug. You can see red blooming. Dorothy in the poppy field, desperate to return home.

"Kam," you croak, and she is beside you in an instant, knuckles white as she grips your hand. "Kam, he just needs her name," you say. "And then he's got her. She's been trying so hard to hold out, but I don't know if she can much longer."

Baker lets go of your hand. It falls heavily to the floor, coming to rest amid the blooming red and white. "You shouldn't let me bleed all over the rugs," you murmur to Kam.

Kam smiles a grim smile, but it is Cynthia who answers, "These rugs were woven by more than just thread and yarn. The root magic of the Weaver lives on somewhere still. Never fear, mortal girl, your blood will not stain."

"My mum made these?" Baker looks from face to face, wondering. A whole history he was never allowed to know.

"Your mum was our Weaver," Ama explains, as she swiftly bandages your wound. "She made rugs, clothes, curtains . . . Xaymaca has never seen her like."

"She would do all of our hair as well," Zahrah calls from where she sits at the bottom of the stairs. "Braids and twists and locs, everything. She could have charged through the nose, but money is not the way of the Perseans and she made us pay in stories instead."

"I remember her stories!" cries little Zuri, as if taking themself by surprise. "I do!" They turn to a woman, dressed in a similar shade of blue with identical dimples and say, "Mother, she would tell me all sorts of tales while she braided my hair!"

"Me too," you whisper. You don't know if anyone hears. You know that Baker does.

"Me, also," says Kam quietly.

"I am Baker," he begins slowly and quietly. "I am the son of Val, the Weaver. I am home. And I remember." Tears fill his eyes and spill. "I remember this place. I remember all of you."

You are so happy for him. Really, you are. But there is so much pain and—*someone, somewhere, is calling your name.*

"So what now?" cries Ama. "Now that we have Val's son here among us?"

"Kill the King!"

"End his tyranny!"

"Free Xaymaca from the dark!"

"I want to smash his pompous little face in!" And you almost laugh at Myrtle, of all people, as she violently mimes the King's death with her hands. You almost laugh, but the pain is too bad.

"It hurts," you make out, through gritted teeth. Ama and Cynthia's eyes meet and their expressions are grim.

"But it's just a graze, you said," Baker says, his eyes darting from one to the other. "Just a little cut."

Ama gives a curt nod. Cynthia's hand is at her throat as she says, "Yes. That is it. A tiny piece of enormous evil."

"What is it?" you ask. "Tell me!" And when no one does you feel your way down your body, sweating in agony. Finally your fingers stop at the spot that holds the attention of the whole room. You pull them away. They are thick and sticky not with red now, but black. A horribly familiar, thick, tar-like substance smelling of damp and death oozes from the wound in your side. Your nail scrapes against something small and smooth but impossibly sharp. When the mirror had shattered, shards of glass exploded across the room, and . . . the King. He got his revenge on you. If you die here in Persea, untethered, then you will never return home.

Baker's hoarse whisper is a, "No, no, no," of denial and he shakes his head, but you are smiling because maybe it has all been worth it anyway.

"Is there no hope, then?" You look from Ama to Cynthia. Their eyes are full and somber. You see the answer there.

"But this is ridiculous!" explodes Kam and you jump. Wince. Yelp. "What do you mean, there is no hope? This . . . this is the very epicenter of hope! Hope lives and breathes in this room! We are Persea! We are powerful once more!"

"Kam, you do not understand," Cynthia says, her voice heavy.

"The kind of magic that lived in that mirror . . . it is the very worst of all that lives and dies on this land. There are kinds of darkness that the light cannot banish."

"No!" Kam is furious, eyes ablaze, hands pulsing with a silvery light. "No, I will not allow this! I will not!" She turns to Baker. "Cousin. The Weaver's power is strong within you. Braid my hair, cousin, and harness your root power. The King's barrier around this place fell when you left him—we all felt it. Weaken him further. Braid the hair of the witches of Persea and return our magic to us. They shall storm the Kingstown Palace Estate. I shall go and find my sister, the most powerful of all of us witches, and she will save our interloper."

Baker releases your hand and you feel yourself sink lower. And Baker, murmuring over the beauty of the green glowing embers at his fingertips, begins to braid. You drift in and out of your present, hypnotized by the quick flashing of his fingers, the dancing shimmering of the green light and soothed by the lullaby, the dream song, that the witches begin to sing.

> *There's a Brown girl in the ring*
> *Tralalala*
> *There's a Brown girl in the ring*
> *Tralalalalala*
> *Brown girl in the ring*
> *Tralalalala*
> *She looks like the sugar in the plum*

As Baker's voice joins the witches' in song, their hair unfurls to claim the skies.

Kam stands. Her hair is pulled back in intricate braids, so delicate you can't believe the short amount of time it took to weave them. Dressed in her leathers, hair twisted and woven off her face, shining daggers strapped at her sides, Kamaka of Persea is a warrior goddess and you understand what *Yaa blessed* means at last.

Her mothers embrace her. Cynthia kisses both her cheeks as she whispers a prayer. Ama gazes into the onyx-bright eyes of the babe that lived within her and says, "Go and do your duty to our coven."

"And how will you find her?" Myrtle echoes her sisters' concern. "And how will you travel?"

"Finding her will not be a problem." Kam is resolute. "Getting there . . ."

"Magic?" Baker asks, flexing his fingers, but they shake their heads.

"The King is a clumsy magician, but he put her somewhere far away and difficult to reach," Ama says.

Little Zuri steps forward. "Kam"—Kam turns swiftly, hearing the hope in Zuri's voice—"Kam, I can hear something."

The room goes quiet, straining to listen. You are too far away to hear anything at all, too mortal to be aware of anything more than Baker's hand, in yours once more, keeping you from floating away entirely, loose and lost as you are. But then, distantly, you hear the thundering of hooves.

"Hooves?"

"A gift." Zuri of Water beams. "Called from the white froth and foam of the Aphra. From the River Mumma herself."

The horse is without saddles and reins but there is a rich sentience in her shining gray-gold eyes, a kindness there. A familiarity. You remember that Zella once told you that no energy can be created or destroyed, only transformed. "No one is ever truly gone," she had said. *Yvane,* you marvel silently. The horse's gray-gold eyes meet yours. You are sure a greeting glows there.

Kam is at your side again, her hand in yours.

"I will save her. For us. For you."

You fumble at your waist and Baker, realizing what you are trying to do, unbuckles Yvane's belt.

Her lips are on your cheek. "You are she who answers the call," she breathes in your ear. "You answered it again and again. You are Yaa blessed, my friend."

You don't think Kam has ever called you her friend before.

Someone, somewhere, somewhere else, is calling your name.

Her warmth is there and then it is gone. The door creaks, shuts, and the clatter of hooves dies on the wind.

And then you don't hear anything else. You don't hear the lament of the witches. You don't hear the animal wail of Baker, the braider, the boxer. You don't hear him calling your name over and over.

You'll never hear your name here in Xaymaca again. Your soul is drifting and the interloper is dead.

Knight in Shining Armour

Kamaka is riding,
tired of always hiding
in a world that's always trying
to say that Black isn't beautiful,
so dance if we tell you to
and teach us how to cook.
"We are strong," thought Kamaka,
at one with her steed,
fingers clinging to the handles and though they might bleed.
"We are so damn strong,
and they think this is wrong and they are scared of us,
because there is so much we can do,
when we beat with one heart.
If we are jealous and fight, see the dark, not the light,
they will win
and erase away the history of our skin."

In-Between Trouble Again

It is peaceful, here in the wherever.

You'd thought you'd be naked when you died, but you're not. You are dressed, absurdly, in your spangly Sankofa dress. You don't have a mirror, but you feel beautiful.

There is something else too. The tang of ethanol in your nose, the feverish cold, calm, clinical voices, those things all feel real enough.

What can you do about them, though? They are there and you are here.

You are holding something in your hand. A shard of glass. You throw the shard across the nothing and it smashes, its tiny fragments fracturing further and further until they became ash and vanish into nothing.

You look back across, throwing out the last of the magic Val gifted you like casting a net and hoping for any small, meager catch. You feel a snag. Got something! You begin to pull, reeling yourself in, until everything is in focus and clear. Zella blooms bright before you, as though she is right beside you, though you know she is eons away now. Her lovely face is alight with a ferocious glow, even as the pitch mist closes in. You cry out, but she can't hear.

"Get back!" she snarls.

Her hair is wild and furious, throwing golden daggers and silver arrows at the twisting, mutating, reeking clouds with the King lurking at their heart.

He laughs in wicked delight. "Well, you are fiery, aren't you, my dear? We'll have to curb some of that language when you're at court."

"How—many—times?" Zella throws a branch made of pure

burning light with each word. "You don't get my name."

"Oh, but I think I will. . . ." The King dodges every attack because, although Zella is strong, far stronger than he, her magic is untrained and you can see that she is as likely to hurt herself as she is him.

"I think I will. If you do not give it to me, I'll wreak such pain and torture on what is left of your little village that the guilt will eat you alive!"

Zella curses again, a half-feral scream of pure rage and her magic flares so brightly in that moment that you wonder the King's retinas don't burn.

Don't lose your temper, you will her. The King is desperate now and desperate men do bad things.

Zella lifts a hand, the forest shifts, and a dazzling herd of shining white horses gallop past her, straight at the King.

The King flips and appears again, this time perched on one of the few soft branches not snaking about in the vicious, burning wind. His magic is waning but he laughs again, his black and blue clothes holding the night about him, his long flowing mane of gold whipping behind and about, seeming to move of its own accord and yet somehow never coming alive like Zella's hair, which to you appears as a physical manifestation of her rage.

She rips the branch from beneath him with another sob of fear and fury, but the King does not even touch the ground.

It ends so quickly that you almost miss it. Zella is hollering a battle cry, magic exploding from her every pore, the mountain around her reverberating with the force of it. The rocks shudder and start to move and shrapnel rains down upon them. The avalanche is small but distracting and, in a moment, the King has pinned her, shadows about her neck and wrists and in her ears. She looks up at the King with such hatred in her eyes that you gasp. If Zella had ever looked at you that way you'd have been running as fast as possible in the opposite direction, but the King merely smiles.

"This was rather fun. A lovers tiff, no?"

She spits at his feet. Shadows snare her ankles as well. She begins to tremble.

"It occurred to me today," says the King, striding to crouch down beside her, "that you are very close to giving in. These childish tantrums are getting you nowhere. Did you know that your family is still alive?"

Zella's face remains unchanged, still twisted in that mask of loathing.

"Well . . . at least for now. But as you continue to defy me, I find my generosity . . . waning." A flicker in her eyes. Then nothing. You feel another surge of pride.

"Yaa will destroy you if you touch them," snarls Zella.

"Well, firstly"—the King leans against a faintly glowing bark, looking as though he could chat like this all day—"I don't believe in your Yaa. So I don't really care what she has to say on the matter. And, secondly, forgive me if I'm wrong, Princess, but as heir, if your mothers died, their power would go to you, would it not? I think the rewards are worth the risk of Xaymaca in chaos. So, come on—the name."

"I would rather die."

The King sighs so heavily that you are reminded of his age. His smooth, unlined face has been rejuvenated by the stolen magic, his golden hair shining without a speck of gray, but that sigh vibrated with decades, centuries even.

"No matter the generation, teenagers are always so dramatic." His boredom is palpable; he's seen all of this before. "But I will win. I just have to wait long enough." His glacier eyes scatter blue light up and down her body, hungrily assessing. He snaps his fingers and his shadows crack like whips, up and away, taking him into a swirling vortex of tar-like clouds, reeking and cold.

Zella closes her eyes. Breathes for a while. Far away, you think you can hear something. A soft rustling, like someone creeping through the forest, soft footsteps, like the padding of a panther. You wonder if it's the King, returning. But Zella does not seem worried.

The Afro forest stills. Zella remains at the center. She regains control of her breathing, her chest rises and falls. A few glowing birds nibble gently at her face before flying back into the overgrowth. A shimmering silver squirrel sniffs at her feet. Her lips begin to twitch as though she is singing, quietly.

Taming

The forest is burning,
    with ravishing gold winds.
        There is a smell Kam thinks she's smelled before,
it fills her like old books and so much more.
She reaches out, scared to touch,
never knew that nature could scare her so much,
and as her hand comes into contact
with what should be wood,
it doesn't feel coarse and scratchy under her fingers,
so she takes hold, her finger lingers.
This brave new world is wild and thick and soft,
it covers the ground and is swept aloft,
forming a downy canopy that twirls and shifts,
a vibrating sparkle twists and lifts
the whole mass, starting somewhere in its core.
It is consistently brown, maybe even brunette,
it spirals and twists, it drifts and mists,
and while her legs know these boughs she cannot climb,
her ears hear a song and her mouth forms a rhyme:
There's a Brown girl in the ring
Tralalalala
There's a Brown girl in the ring
Tralalalalala
Brown girl in the ring
Tralalalala
She looks like the sugar in the plum

And the knowledge comes to her with the sweet tune,
of a past tune,
of a Sankofa moon,
this summerless noon:
Kamaka knows this jungle is a 'fro.
And so
she ventures inside the tumbleweave,
fearing to stay, knowing she cannot leave,
she takes out her pocketknife, intending to cleave
her way through,
but then she knows
that this would cause damage and a ton of split ends
so she takes out black castor oil,
the Afro's friend,
and she begins to braid
her way to the center of this maze
and gazes at the fire that somehow
does not touch her.
Amid it all—
golden birds nesting in the trees,
acorns, conkers, bees,
a family of silver squirrels scurrying along a tangle,
glowing woodland animals shimmering in brambles,
a thousand little eyes watch
as careful hand overlaps careful hand and,
taking from her basket both brush and comb,
and the little pot of avocado oil she'd taken from home,
she takes her time, refuses to rush,
an owl hooted by her, she whispers, "Hush."
She does not need distracting,
in truth she is practicing

an art she has missed, a magic she had lost, each curl lovingly kissed,
not tugged at.
And as she works
the forest seems to sigh
at the woman-child
with the fathomless eyes,
hypnotized
by the steady rise and fall of her hands and feet.
They begin to retreat,
Kamaka's plaits playing,
her steps grow shorter,
the line grows tauter—
she is nearly finished.
The magic flares in her hands until no 'fro
surrounds her,
until Kamaka can see that she has found her.
In a cabin in a wood,
a teenage girl in the doorway stood.
Her hair is the ceiling, the roof, and the sky,
now coiling braids, tapestry wide—
and when she sees her, Kamaka wants to cry—
Rapunzella.
Alone.
Lying weak and exhausted,
blood pooling from her nose,
magic and braids coiling out around her,
like the petals of a rose.
She looks up with speechless eyes
the surprise is too much.
She wells up and staggers forward and the two
girls cling to each other, seeking cover in
familiar flesh and smells,

Kamaka drinking in the sight of her sister,
Rapunzella murmuring how much she missed her.
They speak over each other,
and instantly the world begins to change,
the clouds that threatened rain
become blue again.
"You sang the chariot song," beams Kamaka.
"I heard it and my flesh cried!"
"In slavery, your own hands become manacles,
chaining you to circumstance,
I could not liberate myself with myself by myself,
but there are more of us than there are of him,
have always been more of us."
Rapunzella feels her woven mane,
not tame,
not reined in and
the same as everyone else's,
but powerfully, beautifully, hers.
The pretty face, her full nose and lips and smile,
this woman-child is gorgeous
and as she looks at Kamaka, whose love and care
has turned her hair
from angry revolt against the self to a proud rebellion,
she grins a feral warrior grin.
"I am ready to bear the power of our coven,
I can hear the battle's din."
Kamaka stares into the eyes
of her long lost twin,
looses her magic through her hands,
and begins to sing
the song of the witches
who would kill a king:

There are Brown girls in the ring
Tralalalala
There are Brown girls in the ring
Tralalalalala
Brown girls in the ring
Tralalalala
They look like the sugar in the plum

Freedom Seeker

"Rapunzella of Persea, the heart of Persea, Yaa blessed and prophet sighted, will you allow me the honor of serving you?"

"Yes," Zella says simply and the two girls hug fiercely.

Kam begins to unpack her bag, handing Zella leather pants, a shirt, boots, a jacket, and a belt. Yvane's belt. Your belt. She dresses quickly, saying nothing about the dried blood that has crusted between the brass and the leather.

"There is much to tell you," Kam is saying. "So much that even if we have another five years I couldn't do it."

"Perhaps the faeries will write about us one day," Zella muses, tugging thick socks onto her feet and shoving them into boots. She strides around experimentally, reminding you of how long it's been since you've seen her in shoes.

"Gossiping, pretentious busybodies," Kam grumbles as she runs her hands through Zella's braids, which are still at least a mile long. "I have no patience for those who would rather write the story than partake in it."

"Someone has to bear witness," murmurs Zella quietly.

You will bear witness.

Zella is ready now, dressed in leathers identical to Kam's with Yvane's belt slung around her middle.

Kam helps her sister up onto the horse. She gleams bright and white, banishing the dark, the hissing of the shadows.

Kam mounts in front of her and the horse with Yvane's eyes moves forward and picks up the pace, cantering swiftly down the mountainside. Your stomach lurches to watch their progress over steep declines and narrow outcroppings, but the horse's hooves barely loosen the gravel beneath. They pick up speed. The horse switches smoothly from a canter to a gallop and clears the base of the mountain in a flying leap. The descent has taken almost no time at all and you send a silent prayer of thanks to the River Mumma. Now they are flying, almost literally, hurtling west across barren wastes that lie between Carrion Ridge and the border of Kingstown. Nothing grows here, as though the infestation of evil within the bones of the mountains has infected the land around it and the earth is dull and ashy. Still they gallop on, hooves skimming the gray sand faster and faster, Zella's hair whipping out behind them and Kam's magic stretching ahead, lighting a pathway woven of green and copper and silver as they are pulled closer to the ivory and sandstone of the Kingstown walls.

In a couple of hours that feel like minutes, they have arrived. The battlements are deserted, not a sentry in sight. The twins look at each other. Kam sniffs the air, her nerves thrumming as coils of magic sparkle around her fingers and up her arms like vines.

"Blood. Blood and death and war." Zella's hair waves and swells in response, a tide surging in response to the pull of gravity emitted by the coven, her home.

"Is there a gate?" They cast about.

"I can't see one."

"We could climb?"

Kam raises an eyebrow. "Zella, the damn thing is smooth as a babe's bum."

You feel a pang of longing. There's nothing better than bickering with Saffy.

"I'm gonna be straight with you now—I hate heights."

Zella laughs and then is somber. "You sound just like her when you do that."

They're talking about you.

Kam says, "We fight for her as well as the others."

Zella nods but doesn't say anything. She closes her eyes and faces the wall. Her hair begins to glow again, but it is more controlled this time, a steadily increasing gold shimmer as her braids lengthen, expand, coil through the air until their ends have affixed themselves to the top of the wall, which stands at least six meters high.

"I have heard," whispers Kam, awed, "that the King traverses his tower in such a way."

Zella smiles grimly, her eyes flashing as she tugs on a braid experimentally, before bracing her foot against the wall. "Only a fool would refuse to learn from their enemies. And our mothers raised no fools."

Kam imitates her twin, coiling a glowing braid about her wrist and bracing her weight between the wall and her sister's hair with the balls of her feet. Her answering smile promises vengeance and destruction, as the sisters bid farewell to the horse and start to climb.

*

Cynthia and Ama are armed to the teeth and a violent, violet light cracks the earth with each step they take. Where the earth heats and splits little purple flowers appear, blooms of variety in species and shape and shade, tiny buds of rebellion, as defiant as spring in the face of winter. The rest of the coven follows behind, marching through Kingstown in tight synchronicity, moving and responding to each other like a gleaming shoal of fish, not a uniform army. The mortal and the magicless stick their heads out to see them coming; faces appear at the windows but none try and stop them or get in their way. The coven pass through the streets, noting each brutally pruned garden, the shiny plaques with the King's Conformity Laws embossed upon then, nailed to trees.

"In the name of Persea, our children, and our dear, dear interloper." Cynthia's voice rings out into the new day. "Know yourselves, my sisters. Show them who we are and why we still stand, still sing, still seek freedom!" Her battle cry is picked up by witch after a witch, and as the beat of war is drummed out by their feet and hearts, they surge forward as one, and the dance begins.

The clash of steel on steel sings a song of blood lust as guard after guard falls. The King's men stand at over three hundred, but the witches of Persea move like dancers trained to the same choreography, bonded by the potion that brought you into their lives. Where there is a gap in their unit it is swiftly closed, where a back is left vulnerable, someone else watches it. The five years spent training, hoping for this moment. *Three girls will fight, two will stand . . .* There is total trust, total faith. At the front lines stalks Bedia, her whole body charged with her warrior's affinity; she is Athena reborn and death echoes in her footsteps. She bears a sword and shield across her broad back and seems impervious to their weight as she draws daggers from the straps on her legs and aims, twists, flicks them with chilling accuracy. The guards continue to fall, to drop like flies, and Zella and Kam, standing atop the high wall on the far side of the estate, feel a rush of terror and elation as they watch their mothers annihilate without mercy.

You search for Zella and Kam, and watch now as, having reassured themselves that Zella's braids are gripping the wall securely, they begin a hasty dismount, hand over hand, braid taut and toes yapping in protest at the strain. They reach the bottom and begin to run, sprinting across the estate towards where the Persean witches are gaining ground, pushing the guards back and back, trying to back them against the castle. There is terror in the eyes that widen beneath visors as the guards watch their brothers and sisters fall, and though you cannot forgive them, you pity the lives they have lived, a choiceless, voiceless existence, now ending.

Rapunzella rises like the sun to the east behind her, brilliant and gold and glowing with an earthly fury. She is an avenging angel, running so fast it almost looks like flying, her long braids swishing and whipping, snapping limbs like combs and whipping the guards that come from left, from right, from behind, from left again, lunging at her and the witches fighting around her. She doesn't slow her pace, even at the cries of shock and recognition as the Persean witches behold the heart of their power for the first time in five years. Kamaka is hot on her heels, slashing and ducking, shouting instructions to her twin who seems to anticipate them a split second before Kam's voice echoes across the once perfectly manicured lawn, now muddy, bloody, flowerbeds downtrodden.

"On your left, Zella! Duck!" Zella ducks just in time as an arrow comes whizzing past her. More guards, high up on the castle battlements, are firing, and the air is suddenly full of the sound of whistling arrows and although none find their mark, the distraction for the Persean witches, having to shield from yet another direction, slows the coven's progress. Kam's cry, however, has been answered by more shouts of recognition and joy, and seeing Zella and the shifting, twisting of her braids, like Medusa, had the formidable gorgon been forged in the heat of the sun and stars themselves, has the witches redoubling their efforts. Slash, kill, shield, strike.

Little Zuri is sprinting across the battlefield towards them, tears and blood mixing on their face, but, despite the mess and carnage, they catch Zella in a fierce, swift embrace. They try not to gawk at the glittering white gold braids as they slash and whip, and use their water affinity, swirling their arms and raising a tsunami to keep back the tide of guards bearing down upon them.

"The boy?" Kam calls over the crashing of waves. "And the interloper?"

"The boy returned to the other world. He said he would return, that he did not think he would forget things now, somehow."

"Kam, on your left!" shrieks Zella, and then half-turns her head, not missing Zuri's half-answer, "And our friend?" she presses. She freezes when Zuri shakes their head. Once.

You almost pity the army, nearly upon them at the base of the tower, as Zella and Kam emit roars of rage and grief. Line after line of soldiers fall before their fury.

Suddenly, there he is, standing by the window. He is resplendent in a full suit of armor and the sparkling morning light bounces off the shining metal. His head is free of any helmet and even from where you are—far away and in-between and yet right beside Zella and the witches—you can see the sneer of cold contemptuous fury that sets his face ablaze. His long hair falls from the tower as a shining gold and silver rope, down which his shadows descend, twisting and knotting until they reach the ground, flow across the grass, looking for prey or opportunity.

He looks down into the fray and finds Zella amid the battling guards and witches.

To say that Ama and Cynthia are terrifying to behold would be the mother of all understatements. They are wrath personified. You think of Cynthia, fussing and bringing you tea and wine. You think of Ama's lengthy history lessons, her serious face quiet as she read by the fire in the evenings. And you watch them now, witness the raw power with which they blast and slice and destroy.

You see what the King is going to do a split second before he does it and your cry of warning is heard by no one, nowhere.

The King summons his shadows and he takes a breath. The detonation of darkness that follows is so absolute that for a suspended second all the light in the world goes out. There are screams and panicked cries from both sides but then the darkness is lifting and Cynthia and Ama are standing below the tower, arms out, their entire bodies aglow. The light of life blasts from them, banishing the shadows and keeping them at bay but the King's plan worked and now their defenses are compromised.

Ama and Cynthia are tiring, you can see it in their eyes, and the King, high atop his tower, refusing to get his hands dirty, is smiling because he knows it too. They have been awake for almost two days; they have walked and fought and used up their magic and now they are flagging.

Slowly, Ama drops to the ground. Cynthia staggers.

The King laughs and the darkness grows—and then you see her.

Zella is on fire.

Her whole body is burning so brightly that you can't look directly at it; she is the sun and she begins to glide, her feet seeming to not touch the maroon grass, towards her mothers.

"Who are you?" Cynthia breathes as she squints against the scorching glow.

Zella touches her fingertips to Ama's head who immediately gives a shuddering gasp. Zella turns to the tower, looks up as the King looks down, his golden rope hanging down against the ivory, now still as the witches retreat back from the blinding light of life. He is sneering still.

"I am your daughter," Zella answers her mother calmly, still gazing up at the King. "I am Rapunzella of Life. I am Rapunzella of Persea. I am Rapunzella, the heart of Persea. I am Rapunzella, friend of the interloper who answered the call. I am Rapunzella, King Killer."

"I am her sister," calls Kam. "Kamaka of Persea. I will fight with her."

"And I am her sister," you call, and you don't know if they hear you or not, but you think they do. "I am the interloper, I am she who answered the call, and I will fight with her."

The ground beneath their feet cracks.

Someone, somewhere, is calling your name. Calling your name in a tone and a voice that demands an answer.

You take a long look at your friends, keep the moment suspended there in your mind. Kamaka defending her family still against the remaining guards, Ama on her feet once more, Cynthia by her side, swords raised, the other witches either still engaged in combat or discarding their felled opponents, eyes fixed on the bottom of the

305

tower. Rapunzella, staring up at the King, the end of life beckoning in her eyes.

You want to watch them forever, to dream on. Because you know that once you turn away, you will never turn back. You drink them in. *But someone, somewhere, is calling your name.* There are bright lights and loud beeps and clean smells. *Someone, somewhere, is calling your name*, and it's time you answered.

The End

S aid Rapunzella to the King,
  as he laughed above the battlefield,
  as her mothers and sisters watched and waited,
as her twin still weaved as sword and shield,
"We women can adorn our skulls however we damn please,
and there is not a thing,
no man, no king,
can do to stop us.
We are resurrected because we have elected to believe that
Black is beautiful,
that this land is ours,
and freedom for some is freedom for none,
and with tyrannical monarchy,
Xaymaca is done."
She declared it loud so kingdom-wide,
both magicless and immortal heard it
and every living soul cried.
Rapunzella cast her magic with all her might,
her braids a snare of flame and light;
they captured the King's golden mane,
pale plaster skin flakes falling like snow, he was crumbling,
then tumbling,
trying to escape his ivory stronghold.
His hands were too cold
for the new day sun,
fingers numb,

trying to scale his golden-loced ladder, he tangled—
and it choked the life from him.
And so the King died.
Paleness becomes paler,
frailness becomes frailer,
until he faded into nothing
and was a mound of golden yarn,
ready to be spun into another man's story.

APRIL

The hospital room is nice enough, you suppose, but you're glad you're leaving today.

Your legs are finally strong enough to hold your weight after over a month of not moving at all. Saffy had asked you, after she was done screaming and crying and kissing your face, if you felt rested.

"I had very busy dreams, Saf. So not really, no."

You wince at the memories, the vivid recall of pleasure, pain, and fear, and almost miss the generosity of the hazy forgetfulness.

Baker had grinned at you over the top of his book. He'd been here every day since he'd woken you up. If you think about it too much, it's pretty embarrassing that after nearly dying twice, after stumping doctors with your mysterious "sleeping disease" and nearly breaking your poor mum's heart entirely . . . that Baker saying your name is what woke you.

The clean and bright room is mostly empty now of all the flowers and cards and chocolates that had been scattered across the surface when you first woke, but you still have some gifts—pork scratchings from Mr. Feeney's pub, bulla cake from Miss Annie. Baker had told you, a couple of days after your waking, that Mr. Feeney and Miss Annie had been spotted holding hands in one of the new expensive coffee places on the high street.

"One of the waitresses at the pub was saying that Mrs. Goss did some matchmaking," he'd grinned fiendishly. "Bare sneaky. She took some flowers from her garden and dropped them at Miss Annie's but said they were from Mr. Feeney. Miss Annie sent a card and some bulla cake to say thank you and obviously Mr. Feeney wasn't gonna say, 'Nah, it wasn't me.'"

"Especially if there was cake involved." You'd laughed. "Or anything Miss Annie cooks, to be honest."

"'Xactly." Baker had winked. "What can I say? He likes a big bunda, can't blame the man."

Mrs. Goss had sent you flowers too. Mum and Saffy had taken them home, along with the vintage silk dressing gown that Ife had smuggled out of a haul at the thrift store for you. The thought of home—of your house and room—pulls at you in a familiar way and muscle memory has you searching your vision for the fluffy white clouds. But you are solidly here. Solidly present in your reality.

You shift your legs, so prone to pins and needles these last couple of weeks, and move the heavy stack of textbooks from your thighs to your bedside table. You stretch, yawn, sigh. *It's typical, really,* you think. *Only I would fall into an enchanted sleep during the Easter holidays.*

Cat and Melly had been to visit you almost as much as Baker. After the initial giddiness of your return had worn off, and you'd been caught up on all the gossip—"Monica's still a bitch, Aimee is still a bitch, Amy is still slightly less of a bitch, Paris is still a bitch, Maddie is still a bitch, Hugo still thinks fancying you makes him woke"—you'd been frankly horrified by the amount of work you needed to catch up on before the exams in June. There had been a card from Mrs. Fitzsimons and you'd felt sad that you'd be too busy for extra dance lessons this term, but your legs are still shaky so maybe that's okay. Mostly, you're glad that being worked to the bone will give you less time to think about the inevitable. The incoming loss. The departure that hollows out your insides every time you think about it.

Footsteps ring out in the corridor, a sharp, rapid, familiar *click clack click clack.*

Val's head appears round the threshold.

"Do you mind if I bother you for a second?" You and Val haven't been alone together since you awoke. You wonder if that's deliberate.

"No. It's fine, come in." You sound as awkward as you feel. "Do you want some juice or . . . or a chocolate or something?" You gesture to your bedside table.

"No, love. You're all right."

"Yeah, I am." You are overcome by a sudden boldness. "But I really could not have been, you know."

There is a silence. You look at each other. Val sighs and drops on to the chair next to your bed. "I know."

Another silence. You have so many questions, you don't know which ones to ask first. You decide upon the obvious.

"Why didn't you just tell me?"

She sighs. "I had forgotten almost as much as Baker, little one. You know what crossing does to one's memory. I told you the oil was magic—I knew that much." Her accent sounds different now. Part-Jamaican still, part an echo of Ama's lilting musical voice, and part the quick rap of consonances, a calling card of the high street you call home.

"Yeah, but I was a kid. Come on, Val, if you couldn't remember anything, how could you take that risk?"

Her face is pinched with regret. "I am sorry. You cannot know how sorry. But I knew, as soon as I touched your hair, I knew it had to be you."

"But why didn't you say what you did remember?"

"I was selfish. I admit it." The mingled sorrow and defiance on her face reminds you forcibly of Kam. "I was afraid if I told you my half-remembered truths that you would not want to help. The River Mumma's spell had worked too well. I did not know you would not be able to remember your visits. I did not know I would remember so little. I just knew it had to be you—that you would fulfil the prophecy and

311

make my home safe. I kept waiting for you to come to me, to ask me things. When you did not, I thought . . . I do not know what I thought. That you did not trust me with your dreams."

"But you could have told Baker!"

Val closes her eyes. "The King was arrogant. He believed his mirror to be omniscient—but he was wrong. He heard only part of the prophecy. He never knew about the power of the pear tree. Probably would never have thought that a tree could be the power of our liberation. The prophecy spoke of *a son born of witch and might* who would help the King. So, in his hubris, he decided he would create his prophesized son." She swallows. "He threatened my sisters. He said he wouldn't hurt them if I gave him what he wanted. I never told them. Never wanted them to know of my sacrifice, and feared they would not accept Baker if they knew the truth." There is a heavy pause. The silence sits on your chest. Then Val says, "But out of that horror came Baker. Can you blame me for feeling relief when our memories faded? I did not want to tell him what kind of monster his father was—so, yes, I confess, I did not fight to remember. Do you blame me?"

You reach for her hand. Squeeze.

"I don't blame you, Val. And I would have always trusted you with my dreams."

Val's lip wobbles and her eyes fill. She looks away from you, raises her chin, throws her shoulders back. "You saved them." Her voice cracks slightly. "My family. I can never ever thank you enough."

You nod silently. She's right really. She can't.

Seeing Val cry is deeply unnerving.

"Oh . . . the River Mumma says her debt is paid." Val's eyes widen. "What did she owe you?"

Val's smile is mysterious, her eyes far away. "That's a story for another day." A pause. "So you met her too? Strange, isn't she?"

"Very," you agree. Another silence. But there is a calm spreading now. You are both going home.

"I'll miss you both," you whisper.

"We'll miss you too, little one." You don't tell her you're not so little this time, you just squeeze her hand tighter. Think about all you've seen and done.

"I can't go back, can I?" you ask. You hate the hope that colors your tone.

"I think it is . . . unlikely. Besides . . ." She hesitates. "I think you would be unwise to try. Even if we are able to locate that seed or plant an entirely new tree. Traveling between worlds is risky. You were pulled up and out of the Nothing. I would not advise that you return to it."

You nod. You had thought as much. You stretch again, stifle another yawn. You have been sleeping a lot lately, but waking as if you haven't rested at all.

You take Val's hand again and look out of the window. In a little while Mum will be pulling up in the car to take you home. Saffy will be bouncing in the back seat. You remember the ballet tickets that Val and Baker got you for Christmas. *Swan Lake. I'll take Saffy,* you think. *She'll love it. Magic and princes and fairies . . .*

*

You stare at a weather vane on the top of Mr. Feeney's pub. It is spinning wildly as you walk the route you always walk, wondering when they went out of fashion and why. It seems very useful to know which direction the wind is coming from, to know where it's going. The metal rooster pirouettes; change is dizzying, but he doesn't seem to mind.

And there he is, walking towards you, a smile lighting his eyes but not touching his mouth.

"Hello, Baker."

"Hello, Sojourner."

You used to hate your name until it saved you. Until his voice had given power to your name and pulled you up out of a Nothing into a

313

Something. But now you like the way your name tastes in his mouth, the way it rolls across his tongue.

You meet him on the high street and head to the post office. You made more of an effort with your messy bun today but somehow felt different when you pulled your clothes on, baggy jeans and heavy boots from thrift stores you used to be ashamed of. You wanted to feel like yourself. You've realized maybe yourself is enough for you.

You walk down the familiar road, turning slowly unfamiliar. New places, old places with the shutters down. Val's place.

You talk about Melly and Kwame, and Monica who hasn't even sent a get well card.

Baker smiles. "Listen, yeah, lions don't lose sleep over the opinions of sheep."

"Well, I've blocked her now anyway," you say. "And Hugo." You glance at Baker.

"So what about you? Were you . . . dating anyone? While I was sleeping?"

He looks at you in disbelief. "While you were sleeping I was dealing with all the bullshit that happened because you were sleeping! Your mum and sister needing looking after. I wasn't off flirting with girls while you were lying in the hospital bed."

"You're right. Sorry." You're not. You're thrilled.

"Besides . . . I'm going places."

You don't want to talk about this.

"Well, we all want to go places."

"Yeah. I don't want to go. I don't want to move houses and schools and everything. But I also know . . . that I gotta go home."

Halting silence, uncertainty, a short lifetime of dreams, now remembered. You nod. You understand. You pass a coffee shop, pick up iced coffees, and play a game of remember.

"Remember when your mum ordered too much ice cream at the rec center?"

314

"Yeah, I still can't really eat ice cream."

"I was sick all day! It was fun, though."

"Remember the blue ice pops in Mrs. Goss's garden?"

"Much better than ice cream."

"And that old guy . . . what was his name . . ."

"Giles! I wonder where he is now . . ."

"And the waitress . . ."

"Our peng friend at Bing's."

"She said you were cute once."

"You're telling me this now!"

You laugh. Take a breath. "Baker, do you still dream?"

He knows what sort of dreaming you mean. He nods.

"What's it like there now? Are they all okay?"

He smiles. "They're great. They miss you. Even Kam."

"What will happen now that Persea doesn't have a Seer?" You feel a sweet breeze kiss your neck as you name the coven.

"Cynthia says the land recycles." Baker slurps his coffee. "A new Seer will be born when the time is right. Magic is—"

"Yeah, yeah I know." You swallow. "I wish I could come back," you say in a small voice. "But it's probably not a good idea to try. Given that I died there and all."

He doesn't say anything.

You're in the post office now, helping Baker send off packages of things Val is selling. She won't need them where she's going. Then he hesitates, glances at you, throws a bag of chocolates on the counter, too, and pays before you can say anything.

"Did you get those for me?"

"I got them to share."

"Oh. Right."

You walk together up the high street, walking to the salon, in no particular hurry. Mum and Val are having a girls' night tonight, their last one. You're meeting them to pick up Saffy so they can get ready.

315

You wonder what Mum will think happened. The story of them going back to Val's family in Jamaica won't hold water for long. Not when Val never answers the phone, responds to emails, never invites the three of you—her second family—for a holiday.

This is the last time, you think. The last time you will be alone with Baker.

"Here."

He turns to you as you wait for a gap in the traffic, reaches into his pocket, and pulls out something purple, delicate, beaded.

You eye it warily. "It's a dreamcatcher."

He laughs. "I made this one—and I had proper help. The college does a class on Indigenous American history. There's a professor there with a mother who's Ojibwe—they lived between here and there . . . I had to send a lot of emails but . . . well they understood me. They taught me this word, diaspora. I'd not heard it before but it . . . it fit, you know." His tongue tastes his lip, a nervous nibble, his teeth white against soft skin. "I only have good dreams now. I hope . . ." he catches the words before they're out, then decides to release them anyway, "I hope you will too."

You take it. Squeeze it until the beads hurt your hands.

You cross the corner into the small park beside Bing's and sit on the bench to watch the ducks. He rips open the shiny purple packet and offers you first pick.

You study his eyes, his face, his lips.

"If I dream good dreams, then I'll still see you," you say. "Even if they're just ordinary good dreams, hey, I'm okay with that."

His eyes meet yours and this time he doesn't look away, but probes their depths, searching, memorizing.

You are aware of every second before he kisses you.

And when he does—

It's unlike anything; picture perfect and happily ever after fairy tales are far from this kiss.

This kiss is fireworks and a rushing sound and happy little bubbles popping and fizzing gold like champagne at New Year's, and this boy is Christmas Eve and New Year's Eve and every birthday.

You taste the chocolate. You touch the purple beaded lifeline to your chest.

*

You help Val pack up the last things from the salon. You pause in front of the mirror, in which you have sat, so many times, while Val does your hair.

She watches you watch yourself, Val does. Smoothes out the deep V in your forehead with her eyes, fills your belly with rice and honesty, thinks you're beautiful, thinks you're the smartest kid she knows, has watched you grow and transform in this spotted and smudged mirror, heat rising from the weapons of keratinous destruction and hanging over your head like a halo, like a cloud.

You are liking being yourself.

It is a process.

But you're working on getting there.

*

You lug boxes outside, repeat the walk to the loading trucks. You're slowing everyone down, but you pause to stare at the emptiness for a moment. The usual gospel top forty playlist preacher interruptions are themselves interrupted by an upbeat DJ announcing: *This holiday weekend is going to be the hottest on record.* But you feel cloudy. Or maybe you're just worried about exams starting next week.

You strip and peel layer after layer, like an onion getting closer to raw material. You unhang pictures and posters and certificates mounted in frames until you hit scuffed, whitewashed walls.

Now it is just a room. Just a bare little room Val had once stood in, rotated around, admired like the precious thing it was.

You pack up jojoba, cacao and coconut, castor oils, almond oils, olive, and the empty avocado oil jar and swiftly scoop them back into Val's favorite old box, rough carved and unfinished, but smoothed like a shell from passing through an ocean of many hands.

Val appears through the same door as always, strolling in from the back, collecting the last of her things, running a finger over dust-free surfaces to make sure she didn't leave the place in disgrace. She smiles at you. "I remember when you first came to get your hair done. I washed it so gently and braided up in lickle lickle plaits."

"Yeah." You remember. "They were cute. You pulled them into different-shaped pigtails, said I could wear them one way when happy, one way when sad, like a smile on my head, like a frown on my head."

Baker comes through for another box, sees his mum, puts his arms about her.

"We'll be fine," Val says. "This has been a good place." She catches your eye and sighs. "Your people aren't good at saying proper goodbyes. I've noticed that here. Our people, we know it's just part of life." She cocks her head, scrutinizing you from the doorway. The sun is warm on your face. "Just make sure you're a part of things, a'right? Nuh budda small up yuhself and hide inna da corner. And you'll be okay."

Baker holds out an arm to you, embraces you both. Your mum returns from a lunch run with Saffy. They join in the huddle.

Val goes inside with the others. You stand on the curb, Baker's arms around you. You'll let yourself feel embarrassed by the display of affection in front of your family later, even as Saffy makes eyes at you through the glass.

Nuh budda small up yuhself.

You pack the words away into your vanity, look through the glass at the empty storefront on the busy street. People shopping, eating lunch, walking. No one has noticed this piece of your world shutting up shop.

There's no one left to witness. *But I'm here.* Baker squeezes you tighter.

"Baker." You look up at him. "Can you braid my hair?"

He grins. "Sure," and drops a kiss on your head. Touches his fingers to your jaw. Your stomach swoops and you relish the free fall.

Nuh budda small up yuhself.

Epilogue: Fruit

Wh
hen it was all over and
the King's possessions were split
and sold from the tower,
the gardeners returned to their flowers.
Life flourished in the gloom,
they brightened every room,
for now things were different,
they lived well and wanted for nought,
the laughter was vociferant
and this was the story they taught
their children who came after.
The kingdom was forever changed,
a kingdom it was no more,
for while they no longer needed rulers,
they thanked their Brown queens four.
Kamaka and Rapunzella, Cynthia and Ama,
they threw them a party and at the ball
they raised a glass to she who answered the call.
Their cousin and aunt returned,
amid enormous fanfare,
each with sparkling fingers,
each with beautifully braided hair.
And on a sunny day
in April or May,
fill your heart with their song
and hear Rapunzella say:

"There is more magic in our truth than in all of your fairy tales,
more magic in
our hair, curling upwards and outwards,
snapping pins and breaking combs
because it has a life, it has a soul,
it has a voice of its own,
tones that are both soft and loud,
a heavenly cloud,
it will fight, it will crown, it will break all the rules,
our eyes and our smiles will shine like jewels.
We women,
we Black women,
we are as undecipherable as dark ink on dark pages,
you cannot read the mysteries of each 'fro,
each braid,
each dread locks away
something that cannot be spun by you
from yards of yarn made of gold,
cannot be manipulated by male words,
cannot be controlled
by another Prince Charming in an ivory tower.
Our hands, lined and clever,
tell our own stories, fill our own books,
and are not here to weave a conclusion to your narrative.
We owe you nothing."

Author's Note

At the epicenter of the poor representation of Black femininity in mainstream media and literature, is the discourse that surrounds Black hair. The hair of Black women has, over the last four centuries, been encoded within cultural, social, political, and economic texts, and as such is read, examined, and analyzed. Its narrative is rarely written by the wearer, but is instead constructed by the monolith—our hair is unprofessional, it is untidy, it is too much, and, naturally, so are we.

In writing this book, I thought a lot about the negative portrayals of Afro hair in media, and how I, as a young girl, had dreamed of, prayed on, and cried myself to sleep over "good hair" and my lack of it. I grew up reading fairy tales with their long, flowing, golden-haired protagonists, and felt at best invisible, at worse, unworthy and ugly. And who could blame seven-year-old me for feeling this way? Society, with its Eurocentric standards of beauty, lays this unworthiness on thick, continuously suggesting that our noses are too big, our skin too dark, our voices too loud.

I talk about the straightening of Black hair a lot in this book and wish to make clear that I do not believe that Black women straightening their natural hair is always, necessarily, negative; I love to mix it up as much as anyone. Playing with a variety of hairstyles can be a beautiful mode of self-expression. But I remain fascinated by the autonomy behind our decisions. What do we do to feel beautiful? Who decides what it is to be beautiful? And, in changing the chemical make-up of our keratinous roots, are we damaging our relationship with our genetic ones? These are some of the questions I asked myself as I wrote the first draft of this text as part of my undergraduate dissertation. I returned to it, revisions in mind, over three years later. I had made a complicated sort of peace with the trauma of growing up—and coming into adulthood is, undoubtedly, traumatic—had sat with that trauma for a bit and wanted to continue to interrogate how the anguish of change, the weird, frustrating teen angst affects our ability to call ourselves beautiful.

Over this period I have done much to my hair—relaxed it, braided it, shaved it off entirely. It's been a journey. I hope that, in reading this book, young girls learn to step into their own power, embrace their identity as defined by themselves (not society, with all of its ills and biases), and learn that they are never too much.

*

Writing this book has been a process of writing wrongs, processing rage, and learning many, many things. A few that I'd like to note: firstly, the Black experience is not monolithic. Our experiences are many and varied, based on the intersection of gender, sexuality, ability, and location. This is true of the whole African continent (the experience of an Ethiopian person will be wildly different to a Nigerian person) and is true within the diaspora. Mainstream discourse will often conflate the African American experience with the Afro-Caribbean experience, and with the Black British experience. With that comes a flattening and a reduction of the many things that contribute to these differences, particularly the way in which the colonization of the African continent affected our varying communities.

What I wanted to draw particular attention to in *Rapunzella, Or, Don't Touch My Hair* is the uniqueness of the Black Caribbean British experience. I also knew that I wanted to write something that reflected my experience as a member of a diaspora. There is an expectation that, as a non-white fantasy writer, you will write stories based on "where you're really from." I, however, am not the person to write about Jamaica as it is—I've grown up in the UK. What I know of Jamaica I know through other people's memories, through story and food and song. So I decided to write about that land instead—not the real Jamaica but a land of stories and dreams that those who feel disconnected can feel connected to in order to explore this idea of being from a place and also not from that place. I knew I wanted it to be a place that sat outside of colonization and white supremacy and capitalism—and then to imagine what kind of colonizing force could disrupt it. Above all, I wanted it to be hopeful.

Additionally, I wanted to draw attention to the way in which the colonization of the Caribbean has attempted to separate it from its Indigenous American (the Taínos and the Arawaks) roots. It was incredibly important to me, in paying homage to the West African influences on Caribbean culture, to also pay homage to the Indigenous Americans who first inhabited Xaymaca. Our oppression is shared; the Atlantic slave trade operated in a triangle of violence between Europe, Africa, and the Americas from the sixteenth to the nineteenth century. Slave ships moved manufactured European goods to West Africa to buy enslaved people. They transported these people to the Americas—including the Caribbean—where genocide against Indigenous people was enacted and ship holds were filled with American commodities—sugar, cotton, etc.—before being sent back to Europe.

After doing a vast amount of research, I came to see that there are certain things amongst the African and Indigenous American cultures that have been subject to appropriation. The mechanisms of the appropriation differ but the result—the continued legacy of colonization—is very similar. In *Rapunzella, Or, Don't Touch My Hair*, I link what seem to me to be the most glaring examples—Black hair and dreamcatchers. Dreamcatchers originated amongst the Ojibwe people, who are an Algonkian-speaking tribe and constitute the largest Indigenous group north of Mexico. While dreamcatchers

325

originated in their Spider Woman stories, they gradually were adopted as a symbol of unity across many Indigenous American groups. As the "Pan-Indian" movement flourished across the Americas, dreamcatchers caught the eye of Westerners and a trade of non-Natives producing them proliferated. While cultural sharing and blending can be beautiful, when there is a continued oppression and a vast lack of social, political, and economic equality between two groups, we must question whether our appreciation is not something more sinister. The popularization and commercialization of dreamcatchers has always sat badly with me, particularly when they are mass-marketed, made under poor working conditions, and, as a result, ultimately profit those who continue to benefit from the legacy of white supremacy. I hope that readers of *Rapunzella, Or, Don't Touch My Hair* leave its pages feeling empowered and emboldened, and remembering that true change can only occur with solidarity.

Of many, one people.

Acknowledgements

Whenever I've read author acknowledgements I've always wondered how on earth they began condensing down a lifetime of help and support into a couple of pages. Now that I am here myself, I've still got no idea how to begin thanking everyone, how to decide who is worthy of thanks. Every person, point, and path my life has taken has led me to here—and so this is by no means an exhaustive list of everyone who has contributed to this story. If we've met warmly, if you've loved me, if you've offered friendship, kindness, or advice—thank you. You are here in these pages, even if your name is not below.

I have to start with my mum. Obviously there aren't enough words (and I'm already way over my word count!) to begin to thank you for all you are and all you've done. There aren't enough birthday cards, Christmas cards, or Mother's Day cards to tell you how much I love you and how grateful I am to have been born as your daughter. I could have a lifetime of acknowledgements and it still wouldn't be enough. You are everything I know about being selfless and strong and smart and determined. You make my life happen.

To my little sister, Saffy, DOOD. Your tenacity, your sense of humor, your precocious wisdom, and your scrambled eggs are my sun and stars. Thank you for always answering my millennial language questions and constantly reassuring me that all of this isn't just a fluke. You are my best friend and I love you endlessly.

To Alice and Lara, my cousins, my sisters, my best friends, I wouldn't be where I am without you. Thank you for the long voice notes, for the boozy dinners, and for holding every expression of anxiety with such honesty and compassion. I love you both. To Ingrid, for our

Shawanime Sundays, our deep meaningful chats, for all the fun we're yet to have together, thank you. To Channone, for all of your advice.

To my grandma, my second mother, thank you for your stories, your cooking, your care. You inspired so much of the magic in this book—the spot in my heart gets bigger and bigger every day! None of us deserve you. I love you.

To my Auntie Yvey—for the book recommendations, the TV recommendations, for the long, long phone calls about everything from fan theories to boy trouble, thank you, thank you, thank you. This fantasy nerd would have shriveled and died without your nourishment. I adore you.

To my dad, thank you for the sacrifices you've made, for always being proud of me, and for the many lessons you've taught me.

To my Uncle Melvin, thank you for your generosity, the bounty of opportunity, and your endless love and support. I am eternally grateful.

To my grandma Boswell for reading me *The Dreamcatcher* over and over again, to the rest of my extended family, my wide supply of grandparents, aunts, and uncles—McLeod, Boswell, Morrison, Craven, Haddad, and bubba Leyon—thank you for the love, for the positive affirmations, for always believing in me even when I didn't believe in myself.

To my Auntie Marcie for winding down the windows so we could scream-sing along to Jocelyn Brown, to my Auntie Billie for the Rathfern dinner and wine nights, to my Auntie Dot for being the best fairy godmother a girl could ask for, to my younger cousins, Freja, Cameron, Anna, and Ottilie—every path I clear, I do for you.

To my amazing friends, every person I've canceled on while writing this book, every person I missed during the pandemic, thank you for your love and support. Special acknowledgement to my top ten—Emily, Cora, Hannah, Áine, Charlotte G., Charlotte P., Courtney, Juno, Costie, Sam—thank you for the dinners, the FaceTimes, the tears. You have all been a bottomless well of love and support. Thank you so

To my Michael—words fail. Thank you for it all. More life with you, please.

To all my hairdressers—from Kim at Hype, to Ja'Neal, to Tamara, to Yasmin, and all the hairdressers that are yet to care for me, thank you for making me feel beautiful. Your hands are made of magic.

To all of the amazing teachers I've had over the years. I couldn't possibly name you all but special thanks to Miss Millington, Miss Clark, Miss Wright, Mrs. Jordan, Miss Macleod, Miss Gibbons, Mrs. Sellers, Mrs. Smith, Mrs. Cross, Mr. Hogben, Mr. Chaudery, Maz Evans, Cath Day, Wallace Mcdowell, Jack McGowan, Carol Rutter (read, write, act—change the world!), and of course the late greats, Liz Fitzsimons and Jackie Cobain—taken too soon. You all taught and inspired me more than you know.

To my amazing agents, Steph and Izzy. I remember screaming with excitement the day I received your first email and I honestly can't believe how lucky I've been to have the privilege of your help, support, and representation. Thank you for understanding this story, this world, this writer.

To my Scholastic team and all of the editorial eyes I've had on this book—Ruth Bennett, Sophie Cashell, and Yasmin Morrissey, the first editor to say yes. Thank you for taking the time, the energy, and the risk on a story that sits outside of the way we typically understand genre, plot, and character, and believing in its magic. To Genevieve Herr, you have been my lighthouse through every personal stormy moment. If I ever panicked, I would tell myself, *Well, Gen isn't panicking so it must be fine.* Thank you endlessly, I hope we can do this together for ever.

Additional thanks to Hannah Love for all of your hard work on publicity, and to Liam Drane and Alex Cabal for your stellar work on the cover. She's perfect—you brought my dream to life!

And finally, to all the Black girls who read this book. Thank you. I see you. I love you.